S0-AQL-124

PLAYING WITH FIRE

Peggy opened the door and took the ouija board from its resting place on the top shelf of the closet. Once it was spread before her on the bed, she sat down to talk to Max, but she couldn't. She needed two people to play.

Suddenly, the pointer began to move by itself.

"I am legion," Max spelled out, "I know all and I can do all. . . ."

A GRIPPING TALE OF TERROR
by
Dana Reed
Best Selling Author of
Sister Satan and **Margo**

Other Leisure Books by Dana Reed:

SISTER SATAN
DEATHBRINGER
THE GATEKEEPER
DEMON WITHIN
THE SUMMONING
MARGO

DANA REED

HELL BOARD

LEISURE BOOKS NEW YORK CITY

To my wonderful husband, Arthur,
who stood by my side and
encouraged me to write.

A LEISURE BOOK®

April 1990

Published by

Dorchester Publishing Co., Inc.
276 Fifth Avenue
New York, NY 10001

Copyright © 1990 by Edwina Berkman

All rights reserved. No part of this book may be reproduced or transmitted in any form or by any electronic or mechanical means, including photocopying, recording, or by any information storage and retrieval system, without the written permission of the Publisher, except where permitted by law.

The name "Leisure Books" and the stylized "L" with design are trademarks of Dorchester Publishing Co., Inc.

Printed in the United States of America.

Prologue

Maximilian, Marquis of Death of the First Hierarchy, presented his petition for the bloodied and half-crushed body of Bill Smalls, someone he'd indirectly killed through the ouija board, then he knelt before the Black Master of Acheron, knowing it wouldn't be easy this time. He needed Smalls' flesh to heal the wounds of his pets, but he just couldn't take the body and do with it as he wished. He had to beg for it because actually he didn't kill Smalls. Smalls had killed himself after several sessions with the ouija board and was revived here in Hell!

Smalls, his lips sewn shut to silence him, his eyes wide with terror, cringed in a corner while apelike creatures from the pits stood guard.

1

Using his own blood to write with, Smalls dipped a forefinger into the crimson liquid and wrote a message to Max on a moldy wall behind him. "We were friends," he wrote. "Why are you doing this now?"

Maximilian stared at the message, smiled and ignored it. Paying attention to the task at hand was more important because his wasn't the only petition. But as the spirit in the ouija board, his petitions held prominence over others because Maximilian was a working Marquis, not one to sit on a throne and allow his hatred of fools like Smalls to fester and grow like an untended cancer. No, Maximilian took action.

As he knelt before the Black Master in silence, he heard the sound of a door slamming back on its hinges. Then Maximilian heard deep growling noises, felt himself choking on stagnant breath, and knew that Lycanus, demon prince of werewolves, had decided to oppose him in person this time. Lycanus wanted Smalls' body for the same reason—to heal the wounds of his demon pets.

Turning his scaly, tumor-infested body without rising, Maximilian saw Lycanus, his body covered with clumps of black hair and his wings barely touching the ground, enter with an entourage of equally hideous, demon bodyguards. Lycanus spotted Maximilian and smiled, putrid, black steam hissing from his mouth. Lycanus was amused because Maximilian had also come in person to present his petition.

"You've lost, fool!" Lycanus hissed, motioning towards Smalls who screamed, tearing the leather strips binding his lips. Ignoring Smalls, Lycanus raised a heavy metal sword over his head like a banner, issuing a challenge. He would fight Maximilian for the body of Bill Smalls.

Undaunted, Maximilian rose and bared his own sword. Lycanus answered by spreading his wings while gusts of fetid air rose like a whirlwind.

"This will cease at once!" the Black Master said, rising on two cloven hooves to spread his own wings. "I am in charge here, Lycanus. Do you dare to ignore me?"

Lycanus smiled, baring deadly, white teeth shaped like talons, but Maximilian saw his mouth quiver and knew he was backing down. The Black Master was more of a challenge than anything Lycanus had faced up until now. Flapping his own wings to reinforce his position, the Black Master rose in the air and came down on top of the demon prince. Lycanus was forced to the ground, his breath coming in heavy gasps. When his bodyguards saw their fallen prince, they responded by flapping their wings and retreating to avoid the wrath of the Black Master.

"Now," the Black Master said, his voice echoing with the volley of a cannon, "I will choose the petitioner who gets the body—but first, a test to see who is more worthy." Smiling down at Maximilian, he returned to his throne, and sat down. "Maximilian," he said, "when you deal with victims through the board, how do you earn their trust? And by victims, I mean those who would seek answers by asking questions of the ouija spirit."

"I earn their trust by fooling them into believing I'm their friend. I gain their confidence by acting concerned when they're hurt or angry. Once the humans befriend me, they belong to me—their minds and their bodies."

"And how do you know when they're hurt or angry?" Lycanus asked, getting to his feet, his voice laced with indignation. "You dwell in our world, a dark netherland running parallel to the land of humans—"

"If you have to ask," the Black Master said, his forked tongue snapping like an angry whip, "then your petition is denied."

Both the Black Master and Lycanus were startled when Smalls screamed again and pleaded for Max to help him, but his words were mostly incoherent.

Turning away from Smalls, Lycanus went on with his task. "But, Master," he protested, black smoke billowing from his nostrils, "Maximilian has always been the spirit in the board. He was trained for his role, so naturally he'd know the answers!" After Lycanus spoke, he cringed under the Master's gaze and spread his wings to

4

cover his huge, hairy body lest the Black Master attack him again.

"When the ouija board first came into being in the late eighteen hundreds," the Black Master said, his dark, slanted eyes narrowed on Lycanus, "and humans began asking questions, I used my powers to seek control of the game because I saw an opportunity to control these human fools by supplying a spirit who would live in the boards and whose sole function would be to answer their questions. But before I chose the spirit, I had to be sure it was one who had the mental and physical capacity to deal with each and every ouija board that came into existence. Then I had to be sure it was one who had mastered the arts of cunning, trickery and deceit.

"After all, if the spirit were such that the fools seeking answers saw through him or were afraid of him, we'd have nothing. These fools would turn away from the ouija board. And remember this, Lycanus. I didn't choose Maximilian. He volunteered. You were too lazy to work for the bodies, but not too lazy to come here and petition for them!"

"But I don't see why all of this trickery is necessary," Lycanus said, as his bodyguards left their hiding places against the far wall to stand by his side. "Why not just grab the humans when the pointer is in their hands and their minds full of wonder? Why befriend them first? Why not just materialize and kill them on the spot?"

The Black Master grimaced at the questions Lycanus kept asking as if he couldn't believe this fool had earned the title of demon prince all by himself. "Because, Lycanus, these humans are not ours to take until they welcome us with open arms."

"Why? What do you mean when you say they're not ours to take?"

"Until they befriend us, they are still under the protection of their God, the God of Christians," the Black Master answered, his voice echoing through the Hall of Demons. "If we harm the humans in any way the soldiers of their God will shackle us and we'll all be doomed to spend eternity in the bottomless pits of Acheron. However, once the humans befriend us, their God no longer protects them. Therefore we must wait until the humans accept us willingly before we can lay claim to their bodies. And by gaining their confidence, we make them come to depend on us. They see Maximilian as a friend with their best interest at heart. Once the dependency is established, we've won."

After speaking he held up a clawed hand to silence Lycanus. "Enough with your nonsense. You ask too much. The petition for the body of Bill Smalls is granted to Maximilian, Marquis of Death, to do with as he pleases. As I have spoken, so shall it be!"

Lycanus knew that the same trickery and deceit Maximilian used on humans through his board was a permanent way of life, and it would always be so. Lycanus would lose time and again. Knowing this, Lycanus swore to do better next time, swore to master the ouija spirit's talents, swore to get even with Maximilian the first chance he got.

Silently he watched Maximilian thrust a meat hook through Smalls' back while howls of anguish assaulted his ears. "Yes, Maximilian," he mumbled. "I'll get even. The next body will be mine . . . and the one after that . . . and the one after that . . ."

CHAPTER ONE

When Peggy Rearden saw the fist coming, she tried to duck, but it was no good. She felt knuckles forcing her lips against her teeth, felt the sensation of blood and knew she would damn well spend another week with swollen lips. Only it wasn't so bad. Once the punch had been delivered and her mouth bloodied and distorted, the kids would leave her alone.

Oh, they might hang around to torment her a bit, to call her a loony and make fun because she had fits and messed her pants. They might even start in about her face again and how ugly she was, or about her weight and how she was ten pounds lighter than an elephant. But eventually they'd grow bored and leave.

At least that's how it had gone in the past, but things seemed different this time. No one left, especially not the boy with the fist. He stared at Peggy's blood, followed the stream of it down to her blouse and hit her again, in the eye this time. Peggy's hands shot up to cover her face as the pain and shock of what he'd done struck her full force.

Then she screamed when someone grabbed her hands from behind and held tight so she couldn't protect herself. Hell, this wasn't fair. It was two against one—two burly, bully boys against an overweight epileptic girl.

"Ugly!" someone shouted, and the boy hit her again, connecting with the side of her face.

"Fat bitch!" someone else jeered, and the boy hit her in the stomach.

Peggy groaned and felt the breath being forced from her lungs. "Not fair," she whimpered. She was supposed to be hit once, then the mob surrounding her was supposed to leave. "Not fair . . ."

"Life's a bitch!" the boy with the fist yelled, changing tactics and using his foot instead of his fist. When Peggy felt a steel-tipped boot come crashing against one of her shins and shatter a bone, she screamed.

Then the steel tip struck at the other leg, and Peggy felt the bone crack, the noise resounding in her ears. Looking down, she realized that one eye was almost closed from being hit, but she could still see a sliver of white jutting from her leg below the knee.

"Do it again!" someone else shouted, only this time it wasn't just a voice in the crowd making the request. This time the voice had a name—Nicole Martin. "Hit her again and make her bleed some more," Nicole shouted as Peggy began to slump forward, her legs no longer able to support her weight.

Sinking to her knees, Peggy heard a noise and looked up. Focusing with her one good eye, she saw the steel tip of a boot coming straight for her face. "No!" she screamed as if words alone could stop this—but it was too late.

When the boot connected with her mouth, Peggy heard all sorts of crunching and realized she'd lost her front teeth. Oh God, this was supposed to have stopped with the first punch, but it hadn't. She was being beaten to a pulp, being beaten to death.

And maybe it was just as well, she thought wearily. Life held nothing for her anyway. Besides, she had no choice, since the mob wasn't finished with her yet.

At that point, the hands holding her from behind let go. She saw the ground rushing up to meet her face and heard a dull thud when her head slammed hard against the pavement. She wondered what damage the blow would do to her already imperfect brain, only somehow it didn't matter. She saw the steel-tipped boot heading towards her face again and knew that nothing mattered.

This next blow would do it and she'd die, but, oh God, what a terrible way to leave the world—beaten to death at the hands of jeering classmates in the yard of Philmore High in her home town of Floyd Acres, Long Island. And with no teachers around to stop it.

When the next blow struck her forehead, Peggy felt her skull crack. Rolling slowly onto her back, she stared at the faces hovering over her dying form, then up at the sky, knowing she had to see the sky once more before giving in to the enveloping darkness.

Then she woke up, her body bathed in sweat, her bedroom dark except for the moonlight streaking across the floor.

Sliding her legs over the side of the bed, Peggy caught her breath, thought back on the dream and shuddered, wondering when it would come true. When would those insane bastards at Philmore High kick her to death? Would it be tomorrow, or the day after, or a week from now?

How much longer would she live until her infirmity—her epilepsy—scared and enraged them enough to kill her? God, it wasn't fair.

The bathroom was cold when Peggy stepped from the shower the following morning. Slipping into a terry cloth robe, she tried not to think about how it was late spring with mornings still in the low forties, yet her mother had the thermostat turned down again. Well, at least the water was hot, she thought.

Concentrating on brushing her teeth, dismissing her anger over Mom's frugality, Peggy examined her teeth in the mirror, then frowned. Her teeth were straight and even, so they were not the cause of her depression.

It was her face. She was plain with no outstanding features, nothing to put her in the same category as the other girls at school, the popular ones who didn't sit home on Saturday night waiting for a phone call.

Why hadn't her face changed overnight when she'd prayed especially hard for a miracle? Then again, God could have been busy with others, those whose needs far exceeded her own. Thousands were starving in Biafra, thousands were being brutalized in Central America, and a boy in Miami needed a liver transplant. Compared to these disasters, Peggy's request seemed mundane.

And yet she didn't care. She needed a new face, and she needed it now! If she had a new face, the dreams would stop.

Grabbing the edge of the sink, Peggy felt the room spin and knew she'd worked herself into a frenzy. Now those familiar little lights were dancing in front of her eyes; it was her warning.

"Dad! Oh, God, Daddy," she screamed and waited, knowing Daddy would be here soon. They'd gone through this so many times before that Charlie knew what the panic in her voice meant.

"Dad," she whimpered as he ran into the bathroom. "Help me."

"I'm here, baby. Give me your hands."

"I can't, Daddy. I can't move."

"Peggy!"

"Here," she said, forcing herself to join hands with Charlie. Then she waited. One of two things was about to happen—she'd either come out of this with Daddy's help or have a full blown seizure. Either way, it didn't matter because Daddy was here, and Daddy would help her.

"Hold tight and concentrate," Charlie said. "Try to zero in on your brain, and don't let go of my hands."

Charlie Rearden had been helping Peggy through most of her seizures for years now, ever since her tenth birthday when the seizures increased to 15 a week. Of course Peggy was born this way, with this disturbance in her brain, but nobody was forced to accept an illness.

With this in mind, Charlie found a neurologist who treated seizures with a revolutionary method called biofeedback.

The first time Charlie took Peggy to his office, the doctor had wired her entire head with electrodes. The sight of Peggy with all those wires stuck in her head scared Charlie, but he didn't interfere. Instead, he watched in muted silence as the doctor attached those electrodes to an electroencephalograph machine to measure the intensity and speed of her brain waves.

"Electronic signals produced by the brain are small," the doctor had said. "The electrodes attached to Peggy's head will pass through the EEG machine where they are intensified enough for us to read them."

After getting his reading, the doctor told Charlie that Peggy was producing too many theta waves, which caused a slow state of mind associated with seizures, and not enough beta. Most epileptics usually never had beta waves, which were associated with concentration. Epileptics lacked concentration, and Peggy had to be taught to concentrate, something most people did naturally.

Then began a long series of sessions. Peggy was first taught to recognize the increase in theta waves, signaling a seizure. After this she had to learn to concentrate on something difficult during those periods to stop the oncoming seizures.

"Think about the area of your brain where the disturbance is," Charlie had told Peggy in the beginning. And she did. She looked into herself and concentrated by picturing her brain as a large expanse of land with long ditches, like gulleys, dug into its surface. Sometimes there was unusual activity in those ditches; they moved and shifted, reminding her of the unstableness of the San Andreas Fault. The constant friction caused by movement of the inner crust of the earth along the fault line set off earthquakes, just as the moving gulleys in her brain set off seizures.

Other times she compared her brain to a computer filled with tiny electronic circuits, all interconnected and always in motion. Like the heart of a giant beast, those circuits were working to keep the beast alive. Seizures were caused by glitches in those circuits.

Peggy was good at her games of concentration, thanks to her father, but it was a problem when he wasn't around. When she was in school and the glitch in the computer circuits of her brain caused a seizure, concentrating didn't help then; nothing helped. She needed somebody to talk her through it, to hold her hands and reassure her that everything would be okay.

Nobody in school cared enough.

"Peggy!" Charlie said firmly. "Your hands are still trembling. You're not doing it right!"

Almost immediately Peggy stopped thinking about Philmore High and instead saw a projected image of her brain superimposed over Charlie's face.

She saw tiny electronic circuits and searched until she found the glitch. Once found, she narrowed her attention on the glitch and removed it from its hiding place. The trembling began to subside. When it had stopped completely, she clung to her father and cried.

"Come on, babes," he said, holding her in his arms. "You'll be late for school."

Oh, sure, she thought, mustn't be late for

school. But Charlie meant well. This was his way of making her get on with her life.

"Sure. Musn't be late for school," she said out loud, hiding the bitterness inside and trying to concentrate on something else.

She could concentrate on Charlie and how, standing here in his arms, she suddenly realized they were almost the same height, but Charlie was short for a man. She was as wide as him, though—or fat, in all honesty.

In fact, she was almost a mirror image of him, except she had more hair—long, brown, mouse-colored hair, not ash and lovely like her mother's. The sunlight didn't catch Peggy's hair and throw off a pleasing radiance as it did with Anita's. Peggy's hair was dull and drab, like her life.

"Your mother laid out your clothes," Charlie said, releasing her to follow him from the bathroom.

His shoulders were slumped forward; his flesh looked as though it had been draped across his body by a careless decorator. Her seizures were draining him physically, but she had no choice. Charlie had been helping her for years. She'd never trained with anyone else and often wondered who'd help when Charlie was gone.

Shuddering, she turned her mind to something else. She never wanted to think of Charlie as being gone because that meant death, and losing him was too awful to think about.

Following behind him, she stared at her bed,

at the dress with the white collar laid across it, and remembered what he'd just said. "Your mother laid out your clothes." But when? Did Anita come in here, pick a dress, and leave when Peggy was in the midst of her struggle not to have a seizure? Then Peggy noticed that her bed was made, and so the answer had to be yes. Anita came into Peggy's bedroom, chose the dress, made the bed and left. What Anita didn't do was come into the bathroom and help with the seizure.

Cold hearted bitch, Peggy wanted to scream, but didn't because Charlie was still there. Charlie was waiting for Peggy to snap to and say she was all right. "Dad, dresses with little, white collars went out with high button shoes," she said and laughed, although there wasn't anything funny about it.

After studying her frown, he put his arms around her shoulders and squeezed tight. "Wear what you want to. And by the way, I hate to keep harping, but don't forget the Dilantin and the Tegretol."

"They don't stop the seizures."

"But they do hold them off." The door to the outer hall was still open. When deep-throated whining noises drifted over the threshold, he stopped talking about her drugs and smiled. "Must be your buddy," he said.

To Peggy, this meant only one thing. It had to be Dog, her best friend in the whole world.

Dog was out in the hall waiting to be told that

it was all right to come in. Dog was a large, brown animal, a mixture of Shepherd and Doberman. Charlie motioned him inside and watched him jump on Peggy and cover her face with his wet tongue, then Charlie closed the door and went downstairs to face another seizure of sorts.

Anita undoubtedly was in the kitchen making breakfast, flying about the room in a frenzy to correct any tiny imperfections she saw. Unfolded napkins had to be straightened. A smudge on a plate had to be wiped clean.

Stopping for a moment to sit on the bottom of the stairs because his hands were still shaking from Peggy's seizure, Charlie surveyed the living room in front of him and wanted to choke on the bile in his gut. Everything was in place. There were no errors. No wonder the kid had seizures. True, she'd been born this way, but Charlie saw it as something that could be controlled, whereas the fanatical neatness of this house was something that had long ago gotten out of control.

Still sitting on the stairs, he concentrated on his feet and the way they sort of sank into the carpet. Then he brushed his hair back from his face and noticed there was less on top today than there had been yesterday. His hair was receding, dying, going to hair heaven or wherever the hell hair went when it fell out.

And his feet. He hadn't been able to see his feet in years, unless he was sitting as he was now. Then he could stretch his legs way out, beyond the protruding abdomen, and tell if his socks were properly matched.

He could also see the beige carpet which he hated. Now there was something on which to transfer his frustrations—puky, beige carpet. It was bland and dull, just like his life. He lived; he was; he existed. At times, were it not for the constant motions of his lungs inhaling and exhaling air and his heart beating in his chest, he would have sworn he was dead.

Then again, maybe not. Maybe this was worse than death. At least when you were dead the pain stopped.

"Charles! Margaret! Breakfast is ready!"

He listened to the small voice in the kitchen bellowing its loudest and automatically clenched his fists. Charles! Margaret! It's Charlie and Peggy, he wanted to yell back, but he didn't. Keeping peace was more important than the constant pursuit of a nickname.

Besides, he really loved the woman. He'd married her for better or worse, although things between them seemed worse these last few years. She'd changed after Peggy was born. It was not her neatness, an everlasting fetish. Rather she'd turned bitter and indifferent while Charlie remained in the Land of Oz, forever content to swallow his lot in silence. And born out of her bitterness was a demand for more perfection than he was willing to give.

But he couldn't blame Anita. After their only

child came into the world having seizures life became a nightmare for her. Rearing the child was her job, and Charlie was the breadwinner. Both had assumed their stereotypical roles with a fervor for being the best ever.

Slouching on the steps, he massaged his neck to release his tensions, but it didn't help. Nothing helped when you were depressed—and certainly not lying on the steps staring at the overhead ceiling which only reminded him of how large this house was.

It was a nice house at one time, not that it wasn't now. He was just looking at it from a different angle these past few years, so his feelings about the place had taken a rapid about face.

The house was two stories high, with two bedrooms and two full baths upstairs. Down here on the main floor, there was a living room, a dining room, a kitchen, a half-bath, a utility room, and a family room with sliding glass doors leading to an outside patio where the pool was. And oh, he thought, let's not forget the fully finished basement.

What the hell he needed with a two story house and a mess of rooms he didn't know, especially now when it was too late. He was married to the place, and married to its upkeep as well.

The heating and electric bills, for instance, were killing him by inches.

As for the mortgage payments, Charlie had settled for an Adjustable Rate Mortgage which had been a mistake, because now the bank holding the loan was robbing him blind, legally, without even using a gun. Interest rates were sky high.

Rising from his place on the stairs because his stomach was in knots from thinking about the house, he walked over to the coffee table where neat, little piles of magazines were stacked in neat, little rows. He just stood and stared at them. This setting had always reminded him of a doctor's office—sterile and ultra-clean. It was everything he didn't want. It wasn't a place where a man could drink his beer and fart to his heart's content. It wasn't home, which was hardly fair with him paying the bills while dying a slow death.

Reaching down, he pulled the magazines apart, upsetting their synchronization. No longer were the titles lined up to within one millionth of a micrometer. Not satisfied at stopping there, Charlie crossed to the bookcase by the far wall where each row of books stood like British sentries on guard duty and began pulling one out here and one out there. Now the lines were uneven, he thought, and forced a smile.

And now, thanks to Charlie, the place was starting to look normal. But then, what was normal? Did he still have a grasp on reality after all these years? Or was his conception of what should be out of sync, distorted by his wimpish acceptance of a bad situation for the past 18 years? He really didn't know the answer.

As a final touch, he pulled his shirt up and over the top of his belt, loosened his tie, and went into the kitchen for breakfast.

CHAPTER TWO

After Charlie left, Peggy grabbed the dress from her bed and threw it on the floor of her closet. Then, as an afterthought, she lifted the dress by the hanger jutting from the neck and hung it over the bar. Anita would have a pure fit if Peggy left the dress lying there.

Of course Peggy would be in school by the time her mother found the dress in the bottom of the closet, but Anita never forgot a thing! Never! Peggy would be facing the wrath of the damned when she came home. So it was better to hang it up than to have to listen to Anita.

Besides, there was some satisfaction here. Charlie had told her to wear what she wanted, and he'd help her if Anita threw a tantrum. So

Peggy slid into a pair of jeans, sucked in her breath and pulled the zipper up as far as she could. But there was a space between the top of the zipper and her belt line, caused by her being overweight.

But it was no big deal because a long sweat shirt would hide it. No one would be able to see the space where the zipper wouldn't close or the rolls of fat bunched over the waist of her jeans.

Anyway, the fat wasn't going to be permanent. Peggy was starting her diet today and sticking to it this time, even if it meant convincing herself that all sweets were poisonous—especially those soft, little cakes with the cream filling, the ones she'd kill for. As of today she had to keep telling herself they were the worst, poisonous enough to stop your heart within minutes.

Then she laughed and wondered if this trick would work. Would lumping sweets together in the same category as belladonna stop her craving for them? Nothing else had until now.

She heard Dog making noises and turned to find him stretched lazily across her bed, mussing the pink and gold bedspread Anita had bought to match the pink and gold drapes covering the windows. Peggy swallowed hard and tried not to scream.

She wasn't mad at Dog or upset about him lying across the spread. Dog always lay there. Peggy was getting hyper over all this pink Anita kept shoving her way. Hell, shoving pink at

Peggy was like sticking pins under her finger-nails; she simply hated pink!

Dog rolled over to look at Peggy and whined when he sensed her anger. "I'm not mad at you," she said, crossing to her bed to sit next to him. "You see, Dog, Mom has this fetish for pink. She thinks it's a dainty color and wearing it is gonna make me as dainty as Nicole."

Dog cocked his head to one side, trying to understand what Peggy had said. With large, brown eyes, he stared into hers, making Peggy feel warm inside.

"It would take a miracle to make me look like Nicole Martin. You remember her, don't you, Dog? Thin as a rail with a body like a boy . . ."

Dog whined again, unable to grasp the meaning of her words. Peggy smiled and rubbed his head. "I guess you don't remember. We were best friends once, me and Nicole, but that was long ago, long before I met you. Now you're my best friend. The best ever!" Dog jumped up and licked her face. "You understand that much," she said, "and people say dogs are stupid . . ."

A small voice boomed through the air and shattered the mood; Anita was calling her down to breakfast. "We'd better go, or she'll come up here and raise hell with both of us!"

Peggy listened to the whooshing noises her thighs were making as she walked downstairs with Dog by her side. She was nervous because Anita would have a fit over the jeans, but then

Charlie would be there and help. When Anita had her fit, Charlie would hold Anita's hands and make Anita concentrate on the area of her brain causing the disturbance—

"You're not wearing the dress, I see!"

Peggy heard her mother's voice and traced it to the bookcase. Her mother was fixing the books on the shelves, her tiny hands shaking with a desire to line them up evenly. She'd stopped when Peggy had started down the steps.

"Uh, jeans are more comfortable . . ."

"Put the dog outside please. He's getting hair on the rug."

"Sure," Peggy said, keeping her voice light. Only she didn't feel that way inside.

Leading Dog to the backyard, she kept her mind on what Anita wanted her to do and not on Dog, certainly not on his warm, rheumy eyes or the soulful, trusting expression on his face. She couldn't. She was locking him outside.

Reaching for his leash, she turned to look at his face and stiffened her back. He was a dog, she told herself, nothing more. Isn't this what her mother was forever saying? But Anita was wrong, and knowing this made Peggy soften.

"Come on, Dog," she pleaded, bending to rub the top of his head. "Don't do this to me. You're looking at me like it's my fault. Hell, I only live here. I don't make the rules. So, come on."

Dog put his head down and walked blindly up to the leash, knowing he had to stay in the yard until Peggy came home from school. Of course, most people didn't think dogs were smart enough to be depressed over things like forced banishment and the hours they had to wait to be free again. But Peggy knew they were—at least Dog was.

"I'll bring you a treat," she said, trying to lift his spirits. Then she went into the house and tried to ignore Dog's whining, but it wasn't easy. Dog was her best friend, and this wasn't right no matter what the reasoning. Hair on the rug, indeed!

"What'd she say about the jeans?" Charlie wanted to know as soon as Peggy was in the kitchen and about to close the door on Dog.

"She didn't say much."

"Five points for you."

"What's for breakfast, Daddy?" Peggy asked, scanning the kitchen, her eyes coming to rest on bacon lying on a platter in neat rows and eggs on another platter with perfect yolks like eyes staring back at her. "And she wants me to lose weight—a thousand calorie meal."

"What, honey? I didn't hear you."

"Uh, I was just wondering . . . I'm not really hungry. Can I fix something for Dog?" It was the least she could do under the circumstances.

"Go ahead. I'll keep your mother in here until he's finished eating. And Peggy, I did an awful thing a few minutes ago."

"You messed up her magazines and her books."

"Yes. Only I shouldn't have. She's trying to

make a nice home for us." Charlie rose to his feet and poured another cup of coffee while Peggy heaped bacon and eggs into Dog's dish. "She's just so intent on perfection," he said, "but we still love her, don't we?"

I love you more, Peggy wanted to say but didn't. "I'll take this out to Dog, then I gotta catch the bus."

"Sure, babes," he said, leaning to brush her face with his lips. "See ya tonight when I get home."

Nicole "Nicky" Martin had showered and dressed quickly, so quickly she wasn't aware of her makeup or what she wore. She hadn't checked to see if she was picture perfect. There was no time. If her makeup was smudged, then so be it, she thought. Getting the spirit in the ouija board to cooperate was more important than trivial things like eye shadow or the color of her lipstick.

Standing in front of her closet door, Nicky stared at the chair she'd placed under the knob to keep Max—short for Maximilian—inside although in her heart she knew her efforts were useless. Max, the spirit in the ouija board, had already told her a thousand times that he was legion. Max knew all and was capable of accomplishing the impossible. Doors didn't stop him, nor did locks.

And yet, placing the chair under the knob was the only way she could sleep at night or shower in the morning when her eyes were closed and her guard down. In thinking she had control over Max, Nicky was able to function normally, as if nothing were wrong.

But something was wrong. In fact, a lot had gone wrong these past few weeks. Night creatures moved in the shadows of her home, and furniture turned itself upside down in the dark. Max said her house was haunted but promised to protect her from the evil.

Nicky worked at the corners of her mouth with her hands and wondered, not for the first time, if Max had lied to her, if Max himself was the evil tormenting her family—because Max had changed these past few weeks.

When she first began speaking to him through the ouija board, he'd been a caring, concerned individual, always ready to soothe her feelings and help relieve the hurt when someone treated her badly. This was why she kept going back to the board—for consolation.

Now, though, he'd taken a complete turn and was the opposite of the person she'd grown to love. What had happened to him? *What did I do to offend him and make him almost hate me?*

"Open the door, Nicole."

She heard Max speak and was tempted to ignore him. The door between them made her feel safe, but doors didn't stop him. "Max," she said, her voice soft and reverent, "I'm taking the board to school today."

"Why?"

31

"We've already talked about it. I need the extra credit. Please, Max." Nicky stopped pleading with Max long enough to realize he was doing it again—speaking without her help. If the board was on her lap, spread in front of her, she could have understood this. Even if she'd had the pointer, or the planchette as it's sometimes called, in her hands she could have understood this. But the board was still in the closet, stored on a top shelf.

Spirits from ouija boards weren't supposed to speak until summoned.

But then Max had said his powers were strong, that he could accomplish the impossible. Nicky knew he wasn't lying. "Please, Max."

"If you did your homework this wouldn't be necessary."

"I will, Max, from here on in. I promise. I'll do my homework. But you see, I'm failing a course and I need this. It means taking the board—"

"The board is part of my domain."

"Well, then you'd have to come along. But it's just for today, so could you kinda cooperate?"

"Maybe," he said, his words strangely clear and precise considering there was a door between them. "What do I get out of this?"

"Anything you want," she said, knowing it was no good to make bargains with a spirit. At least if he were human, she'd know what to expect when she promised him anything.

"Close your eyes!" he ordered. When she did, she was surrounded by darkness at first. "Concentrate," he said, "Concentrate and see me."

Nicky saw movement in the shadows of her mind. Then she saw a man move out of the shadows and draw close to her, for suddenly she was there inside of her brain, standing before him. Looking up at him she saw that he was tall and good-looking, with broad shoulders and a slim waist. "Love me, Nicole," he said, but she couldn't; she was afraid. If this was Max he was all-powerful, and the power disturbed her.

"How did you do this, Max? How can you be here inside of my head?"

"I can be anything I desire," he said, his eyes hot coals of passion on her body and face. "I can be a spirit in ethereal form or a man of flesh and blood, or I can be a passing thought in your mind—"

"But how? And you brought me with you. It seems so impossible."

"For someone ordinary perhaps, but I'm not ordinary. I control your senses, your ability to think, to feel, to see. If it's more comfortable for you, I'll materialize in your bedroom in the flesh instead of in your thoughts. Or maybe you'd like to see me as I really am, without the pretense."

"No," she said. It didn't matter where he was or in what form, Max was the spirit in the board and Max was in control because she'd long ago succumbed to the pleasures of the board. She'd long ago traded her soul along with peace of mind for answers to forbidden questions. She was helpless, and both she and Max knew it.

"You said you'd do anything," he reminded her, letting Nicky know that she was trapped in a web of her own doing. She'd tried to use Max and the ouija board for gain, in this case extra points in school, and now Max was using her. "Love me, Nicole," he repeated, his voice husky and low.

Reaching through the mist of her daydream, she stood on her toes and placed one hand around the back of his head, gently pulling him forward until his lips mingled with hers. Somehow Nicky knew this was the anything she'd promised to do for Max, and it didn't surprise her one bit. Nicky was a victim of her own sexuality, of the wanton desires men saw in her eyes.

Hank Brudhle had been using her this same way for months now. Hank was a football jock, and Nicky's main squeeze, which meant nothing because Hank was after one thing like all the others. The faces changed and the bodies changed, but the intentions never did.

Max was rough at first. He pressed his mouth down on Nicky's with such force he heard her moan in pain. Then he gradually let up until his lips were like a soft wind, and she knew he was giving in. He was letting Nicky have her way.

"Yes, I am giving in," he said when the kiss had ended and they were standing apart. "But I warn you, Nicole. No tricks. Understand? Or things will go very badly for you."

"I understand. I'll behave. You'll see."

"Don't mention my name. And don't dare tell anyone about my role as the spirit in the board."

"I won't, Max, I promise."

"And don't let the board out of your sight," he said. Then he left as Nicky sensed he would, leaving her alone in the dark abyss of her brain until she was able to shake herself free and come back to her bedroom, to the warm glow of the overhead light and the sun streaming through her bedroom window. Somehow the light made her feel safe.

CHAPTER THREE

Max left Nicole's side and returned to the board. He knew she was afraid, and that was important. Max thrived on fear and used it to control the spirited ones like Nicole.

Going deeper into a chasm of darkness, into a world beneath the surface of the board, Max walked upright because he was still in the guise of a man, something pleasing to a female like the one he'd left behind. Max had purposely made himself tall, broad-shouldered and slim-waisted because Nicole was a hot bitch who needed someone superficial, yet good-looking, to keep her satisfied.

But now as he approached his living quarters, he felt scales popping through his flesh, felt bulbous, festering lumps return in clusters, and knew he was normal again. At least he was normal for the world he dominated, a world that dwelled in the dream states and nightmares of those who walked in the sunlight, of those who would communicate with spirits of the dead.

He was about ten feet from the entrance to the Cave of the Marquis of Death—his cave—and breathed deeply, inhaling the sweet aroma of rotten meat. It was flesh that had once covered the bodies of souls whose time had run out, souls who couldn't be forgotten by those that had been left behind.

And because the living couldn't let go, Max provided a much needed service. He joined the living and the dead in conversational communion through his board.

Sniffing the air again because the familiar odor of the dead flesh warmed him, he listened and heard their anguished cries. He heard the dead pleading for rest and peace, and he laughed. None of these trapped souls were happy with their lot. None of them were exhilarated because Max had summoned them from eternal rest to speak to the living through his ouija board.

They weren't happy because now they were trapped here in Max's world of darkness for all time to come, guarded by Max's pets from the tunnels of Acheron, trapped by the unreasonable demands of the living to just speak to so-and-so one more time to know that he or she was all right.

Max started into his cave when a mound of unrecognizable skin moved and clutched at his leg. "Master," it said through quivering lips dotted with blackened spittle, "will we have this Nicole Martin now? Will you kill her? My outer crust grows old and rotten."

"Maybe," Max said, stooping to run a caressing claw across the crest of the mound. "But only her mind for now. Her body will remain among the living."

"Why, master?" the mound asked and quivered again. "The point of the game is to gather bodies through the board, is it not? We need her flesh. Why let her live?"

Max saw exposed nerves hugging the ground near its base and knew his pet was in pain. It needed new flesh to cover these raw areas. "Because I'm not finished with her yet. Nicole is basically selfish and cruel. I want to know what it takes to drive someone like her over the edge."

Despite his pain, the creature smiled. "You mean insanity."

"Yes. Someone like Nicole is great sport. Meanwhile, I have an abundance of skin inside. Take what you need."

"Only Nicole's will do," the creature answered, slithering back to the moors surrounding the cave. "She's young and firm. Hers is choice."

"As you wish."

Thus said, Max entered his cave and gloried at the sight of flesh hanging from the ceiling like moss and blood covering the walls like slime. This was his world, the ultimate to a creature such as Max, one who fed on the misery and sorrow of human emotions. This was his home.

"Master."

Max heard a voice that sounded like sandpaper being rubbed against his eardrums and knew it belonged to a nobleman, the Marquis de Sade, who had walked in the world of sunlight from 1740 to 1814, when Death summoned him here to Max's cave.

At the time of his arrival, De Sade, because of his psychotic behavior and lack of conscience, became an entitled disciple of the prince of darkness. De Sade was granted special favors and given the tools to carry on with his work in death as he had when alive.

Max watched him work on a victim tied to a gurney and could not respond when De Sade spoke to him. The man had long ago ascended beyond mere torture. Moving closer to the victim, Max heard deep moaning noises coming from fleshless lips, saw a disembowled, gutted body and wished he had the same talents as De Sade.

"Master," De Sade repeated softly, the flesh of his own body hanging in loose folds, his nobleman's clothing torn and tattered.

"Yes," Max said, not taking his eyes from the victim. "What is it?"

"When might I begin my training as a spirit in the board?"

"Soon," Max said. "But first, be patient and observe for now. When the time comes I will send you in my place."

"And Master," De Sade said, "before I forget, three fools were gathered around the board, summoning the ouija spirit. I knew you were busy with the Nicole Martin so I asked Prince Balberith to go in your place. He's had experience."

"Good choice," Max said, knowing Balberith was the demon prince of suicide. Balberith would talk those three into slitting their wrists or cutting their throats. Then Max could petition the Black Master for their bodies. "Wonderful choice, De Sade. You're learning."

Peggy's home was at the beginning of the school bus route, making her the first one on and the last one off. Today she rode from Anderson to Green to Collier before she allowed herself to acknowledge the other students. Sitting alone, she piled her books on the seat next to her and tried not to think about her classmates, the ones standing in back.

Every seat on the bus was taken except for the one next to Peggy.

She listened to a cacophony of noise and

wished she were a part of the crowd. The noise exploded into a deafening roar when the bus came to a sudden stop a few blocks from school.

Amid shouts of "Hey, Nicky, up here," and "Yo, Nicole!" Peggy stared up front, then turned her head when Nicky Martin got on and started up the aisle in her direction. There was a large, flat box in Nicky's hands, like a game of some sort. Nicky stopped next to the only empty seat on the bus, then continued walking towards the rear.

Nicky was everything Peggy wasn't. She was blonde and beautiful, with clear, creamy skin and the body of a young model. She was Nicole to some, and Nicky to others; she wasn't a Margaret or Peggy. Even her name was exciting.

Peggy bit her lower lip then and fought the images in her mind—two little girls in frilly dresses with bows in their hair. One was blonde and pretty, even then. The other was plain. Peggy prayed for the illusion to end there, but it wouldn't. Every time she saw the blonde and beautiful Nicky Martin, the play continued in her mind for three acts.

She saw two little girls sitting close, up to their elbows in finger paint. Nicky had drawn a house, and now it was up to Peggy to fill in the rest. Peggy drew the sky, all light blue and full of clouds, then the grass in front of the house that stretched up to meet the sky. Peggy covered it all because Nicky wanted no bare spots in their picture.

Then, when Peggy was finished with the grass and the sky, Nicky applied the final touch and put in the flowers, buttercups as Peggy now recalled.

They were classmates in kindergarten, though soul mates was a better description of their relationship. Some even imagined they were sisters because they seemed so inseparable.

Oh, but the memories were wonderful. The first act of Peggy's play was wonderful. Act Two should have been better. Peggy and Nicky should have been inseparable even now; double-dating, sharing secrets in their diaries, talking girl talk. But life never went as planned, and so the play was marred with sadness.

Around the middle of Act Two, a tragedy occurred and things went awry. One of the little girls had been born with a crack in her almost perfect being. There was damage in her brain, a kind of damage that made her do shameful things involuntarily.

She heard music at times and danced like a drunk. Other times she closed her eyes and hummed or screamed obscenities. When things really got bad, when her seizures went into full gear, she sometimes rolled on the floor and messed her pants. It was an awful secret for a child to harbor, and yet Peggy handled it as best she could. She took her medicine, cooperated with her doctor and hid her imperfection from the kids in school.

But it didn't help because as she got older, the

wedge in the crack in her brain grew until hiding it became impossible. And one day she had a seizure in class in front of Nicky.

Of course Peggy had no way of remembering what happened during her blackouts. Whenever her seizures took over, an aura of light generally flashed in front of her and her brain would travel to another dimension. She never knew the shameful things she did until some either well-meaning or outwardly cruel person recounted the facts, leaving nothing out.

Peggy, it seemed, had been sitting on the floor playing jacks with Nicky when the aura flashed in front of her. "Oh, no!" Peggy screamed, went stiff as a board and passed out. When she came to she was in the nurse's office and smelled terrible. She'd messed her pants.

Nicky never spoke to her again.

"It's a ouija board!" Nicky shouted, bringing Peggy out of her trance.

"A ouija board!" one of her friends shouted in return. "You believe in that crap?"

"I don't care to comment. All I know is Ches Quigley's doing this 'Fantasy of the Mind' bit in science class, and I'm looking for extra points."

"Hey, Nicky, you don't have to do this for extra points. All you gotta do is what comes naturally and Quigley'll give you all the points you want."

"Listen, dummy, this is exactly what Quigley has in mind."

"For a fantasy game? Come on, Nicole!"

"Really," Nicky said. "You fantasize with a

ouija board by asking it questions, you know, about things coming up in your future—"

"And it answers you?"

"Yes. It's like having someone to talk to when you're alone. I'm not ashamed to say I believe it really works. Besides, I have proof!"

Peggy listened to the ongoing conversation behind her for a while, wishing she were a part of it, then turned her attention back to the window and the road taking her to school.

A ouija board, she thought. It's a game, but it makes you feel like someone is talking to you when you're alone. Isn't that what Nicky had just said? Nicky was losing her grip!

CHAPTER FOUR

"Daydreams are uncontrolled, unconnected images concocted in the minds of fools. They have no purpose or direction and are often forgotten in an instant," Chester Quigley was saying.

Peggy was in her usual seat in science class in the back of the room near the window, fighting the urge to daydream no matter what Quigley thought.

"Now," Quigley said, going on, "fantasies of the mind are a different story altogether. Fantasies are controlled, conscious images, like pages from a script written in our minds, just the opposite of daydreams."

So what, Peggy thought, wondering under

which heading Quigley would stick seizures if given the chance. While they were uncontrolled and involuntary, they could hardly be termed daydreams. They were real, they were a part of life, and life was painful.

"Daydreams cannot be shared. With no purpose and no direction, there is little content to them, and certainly nothing that would make sense to anyone other than yourself. Fantasies, however, are more formalized. They flow in story form. They're scripted versions of your inner thoughts and feelings. More emotion is expounded in fantasies, and fantasies are something you *can* share with others."

Suddenly taking more interest, Peggy went back over his words and saw the truth in them. She shared her fantasies with Dog. She had directed fantasies in which she was as normal as anyone else, part of the crowd, not an untouchable outsider. For once Quigley made sense, speaking on a topic close to home.

"Another thing I want you to understand is this. Actually there are two more items to add. One, without fantasies of the mind, our imaginations are stifled. It's like sleeping for a year without dreaming. Your mind rebels and stops delivering. Your creative processes are destroyed.

"Now, the second item I want to stress is without fantasies and creativity in your soul, communication is cut off. Conversation becomes a difficult process; you cannot follow a line of thought. Your mind stagnates and becomes inactive."

Following the lecture was becoming harder. Abstract thoughts often escaped her entirely, but she tried. She zeroed in on Quigley's handsome, young face and his British accent, and felt in doing so she could somehow dip into his brain and absorb the meaning behind his words.

Concentrating wasn't easy, though, because there were eyes watching her, eyes with no expression behind them. In fact, it was hard to figure out anything when Derek, a classmate, stared the way he was staring now. Derek was quiet, withdrawn and an outsider like Peggy. Only Derek didn't seem to care; this was the part of his personality that disturbed her most.

Not caring made him a weirdo in Peggy's opinion. Not caring set him aside and made him detestable. Did he think he was so superior that the torment and cruelty dished out on a daily basis were beneath him? What was his problem?

Turning to face him down, Peggy saw the dark hair, the cold blue eyes, the hardened jaw, and felt her heart lurch. Either she was afraid of him, or she was stuck on him. And right now it was hard to sort out her own emotions, let alone try and figure out his when he stared as he was doing now. She decided to ignore him.

"Step one of my Fantasy of the Mind experiments involves fantasizing on your own, then sharing with the class. I want controlled illusions—and I don't mean anything pornographic—"

Quigley stopped lecturing when a cacophony of catcalls rose around him, lingered and died. Then he continued on. "I'm trying to instill a new dimension to your already limited minds, and thereby awaken your creative processes. Once this is accomplished, we move to phase two—a dual sharing of fantasies—then finally, group sharing. Nicole, you said there was something you wanted to show us?"

A ouija board, Peggy thought, a stinking, dumb, old ouija board. Nicky was sure to earn extra points. Peggy wished she'd had the courage to do something similar. Ignoring Derek and his stare, Peggy turned her full attention on Nicky and the ouija board.

"I brought a game in, Mr. Quigley," Nicky Martin said and sauntered to the front of the class with game in hand, her boyish figure looking seductive in a pair of tight jeans and a snug sweater. She tried to talk then, to make her voice project over another chorus of catcalls and lewd remarks, but it was impossible.

"Quiet!" Quigley shouted. Once he had control he motioned for Nicky to start.

"This is called a ouija board, and it's a form of fantasy—"

"Yeah, sure," one of the students shouted. "And it answers questions. And it talks to you!"

"Shut up!" Quigley shouted, bringing order to the class so that Nicky could go on with her demonstration.

"This is usually played by two or more people—"

"Supposen you're alone?" someone asked, followed by laughter.

Peggy saw that she wasn't the only one who was picked on, only it was different with Nicky; this was good-natured kidding. Besides, Nicky was a survivor. She could discount these jerks where Peggy never could.

"Well, if you're alone, you wing it! Anyway, you put the pointer—"

"What's a pointer?"

"This little plastic thing," she said, holding up a white, triangular shaped object with a hole near one tip. "It's on ball bearings, so it moves easily. Now, the board that goes with the game has things written on it. In the upper left corner it has, 'yes,' and in the upper right corner it has 'no,' with 'good-bye' written at the bottom.

"In between the three words you see the letters of the alphabet. You and someone else sit holding your fingertips on the pointer. Then you ask a question, and the pointer moves around supplying the answer. Sometimes it goes to 'yes' or 'no,' and sometimes it spells out the answer by using the alphabet."

"What happens if you can't spell?" someone asked.

"Then you're out of luck," Quigley said while the students laughed.

"Nicole," he said, turning to smile down on her, "thank you for bringing in the ouija board. This is a wonderful demonstration of controlled fantasies."

"How so?" Derek asked dryly, his voice a shaft of cold air.

Quigley didn't answer at first. He just stood and stared contemptuously at Derek. When he answered, his words were clipped and short. "Because you ask predetermined questions. Nothing spontaneous. This makes it a controlled experiment!"

"Are we gonna do this in class? Ask it questions?" one of the students wanted to know.

"Hey, yeah, teach, let's do it!" another student shouted.

Quigley frowned and looked at his watch. "We only have a few minutes before I start pairing you off for Fantasies of the Mind . . . but I guess so."

While some of the students cheered and whistled Nicky sat the box down on Quigley's desk and lifted the lid. Her hands were trembling, and she almost seemed reluctant to go on with this. But then she turned and saw Quigley write ten points next to her name on the blackboard and smiled.

"Okay," Nicky said, her voice filled with the excitement of an extra ten points towards her grade, "to begin with, my spirit said to call him Max."

"Short for Maximilian, no doubt," Derek said dryly.

"Yeah. Anyway, I'll take one end of the pointer and . . . uh . . . Mr. Quigley, you hold onto the other."

It was Quigley's turn to be reluctant. He wasn't nervous like Nicky; he merely looked bored. Mr. Quigley, obviously, didn't believe in ouija boards.

"It's a controlled experiment," Derek reminded him, forcing Quigley to go through the motions with Nicky who was poised and ready with the tips of her fingers on the pointer.

"Here goes," Nicky said nervously. "Mr. Quigley, do you wanna ask a question?"

Quigley stared at Nicky and smiled. "Yes, as a matter of fact I do. Max, tell me, will my class succeed with the Fantasies of the Mind experiment or will I end up failing the whole lot of them?"

Half the students groaned in mock agony while others got to their feet and surrounded Quigley and Nicky. When the pointer didn't move at first, Peggy heard the kids complaining. But after a few minutes it moved with such swiftness that most said it was Nicky moving her hands and not Max, the spirit, answering Quigley's question.

"N . . . I . . . C . . . O . . . L . . . E . . . Nicole,"

Quigley said, trying to hide his boredom. "Max wants to speak to you, kiddo. He's not responding to my question."

"Max, answer Mr. Quigley," Nicky said in too soft a voice. She seemed scared again. "Please, Max."

But the board spelled her name again and again until Quigley gave up and removed his hands. Nicky started to do the same, but the board held her captive when the pointer began to spin in a frenzy as if its actions were controlled by some mysterious force. "I warned you, Nicole. I warned you not to play games," Derek said, reading the ouija's words out loud.

"I'm not," Nicky answered, most of her self-control gone. "I'm trying for extra points. You said you'd cooperate."

"And you said no tricks!"

"Max, please—"

"You gave them my name. You told them all about me!"

"But, Max—"

"I told you it would go very badly for you, Nicole. Did you think I was kidding?"

"Max!" Nicky said, her voice rising, shattering the shocked stillness of her classmates. Nicky was cool. This pleading just wasn't like her.

"Uh, Nicole . . ." Quigley began, then cleared his throat. "Why don't we stop for now? We can do this another time. Meanwhile, I'm adding an extra five points to your grade for your effort."

This seemed to please Nicky. Half-smiling she

packed up the board and returned to her seat while keeping her attention directed on an invisible spot on her desk. Peggy realized at that point that Nicky was purposely staring straight ahead to avoid eye contact with her so-called friends. She'd lost her cool with Max, and she felt foolish. Seeing it reflected in their faces would have made Nicky feel worse than she already did.

"All right, class," Quigley said, checking his watch again, "We have just enough time to choose partners for the dual part of our Fantasies of the Mind experiment. We'll begin with the students in the back of the room. Peggy Rearden. Who wants to be partners with Peggy?"

Peggy slid down in her seat and tried to make herself invisible. This was the part where this game called life usually became a nightmare.

"That thing!"

"Hell, no!"

"She has enough fantasies of her own. She takes all them drugs."

"Yeah. She don't need a partner. She's a team all by herself—"

"I'll do it!"

Peggy heard the voice and realized it belonged to Derek. She didn't know whether to be happy or depressed.

"Okay!" someone shouted. "Peggy and Derek. What a fantasy!"

"That's enough!" Quigley shouted, fighting for control again. He glared at the students until the room became silent. "The rest of you can wait until tomorrow for your partners. I'll do the choosing—and I hope you don't like it! Class dismissed!"

Nicky Martin grabbed her books, the ouija board, and her purse, and ran to her next-period gym class before her friends could stop her. Nicky wanted to get to the locker rooms and change into shorts and sneakers before anyone had a chance to question her about the board and why she had hypered out in class.

If she stopped to explain, then she'd have to go into detail about Max, and she'd said too much already.

The locker room was cool and damp when she entered. Snapping on the overhead light, she rushed to her locker and began to spin the tumbler on the combination lock. But the tumbler jammed, making her hands perspire even more than that awful scene in science class. God, what would she tell her friends about the ouija board and why she got so damned nervous? Certainly not the truth.

Leaning her head against the cool metal of the locker to steady her nerves, Nicky sucked in her breath and tried the lock again. When the tumbler spun loose, she cursed herself for jamming it to begin with, then entered her combination, the one she knew by heart. It was two left, sixteen right, and . . . ?

Damnit, she'd forgotten the last number. But

hell, it wasn't her fault. She was so damned scared of what Max might do. He'd warned her about mentioning his name and his role as spirit in the board earlier this morning, and here she went and did it anyway.

Starting at the beginning again, she entered two left and then sixteen right, but still couldn't remember the final number. She decided to go look for Karen Landis, her gym teacher, who had the combinations to everyone's locks.

But as she turned to leave, the locker popped open by itself, causing her to mumble "Thank God." Then she threw in her books, her purse and the ouija board and grabbed her shorts and sneakers. Nicky wanted to be out of here and in the gym itself by the time her friends arrived for class. There was no talking in gym, which meant she didn't have to go into any explanations about the board, at least not until the following period or the next—if only she could keep one step ahead of her friends.

After taking off her shoes, Nicky slid out of her jeans and gasped when something heavy made a loud metallic noise in the row behind her. Nicky thought she was alone but must have been wrong. That kind of a noise didn't happen by itself. One of the other girls might have come in when she wasn't paying attention. She waited for a moment and slid into her shorts when she heard no further disturbances.

When the heavy banging resounded in the air again, still behind her but closer this time, Nicky picked up her sneakers and closed her locker. She wasn't the least bit curious about the noise, she told herself, and wanted nothing more than to start her workout in gym. But the banging came again, this time from only a few feet away.

Staring in horrified silence, Nicky watched a nearby locker open and slam so hard she feared it would break off the hinges. The only problem was, she was still alone. Nobody had opened it or closed it. Then she began to back away when the locker next to hers did the same, the loud banging resounding so loudly it hurt her ears. She had to get out of there and fast!

Turning with her sneakers still in her hand, she quickly rushed towards the exit but tripped over the wooden bench running parallel to the lockers and fell as the lockers in front of her all opened and closed in such rapid succession that it was frightening.

Then she tried to get to her feet but couldn't. For some reason her legs refused to listen when she told them to move. Crouched behind the bench, as she watched and listened to the lockers booming and slamming, she wondered why no one had come in. The noise was incredible. It should have drawn someone's attention.

With the lockers still slamming all around her, Nicky's heart thumped heavily when something touched her back, the flesh pressing against hers too cold and clammy to be human.

Dropping her sneakers, Nicky grabbed the

bench and tried to pull herself to her feet. Suddenly she felt two rough hands tugging on her shirt. Turning, she saw no one there, only arms reaching to grab her from a swirling mist.

Pulling away from the arms, she slid backwards along the floor in the direction of her locker. But the arms were faster, grabbing her around the waist before she could get away. With two hands firmly holding her Nicky saw herself rising off the ground, her feet dangling in midair until they were swinging high above the benches. Then she felt herself being slammed against one locker after another until she was finally hurled against a bathroom door at the far end of the room.

When she landed against the door in a heap, Nicky felt the breath being forced from her lungs and her ribs aching in her chest. She felt she must be dreaming. This couldn't be happening. Then she tried to get up and turn the knob on the bathroom door when the mist swirled towards her with frightening ferocity.

"Max," she screamed. "Is it you?" This could be him coming to seek revenge against Nicky for not following orders. "Max—" she screamed again, but the words caught in her throat when the arms hauled her overhead again and flung her thin, boyish body in the opposite direction.

When she landed on top of the lockers this time, she felt a deeper pain in her ribs, felt her wrist snap like a rubber band, and prayed that Max was satisfied, that his anger had subsided.

"Max," she pleaded, "please don't hurt me anymore. Please, Max . . ." The white mist swirled around her again, but the arms didn't reach out and grab her this time. Lying still, wondering how badly she was hurt, she waited for Max to speak, to tell her that it was over, but his voice never came, only the darkness as she closed her eyes and thankfully passed out.

Peggy sat in science class until the room was almost emptied before she got up to leave. Derek was close behind her, but she ignored him and walked slowly towards the gym. She also ignored the sound of his voice when he whispered her name and told her he wanted to speak to her.

Why did Derek pick this moment to speak to her when he never spoke to anyone? Derek was the habitual loner who kept to himself and drew energy from the silence around him. He was a strange boy.

Suddenly catching up, Derek stepped in front of her and blocked her path. "Didn't you hear me calling you?" he asked, his eyes riveted to hers.

Peggy sensed the emotional disturbance others had spoken about and felt herself go weak. "No . . . I didn't." He was a head taller, with broad shoulders and muscular arms. Peggy had never gotten this close before, and it was as if she'd never really looked at him.

"I realize we do our own thing to start with,"

he said. "You do your fantasy and I'll do mine."

"Right."

"But we'll have to get together for the partner end of it."

"Sure. In the cafeteria." A crowded place, she thought, somewhere safe.

"Whatever."

She started to walk around him then because in her mind the conversation was finished, but Derek grabbed her wrist though not roughly. There was a gentleness in his touch that amazed her. She looked up at his face and waited for him to explain why he was practically holding her prisoner, yet Derek's attention was locked in on the few students still walking the halls.

Then he shook his head. "I wanted to talk to you alone. Maybe it's quieter by the gym. Come on, I'll walk you there," he said, leaving Peggy to wonder how he knew her schedule.

"You don't need to walk me," she said, hoping he wouldn't get angry.

"Fine," he said gently, but with an awful coldness in his voice. "But before you go . . . You're a lonely person, Peggy—"

"Hey, now that's enough! Who the hell do you think you are? Dragging me—"

"—and you're impressionable."

"Let go of me!"

"I don't want you getting any ideas about the ouija board that Nicky brought in."

"What!"

"I saw your face, Peggy. You were absolutely

fascinated by it. Sometimes a fascination like yours can be dangerous. There are things in this world better left alone, and a ouija board is one of them.''

Then he was gone. He dropped her wrist and walked away, leaving Peggy wondering about their strange conversation. She was not fascinated by the ouija board. No matter what he said, Derek was wrong. Besides, even if she was, how could he tell?

Leaning against the nearest cool, tile wall to steady her nerves, Peggy suddenly thought about her mother, the cold-hearted bitch who had once possessed such marvelously warm and comforting arms. Peggy had suffered through one terrible day so far, and at the moment she longed for Anita's arms to hold her and erase the hurt.

Then she stiffened and dismissed all her memories. The arms she remembered belonged to another woman, the mother she used to have, the one who bore no resemblance to this creature living in her house claiming to be Anita Rearden.

Of course she looked like Anita and spoke like her, but it couldn't be the same person. Anita loved her once, and this woman didn't; that was for damned sure!

Gym class meant sitting on a mat or reading a book for Peggy. Epileptics weren't allowed to compete in Philmore High. Archaic in their thinking, the coaches here equated heavy physical activity with seizures, and Miss Landis, Peggy's coach, was no exception.

Peggy did argue hotly in the beginning, when Miss Landis first told her to sit on a mat and sleep or read.

"Doctors today believe that heavy exercise is good for epileptics," Peggy pointed out. "Exercise supplies oxygen to the brain, so it helps. We can jog, take aerobics, run, swim, even take up karate. Plus, athletes with epilepsy often win big in competitions."

"Good for them," Miss Landis had said. "I'd rather you sat there and left me alone, kid, because if you start shaking and rolling, I'm running."

Later on, after class, Miss Landis called Peggy to her office to apologize. "I'm a dumb shit," she told a shocked Peggy. "Sometimes my mouth runs ahead of my brain." Then, the very next day, she set the gym class straight, telling the girls how wrong she'd been to mock Peggy and how the kids were wrong to have laughed.

God, Peggy thought now, adults sure were complicated people. First they said one thing, then they changed their minds and—

"You okay, Peggy?"

Peggy looked up from her book, her mind still fuzzy from her reverie, to find Miss Landis standing over her.

"Uh . . . Yeah, I'm okay."

Miss Landis bent down to speak to Peggy in

hushed tones, their eyes level, their voices muted by the noise around them. "I thought you were . . . Well, it looked like you were having a small one. What d'ya call them things? Uh . . . *Petit mal*? Yes, a *petit mal*. You looked like you were having one of them." Miss Landis sounded worried.

"No, I was just thinking about something—sort of daydreaming."

"About Derek?" Miss Landis asked, a grin on her face. Peggy thought she was being made fun of until she realized the grin was warm and sincere. "He's one good-looking guy."

"We're just friends," Peggy answered, wondering when Miss Landis had seen her with Derek. Was it in the hall moments ago when Derek had warned her about the dangers of the ouija board? "Honestly, there's no love between us."

"Really? From the way he was looking down at you, I figured the relationship went deeper. Anyway, I'd set my sights on him if I were you."

"Why?" Didn't she know he was an outcast? Then again, maybe she did and felt Peggy and Derek were well-matched. "Why would I wanna make it with Derek?"

"Between you and me, kid," she said, leaning closer to Peggy, "teachers aren't supposed to talk this way, but Derek is more than good-looking. He's about the best I've seen in a long time—in this school and out of it. And he's got some body! Gym teachers are big on good bodies. Plus, he's intelligent. You could do worse, you know."

Miss Landis placed a warm, caring hand on her shoulder. "Think about what I've said. You're at the age where boys are important. Might as well pick one who's sensitive, not like the other clods around here." After that she got up and walked away.

Peggy could feel herself blush. She'd never thought of Derek as handsome or as having a good body as Miss Landis said he did. Whenever he was around, the only thing crossing Peggy's mind was the nearest escape route.

What had Miss Landis seen in the hall outside that Peggy hadn't? How did Derek look at her? What was the expression Miss Landis had mistaken for love? God, Peggy was so confused.

Even more confusing was Miss Landis' suggestion that Peggy make a play for Derek. Easy for you to say, she thought. Sure, she could make a play, if she looked more like her mother than her father, if she had Anita's tiny body and perfectly wonderful ash blonde hair.

Or even if she resembled the beautiful Nicole Martin, she could make a play for Derek. How two little girls who'd began life at the same point in time could have ended up complete opposites was beyond Peggy.

Bored with thinking about Derek and the impossibility of his ever asking her out—despite what Miss Landis thought—Peggy scanned the gym and felt her heart wrench with disgust.

The gym was well-equipped, large and spacious, filled with the latest equipment. There were Nautilus and Universal weight machines. There were free weights for body building. Plus there were parallel bars and other equipment for the serious gymnast.

This place was like gold for someone with a heavy, bulging body, and yet here Peggy sat like a shapeless lump, watching the other girls who were already rail thin working hard to stay that way. There was no justice in this world, none at all.

Getting to her feet, Peggy walked to the end of the gym and went through a heavy, metal door leading to the locker rooms. In her frustration over Derek and his nonsense about the ouija board, she'd forgotten her books. Peggy generally used gym class to get some homework done.

Walking through a narrow hallway, Peggy passed a doorway leading to the boys' locker room and turned left towards hers. The hallway was cool and damp, as usual, and Peggy was fine at first. But somewhere along the way she began to feel a strange fluttering sensation in her stomach, the kind of fluttering she generally got when she was alone but had the feeling she wasn't. She could almost sense someone watching.

Looking back over her shoulder, she noticed the opened door to the boys' locker room and realized with an uneasiness that it had been closed when she passed it moments ago. When she saw someone duck to one side of the opened door, she thought about calling Miss Landis. Her own locker room about five feet ahead of her was empty; there'd be no one there if she needed help. And right now Peggy needed someone.

There was no further movement, giving her the courage to make a run for the locker room ahead. If she could get there first, she could lock herself in until gym was over. Of course she was acting hysterical, running because a door that had been closed was now open, and because someone had been watching her. But still, considering the past problems she'd had with some of the other students, it didn't pay to be careless and ignore the butterflies in her stomach.

Reaching the girls' locker room, she rushed inside and forced the heavy metal door closed, locking it behind her. But she could still see the hall outside from the small window in the door. If someone came here now and put their face up against that window, Peggy knew she'd die. The only solution was to sit on the other side of the room out of view or hide in the girls' bathroom. But first, her books . . .

Rushing to her locker, she spun the tumbler on the combination lock and almost fainted when a breeze came out of nowhere and swirled around her legs. Not like an ordinary breeze, something light and airy, it was more like a heavy substance. It was solid and firm. As her body trembled, Peggy laid her head against the metal locker, closed her eyes and concentrated on the aura forming in her mind. She'd been pushed to the limit with her fears, and now she was about to have a seizure.

But the breeze was ignorant of her physical condition and so it continued to swirl, rising higher and suddenly washing her face in its fury. Opening her eyes, she saw a kaleidoscope of colors surrounding a white mist and knew this wasn't natural. She didn't know why, but something in its midst terrified her half to death.

A creature with strong arms and a hood over his head was carrying an axe!

Oh, God. Oh, Daddy, help me, Peggy screamed inside, forcing her legs to move, forcing her body to back towards the door as she watched the mist follow. Once or twice she tripped over the wooden bench running parallel to the lockers and lost her balance, her body striking metal, backing off, striking metal again. She felt a hand touching the back of her head and tried to concentrate on the aura still forming in her skull. But she couldn't because the swirling mist was getting closer, and now someone's hand was across the back of her head, forcing her to either turn and look or stay where she was.

The hand surely belonged to the person who'd followed her here, who'd chased her the length of the hall, who'd somehow tripped the lock on the door and had gotten in here. She was trapped!

As the breeze caught up with her and began to

swirl up and around her body again, Peggy knew her only alternative was to turn and face the person with the hand behind her. If she got past him, she'd be out the door and on her way to freedom in no time. Sucking in her breath, she turned and saw that the hand belonged to a body that was up on top of the lockers, someone hiding up there ready to pounce on her at any moment. Slapping the hand aside, she ran for the door and saw Derek peering through the window. Derek looked hysterical. He was shouting at her to open the door and let him in.

Knowing he was the one who'd stalked her in the hall outside and that she was afraid of him, Peggy decided to take her chances in the locker room. Turning back, Peggy sunk to her knees in fright when a body dropped from the locker above her.

It was nothing threatening, nobody scary. It was just Nicole Martin and Nicole was unconscious!

"Oh, God, Daddy, help me! Mommy, please hold me."

CHAPTER FIVE

Anita Rearden thought about the scene she'd encountered in Peggy's bathroom this morning —father and daughter locked in a loving embrace. Then she thought about her own frigidity and hated herself for the ideas that came to mind.

Charlie was helping Peggy through a seizure. Period! There was nothing sexual about it, but he had his arms around her while she was wearing nothing more than a terry cloth robe. And Peggy was sixteen now, in full bloom.

Clutching her polishing cloth with more fervor than before, she scrubbed the toaster on the kitchen counter until the entire room reflected off of its surface. But somehow, even when the sun wedged in through the window behind her and hit the toaster, bouncing off in the form of tiny star bursts, she wasn't satisfied.

It still looked dirty and marred; it wasn't clean enough.

She gazed around the kitchen at each and every item she'd just finished cleaning and decided to start all over. She'd start with the floors, remop them and rewax them, then scrub down the Formica around the sink, and when she was through, she'd redo the bathrooms upstairs, then the half-bath down here.

Pushing a lock of ash blonde hair away from her face, she felt her dark eyes burning with indignation. Germs were growing here in her house, germs that could endanger her life and the lives of her family. She had to get rid of them.

At one time Anita had seen something about germs on one of those scientific shows on television—*Nova* maybe. There was a common, household germ growing in a Petrie dish. Someone took a sample, placed it on a glass slide and showed the viewing audience what it looked like through the lens of a microscope.

She shuddered, even now, when she recalled the sight of a moving, shifting, hairy, little thing that was alive and lived in most homes. But not hers, she vowed! She'd wipe the bastards out every chance she got. She'd destroy their nests and leave them no dirt to feed on.

In fact, her clothes were full of germs now. Her shorts and her pullover, her usual cleaning gear, were dirty from cleaning the house, and there had to be germs growing on the fabric. Anita would have to shower and change before she cleaned the house again.

Looking back at the toaster, at a spot she'd missed, she rubbed the damned thing with a vengeance.

"You're wearing holes in the metal," Charlie said, his voice coming from the doorway behind her. She hadn't heard him come in.

"What . . . ?" she began, then decided to let it drop. Her cleanliness wasn't appreciated by Charlie or Peggy, not as it should have been. "You're home early."

"Just closed on a nice, fat contract this morning. Thought I'd give myself the rest of the day off," he said, pulling a pack of cigarettes from the pocket of his jacket.

"Charlie! Have you forgotten?"

"For a minute there I did," he said, shoving the cigarettes back where they were. "I'll grab a smoke in the yard later."

Charlie had placed a package on the nearest counter when she hadn't been paying attention, when her mind had been on those germs and cleaning the house, but now it piqued her interest. Charlie never bought anything without consulting her first. "What is it?" she asked.

"A jogging suit."

"A what?"

"You know . . . for jogging."

"Can't spend your money fast enough, can you?"

"Anita, I'm trying to stay in shape." He was talking to deaf ears by this time. She'd turned her back on him to scrub the toaster again. "My hairline's receding—"

"And this will help you grow hair?"

"No, but it'll make me feel a lot better. I've got this pot belly, or haven't you noticed?"

Anita shook her head. She'd noticed, although she hadn't said much. Now he was taking up jogging. Giving up those extra deserts would have helped. "So . . . go jogging!"

"I tried to get a suit for you—then we could run together—but they didn't have anything in a size one."

"It's okay. If I want a jogging suit, I'll make my own. What amazes me, though, is that you didn't buy a queen-sized one for Peggy. You and she are so close—"

"Anita, why don't you get off the kid's back? So she's bigger than you—taller and heavier— So what! It's all in the genes, honey, all in the genes. And tell me, just why does our closeness bother you?"

Anita never answered. Instead she laid her cloth down and looked at the kitchen clock. It was after two, and she was suddenly famished. "Are you hungry? I'll make something to eat."

"No, I'd rather you didn't. Let's go out and grab a bite."

His eyes were on her now, scanning her small frame in a sensual way. He had sex on his mind as well as food. She didn't—and hadn't for a long time. Going out for lunch would mean not talking her way out of bed.

"I'm going up to take a shower and change," she said. "You stay here."

"Thank God she wasn't hurt bad."

Peggy sat in her usual seat in the middle of the bus and listened while Nicky's friends talked in back.

"They just gotta take her to the hospital for observation. Ya know . . . like keep her overnight." The voice belonged to Nicky's best friend, Connie, the best friend she'd latched onto after dumping Peggy. "And boy, is Nicky pissed!"

"Why?" someone asked. This time the voice belonged to Hank Brudhle, pronounced "brutally," a wonderful name for a huge, ferocious animal who thrived on pain. "What's up?" he wanted to know.

"Well, she's pissed 'cause the accident hadda be reported."

"It was her own fault," Hank said. "What the hell was she doin' on top of her locker. Just hangin' out or what?"

"I don't know," Connie answered, "but Landis called Nicky's old lady, and now her old lady'll accuse her of bein' on drugs."

"That ain't fair!" Hank said. "Nicky ain't no druggie."

"Try tellin' her mother she ain't," Connie said, emphasizing the word "mother" until it sounded like a four-letter word.

Peggy sat and listened and pictured the two of them in her mind—Connie with the red hair, too much make-up, the large breasts and tight sweaters; Hank with the crew cut, the thick neck, and the bull head. They were a pair all right.

And to think they mocked Peggy because she was different.

"I got her stuff from the locker, an' ya know, I was thinkin' of somethin' else, too. Nicky's mother might try an' blame the ouija board—"

"Fer what?" Hank asked.

"For her fallin' like she did."

"Oh, piss off!" Hank spat.

"I ain't kiddin'. Her old lady was yellin' at her fer buyin' this. She said it brings bad luck. She said bad things was happenin' at home and that somethin' bad was gonna happen ta Nicky for foolin' around with the ouija . . ."

"No shit!"

"Yeah. And my old lady's just like Nicky's. Now whadda I do? I can't take it home," Connie said.

"Well, I ain't takin' it home," someone else said. "The friggin' thing gives me the creeps."

"Me neither," Hank said, "in case any of ya's

got ideas about who's takin' it home. And it ain't 'cause I'm scared. I don't like carryin' nobody's shit around."

At this point, as the crowd in back broke into whispers, Peggy tried to concentrate on the passing scenery outside—the small, modest homes, some with shabby lawns, and young children on bikes jeering at the kids on the bus—but it was no good. Those bastards in back were whispering about her or something to do with her.

Why else would they be talking real low if they weren't scheming to pull a joke on Peggy? That's the way it usually went. Connie and Hank were leading the group to a hanging of sorts, and Peggy just knew she was the victim.

Once or twice she overheard the word "rat" being used by the group and wondered if they were talking about themselves. They were rats, all of them, barge rats, pimples on the ass of society.

"I know what ta do," Connie said at last, in a voice that was much too loud. "We'll give it ta Peggy ta hold onto. She likes strange things."

"Yeah. She talks ta Derek, don't she?"

"An' she likes rats," Connie said to Peggy's amazement.

Peggy rode the rest of the way with her nerves dancing under her skin. She didn't want the ouija board either. It didn't scare her. But why do Nicky a favor when Nicky didn't know she was alive?

"Take care o' this!"

Peggy heard a voice come out of nowhere and jumped as something hit the seat beside her. She looked up and saw Hank. "Nicky'll want it back when she gets out tomorrow."

"I don't want it—" Peggy began, but froze when Hank leaned over the seat and put his face close to hers. She could see rage in his eyes and smell hatred on his breath.

"Ya want me ta drag ya off this bus and beat the shit outta ya?"

"No . . ."

"Then do what I say, bitch!"

Peggy put her hand over the top of the ouija board and closed her eyes, knowing she'd have to keep it for Nicky. She listened to the catcalls and jeers following the crowd off the bus and concentrated on her brain. She was on the verge of a seizure.

Leaning her head against the window, she felt the cool pane against her forehead and almost died when Hank banged on the glass from outside and screamed in her face. "Remember what I said!"

But she didn't want to remember. She didn't want to hear anything they had to say, not when it had to do with Nicky Martin. Nicky was dead in her eyes, and now, even from a hospital bed, Nicky was causing her grief.

A ouija board! "Like having someone to talk to," Nicky had said in school. "You ask it questions and it answers. I talk to it."

Nicky was nuts!

When the bus rolled to a stop in front of her house, Peggy rose numbly and got off. Hugging her books in her arms, listening to the whooshing noises her thighs were making in those jeans, she was halfway to her door when the bus driver shouted after her, "Hey, you forgot this!"

She turned and saw him holding the ouija board and felt herself growing stubborn. "It's not mine!"

He was on the bottom steps by this time, his short, stocky frame tight with anger. The expression on his face was telling Peggy she was wrong to have left the ouija board on the bus. "Them other kids gave it to you. I seen 'em."

"It was a joke," Peggy insisted.

"I ain't laughing. I don't want this thing on my bus when I'm driving alone."

Peggy stiffened her body and stared at him. He was at least 40 and appeared to be a cut above the other drivers they'd had in the past, but he was acting like a child. "Why is everyone so afraid of these things?" she asked, approaching him with a seasoned weariness. She felt old at times.

"I'm not everyone! I speak for myself. I don't want it on my bus when I'm driving alone!"

Peggy stood holding the board for a long time after the bus had pulled away from the curb, a funnel of smoke trailing behind.

She thought about the smoke, and how it seemed the bus driver was being pursued by his own fears. A giant yellow beast—the bus—was carrying him to its lair, its billowing, white tail disappearing now, leaving no trace.

It was the same with the swirling breeze in the locker room. After Nicky fell, it disappeared, leaving no trace, causing Peggy to wonder if it had been there to begin with, or if she'd been hallucinating. And the man inside the swirling mist, the executioner—was he real or part of the illusion?

Numbly, she started up the walk again and was almost at the front door when she remembered that she had psychomotor epilepsy. Sometimes her seizures were nothing more than dreamlike states during which she hallucinated and saw visions. True, she'd never seen an executioner before, but there were other instances where the sights she'd envisioned in the midst of a seizure had scared her half to death.

Once, in the semidarkness of her bedroom, she saw a man wearing a hockey mask like the psycho in a series of gruesome murder movies. He was sitting on the side of her bed with an axe in his hands. Peggy murmured to him, asked him why he was there.

It seemed he wanted her head for a souvenir. He even brought his own axe in case she had none. "I don't want to be a bother," he'd said, unlike the psycho in the movies who never talked. "No bother," Peggy answered.

Then she screamed and Charlie came running. When Charlie snapped on the lights, the psycho was gone. It was only a hallucination.

No wonder she'd seen that gruesome creature in the locker room. Peggy had suffered through a small seizure and had seen a vision—a horrible one, but a vision just the same.

CHAPTER SIX

Nicky Martin shivered when the nurse rubbed an alcohol-soaked, gauze pad over the spot where the needle had been stuck only seconds before. Nicky hadn't wanted the needle because it was loaded with Demerol—50cc to kill the pain from multiple bruises, contusions and a sprained wrist.

Protesting, she told the nurse she'd gotten hurt before and hadn't needed drugs. But the doctor had ordered it, so Nicky took her shot, knowing the Demerol would render her helpless in the face of Max's wrath.

Not that she could fight him even when she wasn't drugged. Max was capable of the impossible. But at least if her head were clear, Nicky could see Max's revenge coming before it hit. She had to see it coming, had to be ready. Nicky didn't want to die in her sleep.

"It won't happen in your sleep, Nicole. Besides, what makes you think I'm out for revenge? Did you do something wrong?"

Nicky heard Max's voice coming from somewhere close by and looked around. She had a small private room with her own bathroom, a closet and a night table. There weren't too many hiding places in here.

Starting with the bathroom, she moved to one side of the bed and propped herself on an elbow to look inside. There was a shower stall, a toilet and a sink, but no Max.

Lying down again because her head was throbbing, Nicky figured Max might be hiding in the closet. That's where Max hid at home. But the door was closed, so if Max was in there, then so be it. She didn't have the energy to get up and look. She also didn't want to die in her sleep. Perhaps if he showed himself, Nicky could reason with him.

"Where are you?" she asked and listened to the sound of silence hovering like a blanket of dread. Max wasn't answering; Max was acting stubborn.

Then she wondered if he was really there, or if she was acting hysterical. "Max," she pleaded, her voice slurred from the drug. "Answer me, please?"

"Where's the board?" he asked. Max had finally decided to talk and she should have been glad, but he'd asked a question that she couldn't answer. Max was still in control, and Max was still hiding.

"I don't know," she said quietly. "I think it's in school."

"You think? Don't you know?"

"Well, after you slammed me around I passed out! They brought me here. How the hell was I—"

"Stop right now! I don't like your tone!"

Nicky swallowed hard and forgot about being defensive. Max only responded to kindness, not wrath. "I can get it back. One of my friends must know where it is. Max, the drug is working. I can't stay awake much longer. Please don't hurt me in my sleep."

"I won't," he said. "In fact, I just might join you in sleep to collect on the promise you made this morning. Remember? You said you'd do *anything*."

Nicky remembered the promise. She also remembered what he said he could do with his body. Max could appear in solid form, like a man, or he could be an ethereal spirit, or he could make himself enter her mind as a thought where she could see him and touch him.

"Yes, Max, you do that. Come to me in my sleep." Nicky wasn't sure she liked this. She'd never made out with a spirit before, and certainly not in her sleep. And yet, after the clumsy efforts of Hank Brudhle, she might even come to enjoy Max. Closing her eyes, she was surrounded by darkness at first.

Then, in the mist of her dreams she saw a man coming towards her—a tall, broad-shouldered, good-looking man. Max! Raising her lips to his, as if he'd silently told her to, she kissed him and waited, wondering how far Max intended to carry this.

"All the way," he answered softly. Max had obviously dipped into her brain and knew what she'd been thinking. "I want everything. Then maybe I'll tell you where the board is, and who's keeping it for you."

"Who's keeping it for me? Max, you know where it is?"

"Yes," he said, pulling her close so that she could feel the heat of his body, the firmness of his desire for her.

"Then why are you—"

"Giving you a hard time? To teach you a lesson. Now, do we have a bargain between us or not?"

"Deal," Nicky said, although she had this feeling about making deals with spirits. Max had hurt her once, so he was capable of cruelty. But, in all fairness, he'd warned her not to play tricks with the ouija board or with him.

"Close your eyes," he said, "and just go with it."

Nicky remembered Max kissing her passionately after that, his lips soft and hungry against her mouth, his hands probing her body, exploring the sensuous parts, driving her crazy with their demands. She also remembered Max pulling her gently to the ground, fumbling with her hospital gown until they were naked and joined as one.

And the dream should have ended there, but it didn't. Oh, no! There was so much more to Max's lovemaking, so much more that Nicky didn't want to remember. But she did.

There were beasts with cloven hooves and spear-shaped tails in the darkness of her mind, beasts who stood over their writhing bodies locked in passion and told Max to hurry up. They were demanding their turn with Nicky. There were hideous masses of reeking flesh with no faces, who left trails of slime when they crawled and who wanted their turn with her as well.

The worst of the beasts, though, were the creatures who walked upright, their winged bodies coal black and lumpy. One of them spread his wings in his excitement displaying a pair of transparent, vein-covered appendages that reminded her of a bat. She felt her stomach trying to force its way to her throat in the form of bile.

As for Max—Max had been so handsome and alluring in the beginning, when he first started making love.

But it didn't last! Once it was over and Nicky

felt his body shuddering with release, she wanted to reach that pinnacle as well, but she couldn't. Those beasts had gathered behind Max, and she was afraid that Max would let them have her.

"Max," she pleaded, but he crawled off of her body and got to his feet. Staring down at Nicky, Max assumed the authority of a conqueror with a black hood over his head, a conqueror with an ax in his hands, a conqueror with the body of a beast. His body was green and covered with scales. A putrid odor oozed from his pores.

Anything! Nicky had promised him anything, hadn't she?

But it was no good to make deals with spirits!

Max had wanted to show her what he really looked like this morning, without the illusions he projected. This was the real Max—a horror —and she had slept with him, allowed him to enter her body and leave the juices of his passion behind. She wanted to die.

"Max, why?" she murmured. "Why were you so good to me in the beginning? You don't even resemble the Max I knew then. Why did you change and begin to hate me so?"

"I've always hated you," he said, black fluid flowing from between his lips when he spoke. "My kindness was all part of the game. Now, turn over, bitch! I want more, only this time we're doing it my way. Then my friends can have you."

Nicky screamed and kept on screaming until

an orderly came and shook her awake. She saw a face up against hers and heard someone human speak her name, but she couldn't stop screaming. Not even the light from an overhead lamp could quiet her.

It didn't matter that she was free and no longer in the passionate, painful clutches of beasts who shattered your worst nightmares. Nor did it matter that the sun was still shining, drowning the darkness in her brain. Max could reach her any time of day. Max didn't need the cover of night to hide in. Max was legion; Max could do all.

"I want my ouija board," she screamed, hoping the orderly would understand. "I want to burn it! Do you hear me? I want my ouija board, and I want it now!"

"Sounds like you did all right," Charlie said. "You beat it by yourself."

Charlie had been in his leather recliner with his legs propped up when Peggy opened the front door. He was wearing a sweat suit like he was ready to jog or work out, but he was also reading a magazine which confused her. People read magazines to relax, usually not to set the mood for any kind of exercise session.

But she was so surprised and happy to see him home this early that she ignored the contrast in his clothing and actions because now she had someone to talk to besides Dog, someone to discuss her seizure with.

"I'm proud of you, babes."

"So am I," she said. She'd told Charlie about the seizure and how she'd licked it by herself, but she didn't describe the miasma of colors or the rest of what happened. "Where's Mom?" she asked, anxious to change the subject.

"In the kitchen—cleaning. I suggest we leave her be."

He sounded disgusted. Peggy knew her parents, like most married couples, had been having problems caused by the pressures of paying bills and raising kids. Only lately things seemed worse between them. "Why, Dad? What's wrong now?"

Charlie sighed heavily, then he picked up the magazine lying folded across his lap and threw it towards the coffee table. It landed on the floor. "Close enough," he said and turned back to Peggy. "I came home around two and took your mother out to eat."

"Oh, how nice. Then why is she mad?"

He sighed again. "I took her to a nice place—a converted diner."

"You took us all there once if it's the same one I'm thinking of." Peggy remembered the polished wooden tables and chairs, the red carpet that swallowed your feet to the ankles, the steak dinners served on cutting boards. "It was really something."

"It still is. Only there was a hair in your mother's food—"

"A hair?"

90

"Yes. And it wasn't hers or mine, not that it would have made any difference."

Peggy wanted to laugh. Of all the people in the world, this had to happen to her mother, the germ buster. She bit her lower lip to keep from laughing. "She must have yelled like hell."

"That she did. Now, let's change the subject."

"But, Dad, you think I should ask her if she needs help in the kitchen?"

"Why?"

"'Cause then maybe she'd stop being mad."

"Forget it. She's on a roll!"

Crossing in front of Charlie, Peggy went over to Anita's chair, the one with the doily covering the headrest, and sat down. "I never saw you in a sweat suit before."

"And you probably never will again," Charlie said, nodding his head towards the dining room door. Anita was in the kitchen beyond the dining room in the back of the house, but he still spoke in gestures rather than words as though he was afraid she'd overhear. "I spend my money foolishly, you know."

It's yours to spend since you earn the stuff, Peggy wanted to remind him, but didn't. "What'dya buy it for?"

"To jog in. I've been sitting here trying to talk myself into it. Seems like a lot of work."

Peggy put her books on the floor along with the ouija board. The whole time she'd been speaking to Charlie she'd forgotten she even had the damned board. "Jogging is good for your heart, Daddy. You oughta do it. Never mind what you paid for the suit.''

Peggy was anxious to let Dog inside and take him up to her room. She wanted to tell Dog about school today—the whole story—just to get it off her mind.

"What the hell are you doing with a ouija board?" Charlie asked, bringing her thoughts back to him.

She followed his gaze down to the board at her feet and tried to figure out what to say. Everyone else had been so damned uptight about the thing. She wondered how Charlie felt. "Uh . . . Nicky brought it to school for science class."

"A ouija board? What's so scientific about that?"

Peggy turned away for an instant, then looked at him again. "Are you sure Mom's in the kitchen? She never understands."

"Well, suppose we talk in scientific terms, in case she hears us."

There was something odd in his expression, something resembling anger. Either he was disturbed about the game, or about Anita and the possibility she'd overhear them discussing the ouija board.

Peggy picked up the board and explained about the Fantasies of the Mind project, and why Nicky Martin had brought the ouija board to school. Then she explained how Nicky had fallen in the locker room and bringing the board home was being done as a favor to Nicky.

"Nicky hasn't been your friend in years. Why put your ass on the line for her?" Charlie asked.

He sounded bitter, but he had every right. Nicky did drop her cold when she found out about the epilepsy. "I don't know," she said, shrugging her shoulders. She certainly couldn't tell him about Hank Brudhle and how the board had been forced on her.

Charlie was in his forties and kind of soft when it came to facing up to her mother, but he was no pushover. If he knew that some bully had scared his kid into doing something she didn't want to, Charlie would have gone to school looking for Hank. Charlie would have killed Hank, then he'd probably spend the rest of his life behind bars. Peggy couldn't be responsible for anything bad ever happening to Charlie.

"I just couldn't say no."

"Then I guess you're stuck with it—until tomorrow at least. And listen good, Peggy. I want you to put that son-of-a-bitch game someplace where you won't be tempted to use it."

Peggy studied the fluttering motions of his mouth. "You're nervous about this. Why?"

"Ouija boards have stigmas attached to them," he said, raising a hand to stop her from interrupting. "And don't ask why. They just do."

She'd never thought much about a ouija board until now. However, the mystery surrounding the game was beginning to pique her interest. Everyone was so damned scared of the thing. "It's only a game. You ask it questions."

"From what I know, there's a spirit inside who answers those questions. And don't laugh, it's true."

"A spirit?" She remembered the incident with Nicky in school today; Nicky had called her spirit by name. And yet this was her father talking, not some teenager. How odd!

"You have to be a sensitive person to talk to a ouija board. Some say you almost have to have spiritual powers like mediums or it doesn't work."

Peggy busied a hand making small circular marks in her jeans. "Mediums talk to dead people."

"Yes. Through spirits from the other side. Mediums summon up spirits who supposedly have control over the world of the dead to communicate with dead people. It's dangerous. You might even summon up something you can't get rid of . . ." Charlie's voice trailed off then, and Peggy saw a haze pass over his eyes.

"You can't talk to dead people, Daddy," she said, not sure if he was still listening. "Besides, only God has control over the dead."

After Peggy finished speaking, Charlie seemed himself again. "Not everyone who has died is in God's control, honey. Some of them are . . . never mind. It doesn't matter." Charlie pushed a button on his recliner and lowered his feet. He was getting ready to run from her, like he usually did when he couldn't follow through on an explanation.

"Daddy, how come you know so much about the ouija board?"

He stared down at her hand, at the circles she was drawing on her jeans, then his eyes traveled to rest on her face. "Because I fooled with it when I was your age. Me and some friends . . . One of them was an occult nut who had studied all kinds of things, from mind exercises to casting spells to summoning up the devil."

"Wow! And I thought the kids at Philmore High did nutty stuff."

"Yeah . . . Well, this boy had a real fascination for the supernatural. Normally when he started his nonsense we stopped him cold. We weren't interested. But then one night . . ."

As Charlie spoke, the scene unfolded before Peggy's eyes. She could envision the encounter as though she'd been there. She saw four teenagers sitting in a boy's bedroom.

There were model cars and planes covering a desk on one side of the room. She saw a half-opened closet with clothing overflowing onto the floor outside. She saw an unmade bed. It was her father's room all right. Charlie was basically messy.

The boys were sitting around a folding table that Charlie had dragged up to his room moments before. There was a ouija board spread out in front of them.

A single candle flickered on the dresser behind him, casting an eerie glow over the faces of the other boys seated around the table. Charlie's hand was busy digging trenches into the surface of his jeans. He didn't like this, not one bit, but the other boys were laughing. All except one—the occult nut.

"Get serious," the one who wasn't laughing said, "or it's no good."

There was sudden silence when the boys stopped laughing, a silence that Peggy found disturbing.

Peggy watched them all place their fingertips on the pointer in the middle of the board. The pointer was still, waiting for a command to start. "Oh, spirit of the Ouija," the fourth boy began, "listen to us and answer our questions. We wish to summon forth the dead—"

"Charlie! What is going on!"

Peggy heard the voice and struggled to recognize it. She saw her grandmother, Charlie's mom, come into the room and snap on the lights, scaring hell out of the boys at the table.

But then the voice boomed again, making Peggy realize it was her own mother, Anita. The sudden intrusion of light had come when Anita's voice jarred her back to the present.

"What're you doing? Hasn't she got enough problems without you telling her stories?"

Anita stood over him, her tiny body looking tall and majestic because she knew she was in charge. "And what is this?" Anita asked, pointing to the ouija board still in Peggy's lap. "Why is that thing in my house?"

Charlie started talking fast, explaining what

Peggy had told him about Nicky Martin. But this didn't satisfy Anita. "I want it out of my house!"

"I don't like it either," Charlie said, rising from his seat to tower over Anita. "But she made a promise and she's got to keep it."

"The hell she does," Anita spat, not intimidated by his height.

"Take it up to your room and put it away," Charlie said to Peggy, then he turned back to Anita. "She has a hard time making friends as it is." His voice was softer now, full of reasoning. "She can't go back on her word. Besides, she's not stupid enough to fool with that thing."

Peggy went on out to the kitchen with the ouija board and her books and let Dog in. She couldn't go up to her room without Dog. Crossing back through the dining room, she entered the living room again and heard them still arguing. Anita might win, yet Charlie was holding his own.

"Come on, Dog," she whispered, climbing the stairs with him beside her, his paws almost silent on the runners on the steps. "You're the only one I have to talk to—except for Daddy, but that's only once in a while. Like today, when he came home from work early and we talked. But she ruined that, just like she ruins everything else."

All this stupid, bitchin' nonsense about a game, she thought to herself.

CHAPTER SEVEN

Put your paw on the pointer, Dog."

It was late. Dinner had been eaten hours ago. After dinner, Peggy retreated to her room; it was either that or watch television, which bored her to pieces. Listening to her parents squabble was just as boring.

Her room was the only safe haven in the house. Besides, Dog was up there, waiting for Peggy to finish telling him about school today. Carefully going over each and every detail, leaving nothing out, Peggy told Dog about science class and about gym and about Derek and how Miss Landis felt he had a crush on Peggy.

Then she told him about Nicky Martin and how Nicky had fallen from the top of a locker.

She even told him about the swirling breeze and the man in the midst of it. She told Dog everything because Dog was the only one she could count on to listen and not go blabbing her secrets to her parents.

Dog was tight-lipped. Maybe because he was a dog, she thought and laughed. Stripping her bed of the pink and gold frilly spread, Peggy laid out her books after telling Dog about school and hurried through her homework.

But why hurry? What was the difference if she finished her homework at eight or nine or even ten? She wasn't going anywhere. She wasn't in a hurry to finish so she could run through the front door and rush to the mall to meet the gang. So why hurry?

But then the answer was simple. Dog had nothing to do for those few hours she spent on her homework. The poor thing lay at her feet and waited until she was done, his boredom reflected in his rheumy eyes. And hell, he'd already spent most of the day chained in the yard outside waiting for Peggy to come home from school, so it wasn't fair to keep him waiting now. Friends just didn't treat one another so poorly.

Peggy let him lay on her bed, ignoring Anita's command to keep the damned dog on the floor where he belonged! And Peggy did her homework on her bed to be near Dog so he wouldn't feel lonely, ignoring the desk and chair Anita had bought her. As far as Peggy was concerned, there was too much furniture in her bedroom, some of it put there to keep her from getting close to Dog.

"Listen, Dog," she said when her homework was finished. "I wanna try out this ouija board thing."

Dog cocked his head to one side as though he felt she was losing her mind.

"You, too? Another one who's afraid of a game. Well, we're playin' it, but not before I get into my pajamas. And you know what that means."

While Peggy quickly undressed, Dog lay his head out flat and covered his eyes with his paws. Peggy had taught him this years before, mainly because Dog was a male, so it wasn't proper for her to undress with him watching.

Then she climbed into a pair of powder blue, silk pajamas that Charlie had bought in Chinatown in New York City last year. She liked the color, and she liked the oriental-style collar on the jacket. Charlie, it seemed, had better taste than Anita; he felt that blue was her color and never bought her anything pink. Blue, he said, blended well with her dark hair and added radiance to her eyes.

She buttoned her jacket to the top and left her clothing lying in a heap on Anita's precious slipper chair, the one Anita had bought because it was pink and went so well with the rest of the frilly garbage in Peggy's room. Peggy kept it shoved in a corner near her closet just to keep it out of sight.

Glancing down at her clothing, she hoped she'd remember to put her jeans and sweat shirt in the hamper before Anita came in here to make her bed in the morning. Otherwise, all hell would break loose. Leaving dirty clothing lying around was forbidden.

Peggy soon forgot her dirty clothing, though, when the wind began to whip up outside. She listened to it for a moment, then went to her bedroom window to stare at tree branches swaying in the wind, at the shadows they cast on the lawn in front of her home, and at the other homes on the block as well.

The scene was warm and familiar, and Peggy took comfort in the familiar, in knowing she was home where it was safe, where the normal turmoil in her life had been left behind. The kids at school couldn't reach her here. Their jeering, mocking voices couldn't be heard on this block. This was her safe hiding place.

Then she remembered that Dog was still lying on her bed, waiting for her to get undressed. "I'm decent," she said and laughed when Dog pulled his paws away to uncover his eyes and curled his upper lip in a grin. Most people thought Dog was snarling or getting ready to attack when he showed his teeth, but not Peggy. Dog was definitely grinning. "I'll get the board," she said. "You wait right there."

The ouija board was hidden on the top shelf of

her closet, under a pile of old movie magazines. Peggy had once followed the trials and tribulations of the Hollywood stars until she'd discovered the truth about those magazines; most of the stories were made-up, fantasies of some reporter's mind. About the only thing they were good for now was hiding the ouija board.

But why hide the ouija board when Anita knew the game was in her room? Unless subconsciously she was hiding it from herself.

Shrugging, she took the board from its hiding place and carried it over to her bed. There were instructions written on the back of the game, and she read them to Dog. "One person at a time should ask questions and those questions shouldn't be frivolous or ridiculous. Also— listen to this, Dog—the board should be kept dust free or the pointer won't glide over the surface."

Peggy was getting excited. She hadn't played games in years and missed that phase of her life where spinning a small, cardboard wheel or throwing some dice meant entering the magical kingdom where nobody ever got sick, and certainly not sick with epilepsy.

Opening the lid on the box, Peggy took out the folded board from the box and spread it on the bed between Dog and herself. "Put your paw on the pointer," she told Dog. But he didn't understand. She watched him sniff the board and run his tongue across the pointer.

"Look, two people have to play for this to

work. And I know we never played with the ouija before, so I'm trying to be patient. Here, give me your paw and I'll show you how." Immediately Dog offered a paw to Peggy. Not that he understood, but he'd been trained as a puppy to offer his paw. Peggy grabbed his paw and placed it on the pointer, holding on when he tried to pull it away. "Stop it!" she said. "Do as I say."

Dog listened and left his paw on the pointer. But he didn't like this one bit, she noticed, because he was uncomfortable. Sitting up wasn't easy when he had only one front paw left to balance himself with. But since this was Peggy talking to him, telling him what to do, he tried.

"One person asks a question at a time. I'll go first." Her hands were trembling, though not a lot. In fact, she hadn't realized she was nervous until she looked down at the pointer and saw it vibrate beneath her fingers.

You're really tough, she told herself, breaking into a half-smile. Everyone else is afraid of this, but not you, not Peggy.

Dog's whining brought her to; he was impatient to get on with this. She had to ask a question and not just sit there and torture the poor animal to death. Dogs couldn't be still for a long time. They were naturally fidgety and nervous.

In fact, she was feeling fidgety and nervous, too. The wind outside was still whipping the trees, still making them dance in what had become a nightly ritual, especially at this time of year when the wind was stronger. She listened to the rustling of branches against the glass of her bedroom window, but didn't feel warm as she had before. There was something eerie about the scraping noises the branches were making now.

Taking a deep breath, she stared at the board and seriously considered her first question, feeling a sudden reverence for the mystery behind the game. And if it wasn't a reverence, it sure as hell was a healthy respect—or fear.

As she well knew, the ouija board was supposed to answer questions about the past, the present, and the future. Peggy had a question about her future, the most important one she could think of on such short notice. "Will I ever be beautiful?" she asked, and the pointer moved, and the branches scraped against the window again.

Pulling her hand away as if she'd just touched something hot, she watched the pointer glide across the board, driven by an unseen force. Dog still had his paw where she'd placed it. He was staring at her now, his large, brown eyes full of wonder.

"I don't know what's going on," she said to Dog. The pointer was moving so she had to concentrate on that and not on Dog—and not on the shadow she saw from the corner of her eye sliding across the slipper chair by the closet, as though someone were about to sit down.

The pointer, she noted, went straight up to the

letter O, then it slid back to N, then to L, and at last went to Y, and hesitated. "O . . . n . . . l . . . y . . . Only! It's talking! Dog, it said only. It's answering my question."

Forgetting her fear of a moment ago, Peggy put her fingertips back on the pointer. The ouija board was talking to her, and she didn't want to screw this up. She had to cooperate. Besides, she was too fascinated to be scared—of the game at least. She was a bit nervous, though, about the noises outside. The wind was beating the trees into submission, the trees groaning in protest. The familiar had suddenly become something strange and ominous.

The shadow across the slipper chair made her nervous as well, but only because the shadow didn't belong there. While it was true that Peggy was using her bedside lamp, so the corner by the closet was bathed in semidarkness, the area over the chair seemed darker than the rest.

Turning back to the ouija board, Peggy saw the pointer move again, completing the answer to her question. "Only if you stop eating sweets," it said.

God, this was incredible. It was telling her the same thing Anita had been saying for years. Peggy had to lay off sweets to lose weight and to get rid of those pimples on her face. Being beautiful meant giving up Twinkies.

Then she wondered if Anita had somehow programed the game like you would a computer. It was answering her with Anita's thoughts in mind. "What sweets are we talking about?" Peggy asked, her eyes narrowed suspiciously and watched the pointer spell out "Twinkies."

Oh, God! Her brain reeled from the answer it had just given because it was right on the money. Twinkies were her all-time favorite. She'd kill for a Twinkie. "How do you know?" she asked.

"I'm Legion. I know all," the Ouija answered.

Peggy pulled her fingers away again. Nicky Martin had said this was like talking to someone, like having a conversation, and Nicky had been right. Peggy had the feeling that the board was alive, a breathing entity with a brain. It could think, reason, speak. But it was just a game, she kept telling herself, even though its answers had been accurate to a frightening degree.

"Is there anything you wanna ask it, Dog? 'Cause if not, I'm puttin' the damned thing back in my closet. Enough is enough."

Peggy glanced at the closet then, as if drawn there because it was open. Strange, she'd closed it a while back when she'd taken the ouija board from its hiding place.

And the pointer was moving again—by itself.

She tried not to think about the movements or about why it was doing its own thing—moving without her asking a question! She also tried not to think about the wind outside and why it was howling in voices. In fact, there were many things she was trying not to think about at the moment, one of which was the seizure she'd had in school today and the swirling breeze and the man, the executioner, standing in its midst . . .

Because a moment ago she'd spotted something from the corner of her eye, something that was maybe there, and yet maybe wasn't. She'd seen someone sitting in the slipper chair, someone with a black hood over his head like an executioner, and that someone had been wearing her soiled clothing, and that someone had been staring at her.

And this vision of the executioner in her slipper chair had to be one of two things. Either Peggy had thought too hard and for too long about the nightmarish creature in the swirling breeze today and was seeing him because of that, or he was really there. He'd followed her from school. No! It was just an illusion, she told herself, and repeated it over and over until she was almost convinced.

One of her hands was making small, circular movements on the leg of her pajamas, wearing a shiny spot in the fabric. The color was lighter inside of the circle; not quite powder blue, it was almost white. Well, she thought, at least it wasn't pink! She looked down at the board, and spelled out what it was saying, the pointer moving at a furious pace, rushing to complete its thoughts.

"Not yet," it said.

"Not yet what?" she asked, still wondering why the board was speaking when she hadn't spoken to it first.

"Don't put me away!"

"Why not?"

"I have something to say."

"I don't wanna hear it."

Peggy was frightened beyond belief. Charlie's words came back to her, overriding her fear. "Some say you almost have to have spiritual powers like mediums for the ouija board to work." Then she recalled her answer as well. "Mediums talk to dead people!"

"You're not a medium," the Ouija said, although Peggy hadn't spoken out loud but had kept her thoughts to herself. "You're a lovely, young girl—and Charlie's right, blue *is* your color!"

Peggy woke up early the next morning, dressed and was on her way down to breakfast with Dog at her side when something made her stop in the middle of the stairs and listen. Charlie and Anita were in the kitchen in the back of the house, quarreling over the ouija board.

She held onto the railing, the heavily varnished wood warm and familiar against her flesh, and went no further. There was no way she was about to go out to the kitchen and get in the middle of their fight.

"Oh, so now it's reverse psychology," Anita was saying. "Aren't you the expert."

"Stop it, Anita. What I meant was that Peggy agreed to hold the ouija board for a friend. She doesn't have many friends. How could I say she was wrong? I couldn't even tell her to keep her hands off it. Then I know she'd be up there playing with the damned thing.''

"So you tried scaring her with your ghost stories.''

Peggy sat down on the steps and stared straight ahead.

All this dumb bitchin' over a game, she thought. Sure it had scared her last night, but this was the morning after, and nothing was ever scary the morning after.

"We have to wait till they stop fighting to eat,'' she told Dog, although she shouldn't have been speaking to him. She should have been mad at Dog, mad enough to whack him, but Dog was the only friend she had. Sensing her annoyance, Dog lay down next to her and put his head across her lap.

"You just had to dribble on the board, right?'' she scolded. "You had to mess it up so I can't give it back. Now I gotta buy Nicky a new one.'' Moving Dog off her lap, she fumbled through her pockets and came up with a handful of change and a few folded bills. There was a department store about halfway between home and school. They must sell ouija boards.

Meanwhile, Nicky's board was back in Peggy's closet, hidden under the movie magazines.

"Why would I condone it after what happened to me with the damned ouija board?'' Charlie asked. He was still shouting, but his anger was almost gone, replaced by a pleading quality.

"And tell me . . . Just what happened to you?'' Anita asked.

"You want me to go over it again? I've already told you—"

"Yes, you did, but I didn't believe you then and I don't now. About the only thing I do know is that Peggy's inherited your imagination!"

"What's that supposed to mean?" Charlie asked, his tone harsh and angry again.

"Peggy sees things, too. Only she has an excuse," Anita said. "She's epileptic!"

Yes, Mother, I am, Peggy thought to herself. I'm epileptic and I see things. Yesterday I saw an executioner inside of a swirling mass of color. Last night I saw the pointer on the ouija board spell out answers to questions I had in mind, questions I hadn't spoken out loud. And today I'll probably see something else.

"You hungry, Dog?" she asked in a loud voice, knowing Charlie and Anita would hear. She was suddenly anxious for their company, because thinking about the ouija board brought something back to her, something she was trying to forget. The spirit in the board had known Charlie's name. How?

Then the spirit mentioned the color blue and how blue was Peggy's color while Peggy had been wearing blue pajamas. It was only a game. How did it know?

The next question running through her mind was the most disturbing of all. Why did she sense a closeness to the spirit in the board as though it were human and really cared about her? It was only a game, she repeated to herself; it wasn't flesh and blood. So why did she feel as if something or someone in the Board was her friend? She was beginning to sound like Nicky Martin.

"Come on, Dog. Let's go eat before I miss the school bus."

Peggy's first period class was science. Sitting in the back of the room, she tried to make her sometimes muddled brain concentrate. Mr. Quigley was going over his Fantasy of the Mind experiment. She had to pay attention; she had to know what was involved.

Derek was staring at her again. Actually, though, glaring was more of a description for the cold hardness she sensed in his eyes. Derek was staring at her as if wishing she'd fallen from the top of the lockers instead of Nicky. The bastard was stuck on Nicky and not Peggy, as Miss Landis had said he was.

And yet, this wasn't fair. Nicky wasn't badly hurt, so Derek should be keeping his old, cold looks to himself!

"Let's go back over what we learned yesterday," Quigley was saying in the British accent so soothing to her ears. He was tall and dark and rail thin—decidedly British. He was handsome, too, standing at the front of the class, leaning against a podium in a kind of casually sexual way.

"As I've already told you, daydreams are misdirected flights of imagination, too fleeting and too intimate to share with another person. Fantasies, on the other hand, are conscious expressions directed by your mind. Directing fantasies can be compared with a writer creating a script, thus adding depth to your creative energies—"

"What the hell are you talkin' about?" one of the students shouted, causing a crack in the proper facade of Quigley's proper British face. Peggy watched a line form across his forehead and the twitching motions of his mouth, and she knew he was pissed.

"What I'm saying is this. Basically, man employs such a small area of his brain to function on a daily basis that it's both frightening and ridiculous. We do not work our minds to full capacity, and this is because most of our thinking is done for us through television, newspapers and computers. I'm endeavoring to force you to exercise your brain, to use it as it should be used before we all lose the ability to think for ourselves!"

"Nicky uses a ouija board to do her think—"

"I fail to see the humor in your statement! Now, you will participate in this experiment, or you will all fail the course!"

Quigley stepped back to the drawing board behind him. Fingering a piece of chalk, he began to write and speak at the same time. "I want you to create stories in your mind," he said, and wrote Directed Flights of Fantasy. "I want you to begin by picking a subject or an object and building from it.

"You see, what you kids fail to realize is that

your mind affords complete freedom. You can be anything and you can do anything in your mind. And to illustrate this point, I'll tell you a bit about my own fantasy games.''

Peggy watched him working the chalk between his fingers and allowed her mind to wander back to her biofeedback lessons. She had learned to create scenes in her head following an aura to stop her seizures. Quigley seemed to be heading in this direction, only for different reasons—not to stop seizures, but to expand their brain power.

She scanned the classroom and saw jackets with cutoff sleeves, spiked hair in various hues of pink and purple, clothing in outrageous colors, and knew that Quigley had his work cut out for him.

"I wrote a script in my mind years ago," he said, "where I was able to explore space along with the astronauts who went up in their rockets to orbit the Earth and land on the Moon. I also rode in our space probe Voyager as it traveled to the outer hemisphere of our galaxy—"

"Hey, Teach, ya act like ya were really there," a student remarked, while the others laughed.

"I was."

"Did ya wear a space suit?"

"Of course not!"

"Then how did ya breathe?"

"By stopping my heart first. Then I didn't need to breathe."

Peggy listened to the sound of shocked silence

hanging in the air and felt he must be kidding. Quigley stopped his heart?

"I thought that would get your attention. You see, I've taken this experiment to higher levels after reading about Buddhist monks who have the ability to stop their own hearts and enter a state of suspended animation—limbo. In order to accomplish this, I frequently perform what's called self-induced hypnosis, during which time I stop my bodily functions—heart beat, breathing—and reach heights of awareness you've never dreamed possible."

"Isn't that dangerous?" Derek asked. Derek had been quiet throughout Quigley's lecture, just listening and absorbing. When he spoke his face was slack, his eyes wide and unbelieving.

"Yes. You have to be trained, so it is dangerous. Therefore, I'm not asking my students to attempt anything this advanced. I just want you to fantasize for now, and this is how it's done. And remember, all conditions must be perfect or it won't work. First you pick a dark, quiet spot—your room at night perhaps—then you close your eyes and breathe deeply. Just let go. Release your inner inhibitions. Let your imagination soar, but only while under your control."

"Are you gonna teach us the rest of it?" a student asked quietly. "Are you gonna tell us how to animate our bodies in suspension?"

The student had his explanation backwards, but Quigley answered without a reaction. "Perhaps. It depends on how well you do with the first step. Stopping your heart isn't easy. The really hard part, though, is getting it beating again."

"You don't expect half these kids to pass your course, and yet you intend to teach them something complicated like stopping their hearts?"

Derek's words hung between him and Quigley like an old-fashioned challenge to a duel. Quigley glared at Derek, then glanced at his watch and smiled. "Sorry, my boy, but time's up. We'll have to discuss this tomorrow. Class dismissed!"

Peggy didn't know many of the students in her class by name and normally didn't give a damn about them, but it was different now. They were impressed by Quigley. And Quigley sounded as though he'd lost control, as if his brain had traveled to la la land and not outer space as he'd claimed.

Stopping his heart! Causing his lungs to cease their movements! Halting the pumping motions of his blood through major arteries! Either he was completely insane or the best damned liar she'd ever met.

Now she wondered if Quigley would teach the students what he'd learned from those Buddhist monks or if he'd be stopped before he blew their coke-popping brains to hell and back.

Derek was behind her as she left the class; this was turning into a pattern, one she could live without. Walking as fast as she could, Peggy headed for Home Economics and hoped he wouldn't catch up. She didn't care to listen to his nonsense about Nicky Martin, and how it was a shame she'd fallen.

Derek stepped in her path just then, derailing her train of thought. "Get out of my way," she said, trying to push past him. But Derek's body was firm. Bumping into him was like walking into a solid mass.

"We have to talk," he said.

"Not if it's about Nicky Martin!"

"Nicky? Why the hell would I wanna talk about her?"

"'Cause you're stuck on her, Derek. That's why!"

"My, my, don't we have an imagination."

Yes, she thought, don't we? Don't I? Even her own mother knew of her vivid imagination. Consciously pulling at her blouse to work it down over the top of her jeans, Peggy was aware of Derek, of the muscular tightness of his body and how appealing it was. "What'dya want?" she asked, feeling homely and inadequate.

"I heard you got stuck taking the ouija board home. Don't fool with it, Peggy."

"Yeah. Yeah," she said, looking past him, wishing she was in Home Economics this very minute. Derek *was* the best-looking thing around here; Miss Landis had been right about that. Only now, his being gorgeous made her feel homelier than ever. Standing there in front of him, she felt overwhelmed by her weight problem, by the blemishes on her face, and by the awful way she dressed as if she didn't care what she wore to school. "Why are you so concerned?" she asked.

"Because we're both outcasts, part of an elite group. We have to stick together." Derek was right. They were both outcasts, although Derek didn't have to be. He was an outcast by choice, and because of his choice, they had to stick together as Derek said they should and be friends.

But Peggy suddenly yearned for more. She felt herself growing attached to him in a giddy way, which was hopeless and stupid because Derek was too good-looking for her. Derek belonged to a world of beautiful people, a world running parallel to and in contrast to her own.

And so she had to be content to accept his friendship and long for nothing more. Also, she had to drop her awful attitude towards him and learn to deal with his advice. "I guess you're right," she said. "We do have to stick together. But tell me, why is the ouija board so dangerous?"

"I'll explain when you can give me about an hour of your time. Meanwhile, please do as I ask."

Then he turned and was gone, his tall, muscular form lost in the crowd as though he'd never been there. Peggy remembered his eyes just now when he'd looked down at her, how warm they'd seemed in comparison to how they normally were. Even Derek's tone of voice had been different. He'd sounded angry when he first stopped her but only because she had Nicky's ouija board. Then his voice had changed and turned all soft and caring.

But caring in a friendly way, she told herself sadly, and went on down the hall to her next class.

CHAPTER EIGHT

Connie was waiting for Peggy in Home Economics class. She was waiting with a group of her friends to back her up, not that she needed backing up; she was a bone crusher on her own. But there was safety in numbers, so these female felines preferred traveling in litters.

Peggy caught the expression on Connie's face when she was halfway through the door and looked for the teacher. She saw Formica counters with built-in stoves and she saw wall ovens, but no teacher. The bitch was always late, Peggy thought, and walked in casually in case she was wrong, in case they were waiting for someone else.

"Where's the Ouija?" Connie asked, her breath heavy with the odor of cigarettes. "Did ya bring it?"

"No."

"Why not?" Connie asked, while the others formed a tight ring around Peggy. "I told ya to have it here today. Nicky's supposed to get outta the hospital. She wants it ta keep her company."

To keep her company. Peggy was able to relate to that. It was like talking to someone human when you talked to the Ouija. "I'll bring it tomorrow."

"Ya'll get it over ta Nicky's when school's over, understand, dummy? Otherwise we gotta come to yer house and get it!"

"I could go home with her and make sure she does," one of the other girls suggested. Her name was Tracy, and she was as awful-looking as Connie with the same red hair, but there the resemblance ended. Tracy was bigger, huge in fact, almost in a class with Hank Brudhle. Not only did she tower over Peggy, but she lifted weights and had muscles that would make the Hulk turn pale. "I could get her to get the board and bring it over ta Nicky's," Tracy volunteered.

Connie smiled. She liked the idea. "I can go ya one step better. Why don'cha cut outta school and go over to her house and get it now. Her old lady'll give ya the Ouija."

"Sure," Tracy said, happy to oblige.

"And you, bitch, call yer mother and tell her we don't want no trouble. Alls we want is the board, an' if she don't give it to us, Tracy here is gonna beat her face in," Connie said while she poked Peggy's chest with a pointed finger.

"I can't," Peggy said softly, feeling her fear turn to anger, filling her with a false courage she didn't think possible. "The game is ruined. My dog—"

"Oh, yeah! Sure!" Connie yelled. "Tell me yer dog did somethin' to it. Like he ate yer homework too, right."

"I have the money to pay for it. I was going to buy another one after school."

"Give it ta me! I'll get it fer Nicky. I don't want yer dog pissin' on it again."

"He didn't piss on it! I never said he did!"

"Just give me the money and shut yer friggin' mouth," Connie hissed. "I don't wanna hear nuthin' outta you."

Peggy handed her the money and watched Connie pocket it, wondering if she'd really replace the game. Or would Nicky come back to school and start harassing Peggy for the ouija board? But Peggy had no choice but to trust Connie.

After Connie and Tracy and the others walked away, and Peggy was alone by the door, she breathed deeply and concentrated on her brain. An aura had formed in front of her eyes when she'd been arguing with Connie. Now she ws doing everything she'd been taught in biofeedback to fight an oncoming seizure. She was training her energies on the imperfections in her brain, making repairs where she could. The aura flashed a moment longer, then it disappeared.

When it was over, she looked up and saw the Home Economics teacher standing in front of the room, her face twisted, her cheeks flushed. "I told you girls repeatedly not to stand around and talk. I want your projects started as soon as you get here. We don't have all this time to play games."

Peggy sighed heavily and slowly went to her station. She couldn't rush or the aura would come back. Scanning the faces of the girls in class, she fought an inner rage, she fought a seizure, and she fought against her imposed loneliness as well.

Peggy was the only one in Home Economics who worked alone, struggling through the recipes by herself. There had been an uneven number of girls in the class when the term began, so when partners were chosen to work together, Peggy was left out as usual. She placed her books under the Formica counter and searched for a pot.

They were making chili today, and somehow or other, her supplies always turned up missing.

Tracy was at the station next to her with another of Nicky's pals, both with cold smiles on their lips. Tracy watched Peggy search for the pot, then she flexed her muscles for Peggy's benefit and reached beneath her own counter and took out a pot. Peggy knew it was hers. There was a dent in the side of it where Peggy was supposed to have slammed the pot against the stove during a seizure.

Peggy couldn't swear to the truth of the story about the dent since she generally blacked out. But since everyone said it happened, she swallowed the majority vote and didn't argue.

"Here," Tracy said, walking over to lay the pot on the counter in front of Peggy, leaving Peggy to wonder why Tracy had given it up without a fight. "Nicky wanted us to give you somethin'. It's in the pot."

Peggy stared at the pot but didn't remove the lid. She had this awful feeling. If this was a gift from Nicky it had to be bad.

"Tracy, get back to your station!" the teacher demanded, her voice cracking the silence hovering over them with the force of a whip.

Tracy jumped but got herself together and spoke with her usual, phony, little girl voice. "Peggy always works alone," she said. "I just wanna help her."

"Okay, dear, but your own project has to be done before class is over."

"Right," Tracy said, then she turned to Peggy again. "Nicky's been hurt in gym before, but none of the teachers ever wrote it up. Did you know she's in trouble 'cause the accident was reported? Her mother's thinking of pullin' her outta gym. An' she's havin' Nicky tested for drugs.''

"So?"

"If the accident wasn't reported to the nurse, she coulda talked Landis into forgettin' it happened.''

"So?" Peggy had no idea where this was leading.

"Listen, bitch," Tracy spat. "don't keep playin' dumb. You sent Landis to get the nurse! It's yer fault!''

Peggy couldn't believe she was hearing this. "Miss Landis got the nurse because she heard me screaming way inside the gym and thought I was having a seizure."

"Liar!"

Peggy saw the cold, brown eyes, the thin line that passed for a mouth, the heavily muscled biceps, and felt an aura forming. To make matters worse, Tracy wasn't alone in this. The rest of the girls in the class were in on it, too. From the looks of them, they were absorbed in their work, but it was only an act. "I'm not lying. Ask Miss Landis."

"We don't hafta! We know a rat when we see one. And this's for you, squealer!"

Peggy didn't want to look into the pot when she lifted the lid, but Tracy grabbed her by the neck and forced her head down. Peggy wondered why the teacher didn't stop this, but then Peggy heard one of the girls across the room ask the teacher a question to get her attention away from Tracy.

Closing her eyes against the horror she felt must surely be in the pot, Peggy refused to look. But Tracy squeezed the back of her neck with an iron hand and whispered threats until she opened her eyes again and looked down into the pot through the brightened ring of an aura and saw a brown, furry body with a long tail and long, sharp teeth. It was a rat. From the way it was lying all still and stiff, Peggy knew it was dead.

"We broke its neck," Tracy whispered. "This's what we do to rats!"

Peggy was numb and wanted to scream, but her throat was tight with shock. The rat smelled terrible, its body reeking with the nauseating stench of death. Oh God, but these girls hated her, otherwise they wouldn't be doing something this cruel.

But now the rat was beginning to disappear, its hideous form overpowered by the white, hot light swimming before her. It was the aura preceding a seizure—and it was strong. The seizure was coming fast, too fast for her to concentrate on her brain and repair the glitch in the computer of her mind, too fast to search for the fault in the gulley and close it.

It was too late for games.

In fact, the seizure was almost at its peak by the time Tracy released her, but Peggy didn't mind. For once in her life she welcomed the oncoming seizure because it was a way of escaping the horror around her, a way of escaping the nightmare of being an outcast. The seizure afforded a sense of relief.

Closing her eyes, Peggy willingly let herself go and drifted with it, let herself surrender without a fight, let her body collapse to the floor and shake with stiffened spasms. Then everything faded to black and Peggy was on safe ground.

Again Peggy said nothing to Charlie—nothing about Connie, nothing about Tracy and nothing about the rat. "The seizure just happened, Dad," she'd told him, and Charlie believed her.

Uncontrollable seizures had knocked Peggy down before. This wasn't anything unusual, and there certainly wasn't much Peggy could do to stop the uncontrollable once it started. So Charlie accepted Peggy's story.

But Peggy still wasn't satisfied. It made her angry to think she'd covered for those bitches, the same as she'd covered for Hank Brudhle. They had caused the seizure—Connie and Tracy had—and she wanted to scream. Only Charlie would have gone after them, and Charlie would have landed in jail. She couldn't hurt Charlie.

Another reason Peggy had kept quiet and not told Charlie the truth was the idea of reliving what happened, and by reliving the experience, reliving the pain as well. Those girls hated her and she couldn't bear to live with so much hatred directed her way, so she stuffed the memories deep inside of her subconscious along with every hurt she'd suffered over the years.

Then, and only then, could Peggy go on as though nothing bad ever happened in her life.

Peggy had been in bed when the memories of the day were temporarily dismissed, and Peggy was bored to death. Dog was out in the yard at Anita's insistence, so she had no one to talk to, not even Charlie. And damn, Dog didn't upset Peggy when he was up here in her bedroom. Why lock him outside when he'd never made her hyper? This was bullshit!

How would Anita like staying in here with—

Peggy heard a noise in the hall and turned on her side to stare at the door. She longed for company and anxiously watched the knob turn. When at last the door was open, she still didn't see anyone, but then Dog came leaping into the room with Charlie right behind him.

Charlie must have read her mind and sensed her loneliness.

"Okay, boy, lay down," Charlie said. "I promised you'd be good. Otherwise we're both in a whole lotta trouble."

"Thanks, Daddy, for making her let Dog in."

"No problem. Sleeping on the couch for a week won't be so bad."

Peggy's face crinkled into a smile. Charlie had to be kidding. Then again, maybe he wasn't. Anita could be a bitch when someone bucked her.

"How ya doin', babes?" Charlie asked, bending to brush his lips across Peggy's cheek.

"Okay. I'm doin' just fine."

"Do you wanna talk? Maybe go over what was happening around you before the seizure?"

Doing this was important to Charlie. Reliving the incident might prevent another seizure from taking place. But Peggy couldn't be honest with him, not when he felt so protective towards her. Charlie would get himself into a pound of trouble if she leveled with him.

"There's a boy in school. I like him very much," she said, grabbing onto the first thing to enter her mind. "But I don't think he'll ever feel the same about me—and it hurts. It was on my mind when I freaked out."

Charlie was quiet for a moment, his expression telling her he'd been waiting for this. She was at that stage now, and all of the biofeedback lessons in the world might not help when her sexuality was awakened. Still, being epileptic didn't mean she had to remain celibate.

"To begin with, I can't imagine this boy not liking you back, so don't let this upset you . . ." He stopped talking then and fingered his chin. "Babes, when you were taught to control your emotions so you wouldn't have seizures . . . well, it covered everything."

"You're talking about boys and what I feel inside for this one?"

"Exactly. Whether the emotion you feel is hatred or fear, or even if it's sexual, they're all handled the same. You can live a normal life, not that I want you going to bed with him. This isn't what I mean. It's just . . . When you really like someone, your body goes through some serious chemical changes. Your heart beats faster. The blood in your veins pumps harder. Your adrenaline flows heavier."

"What you're saying is, I should try to handle this like I handle everything else when I get excited."

"Yes," Charlie answered, concentrating on his feet. He was embarrassed.

"We're not going together, Daddy. He's in one of my classes and I see him every day."

"And you like what you see?" Charlie asked, sitting on her bed, his shoulders slumped.

"His name is Derek—"

"Derek! What's his last name?"

She watched Charlie get up and raise himself to full height. She couldn't be certain, but his body seemed to stiffen at the mention of Derek's name. "I don't know—"

"Find out! Ask him what his last name is and let me know. Meanwhile, hang loose with this guy!"

Then he was gone. Charlie had walked out on her so abruptly she didn't know what to think, and he slammed the door behind him. Charlie actually slammed a door. What the hell was wrong?

But then Dog was there, lying on the floor near her bed, and she had so much to tell him about what happened at school that she quickly forgot Charlie and the way he'd gotten upset at the sound of Derek's name.

"Here, Dog," she said, slapping the side of her bed, motioning for him to climb up next to her. "Get up here and lay down."

Once he was settled, Peggy propped up her pillows and told Dog everything that happened in school, leaving nothing out as usual. Funny how she could tell Dog things she held back from her parents. Funny too how the nightmares in her life never hurt when she recalled them to Dog.

She guessed it was because Dog couldn't talk, and since he couldn't talk, he also couldn't react. He couldn't tell her how sorry he was that she was an outcast, and because he was this way, Peggy was able to lie to herself and muffle the hurt.

"And then I just blacked out, but it wasn't so bad," she said, finishing the story, wishing there had been more. Because once the story was over there wasn't anything to do. Anita wouldn't let her go to school for a few days, so Peggy didn't have to bother with homework.

There was just nothing to do.

She lay in bed and rubbed Dog's back and listened to the wind outside starting its nightly ritual. Make the trees dance, she thought, make the branches sway and throw moving shadows across the lawn. Then she tried to picture the scene she'd just wished for in her mind; it was such a comforting sight. It was familiar and safe.

Nothing could touch her here on this block, not while the wind blew and the trees danced and shadows moved on the lawn. Nothing.

"Okay, Dog, what now?"

As if in answer to her question, Dog jumped down and ran to her closet. Then he stood by the door and whined. There was something inside that stirred his interest, making her curious.

"Is it animal, vegetable, or mineral?" she asked. "Does it walk and talk?" She couldn't imagine what was in there, and suddenly thought it best not to try. Dog was whining at something. Last year a squirrel had gotten into Anita's closet through a small opening between the roof and wall of the house. Some squirrels carried rabies. "Come here, Dog" she commanded.

But Dog didn't listen. He stood by the door and continued to whine.

"What's in there?" she asked, as if he could answer. Then she slid her legs over the side of the bed and got to her feet. She had two choices concerning Dog and the closet. She could either ignore his whining or she could open the door and settle her curiosity.

Studying her first choice—ignoring Dog—she realized that was a terrible idea. Dog's whining would soon reach Anita's ears, and Anita would come up here and throw him out. That left choice number two.

Not that she was anxious to free a rabid squirrel from the confines of her closet, if it was a rabid squirrel in there. It was just that she didn't want Dog thrown out. Dog was a friend, and friends didn't treat one another so badly.

After approaching the closet with caution, Peggy stopped and listened at the door for the telltale noises a squirrel would make, like scurrying or scratching. Hearing nothing, she sucked in her breath and pulled back on the knob. "Well, it's open," she said to Dog and waited.

Dog stuck his head in, and when he didn't get bitten, Peggy swung the door wide and peered in herself. "What is it?" she asked, staring at Dog, waiting for him to do something. But Dog ignored her and went on in, his attention focused on the shelf above the rack.

Peggy felt herself go weak and raised her eyes to look on the shelf. She was afraid that the rabid squirrel might have been up there, ready to pounce. But before she had a chance to look, Dog whined again, louder this time, scaring her badly. "Damnit, what the hell do you want?"

But then the answer was obvious, and yet, was it? The only thing on that shelf besides the movie magazines was the ouija board. Dog couldn't be barking because of that. Was it possible he'd remembered it was there? And if so, why was he barking?

Peggy reached up and took the ouija board from beneath the magazines and wondered at the noises the trees were making outside of her window. She heard whooshing and squeaking and groaning, and those noises weren't normal, nor were they as pleasant and familiar sounding as they should have been.

Somehow the trees weren't dancing or the branches swaying softly in the wind. Somehow it sounded like the trees were moving in a wild, frenzied, almost psychotic way.

Dog barked impatiently, triggering Peggy into action. Peggy grabbed the ouija board to her chest and ran from the closet, slamming the door behind her as though heeding the warning in Dog's voice. "Stop that!" she yelled at Dog. "You scared the hell outta me."

But Dog didn't bow his head and act ashamed because Peggy yelled at him. Instead, he ran to her bed and back again. Then he made another trip. He seemed anxious to begin playing the game.

"What's gotten into you? Last night you were annoyed 'cause I made you keep your damned paw on the damned pointer. Now you can't wait to play."

When Dog barked impatiently again, Peggy held her fingers to her lips. "You keep this up and you're outta here! Mom'll throw you out!"

Following Dog to her bed, Peggy kept talking to keep her mind off the squealing noises the trees were making outside, their branches driven to madness by the wind. "I mean, are you so bored, Dog, that you wanna play with this thing? I'm bored, too, and you don't see me carryin' on."

Laying the ouija board on the bed, she sat on one side while Dog jumped up and sat opposite her. But then her attention drifted to her bedroom door. What if Charlie or Anita should happen to walk in and catch her playing with the Ouija? She rose and locked the door, knowing she was locked inside with those horrible tree noises as well as the alleged spirit in the board.

But the tree noises didn't matter, she told herself, while Anita's words from this morning came back to her. Anita had accused Peggy of having quite an imagination because of the epilepsy, and Anita had been right. Peggy did hallucinate at times and tended to blow things out of proportion.

The noises were no different tonight than they had been last night and the night before. The intensity was all in her mind.

"Put your paw on the pointer, Dog. Or the planchette. It's called a planchette, too."

CHAPTER NINE

Peggy sat with her hands folded across her lap, her fingers drawing circles on the fabric of her pajamas. Dog was by her side, his paw no longer on the pointer. Peggy had called him over when it started again, when the small, white, triangular object began to move by itself.

Staring down at the board, Peggy watched it go frantically from one letter to another, as if it couldn't move fast enough. "Hello, Peggy," it said. She didn't wonder how it knew her name. Yesterday it had known about Charlie and the color blue. Today it knew her name. So what?

Wasn't this supposed to be the same as talking to someone human? Then don't question its knowledge, she told herself. Besides, it already told her that it knew all.

"Answer me!" it commanded, its words storming through her brain, muffling the sound of the wind beating against the trees outside.

"What'dya want me to say?" she asked, the small hairs on the back of her neck bristling with anxiety.

"Say, hello."

"Hello." The voice she'd just heard wasn't her own; it belonged to someone else. Her voice wasn't low and squeaky, at least not until now.

"How was your day at school?" it asked.

"Fine. Just fine."

"Liar!"

"What!"

"Lie to yourself, Peggy, not to me. I know the truth."

Dog whined and brushed his nose against her hand. She jumped when the sensation of something wet and cold touched her flesh. Oh Lord, this was scary. "You know the truth about what?" she asked.

"About those girls—Connie and Tracy—and the rat."

It knew those girls, knew their names and what they did to her. But how?

"Don't bother to explain it again," she said. "You know all, right?"

"Right!"

"But I'm not lying to you. School was fine."

"Sure! Just like you're sitting here playing with a game while pretending nothing is hurting inside."

"I can hack the pain. I've gone through this before."

"What you mean is you've lied to yourself before. You've been covering the hurt and pain of your loneliness for so long now, you just automatically do it. You've been lying in bed for hours now, pretending you were bored and trying to act as though nothing bad happened in school. Like when you were younger and got punched in the mouth at least once a week. Not only did you hide the truth from Charlie and Anita, you hid it from yourself as well."

"Ouija, this is part of my biofeedback training. I can't dwell on the bad in my life, only the good. If I don't bury it, I'll have seizures."

"Bullshit! And don't call me Ouija."

This was ridiculous. Here she was, having a full-blown conversation with a game. Talking to Dog was bad enough. Then it dawned on her that the Ouija had known what happened when she was younger and about the swollen lips each week. Peggy was overwhelmed. "What should I call you then if not Ouija?"

"Derek."

"Come on, now! You're being stupid. Your name isn't Derek."

"But you like him," the pointer spelled out. "So, if you call me Derek, you'll like me as well."

"Is my liking you so important?"

"Yes!"

Peggy felt good inside. Someone—or something—actually cared if she liked them. Nothing this wonderful had ever happened before. "What is your name?" she asked again, expecting the truth this time.

"Maximilian. But you can call me Max!"

"What an exciting name! Just like the Roman Emperor!"

"You really like it, huh?"

"Yes."

Now Peggy had someone named Max to talk to, along with Dog and Charlie. Her circle of friends was growing, something she never dreamed possible. Then she felt silly; she should have remembered the Ouija's name. Nicky had called the spirit in the board Max the day she'd brought the game to Mr. Quigley's science class.

"Getting back to the hurt and how you cover it up," Max was saying, the pointer still moving at a furious pace, "I want you to tell me how you really feel inside."

"I can't. I'll have a seizure."

"No, you won't! Now stop this! Those girls forced your head down into a pot with a dead rat. You should be in total shock. I want you to experience the shock. I want you to dig it out of your subconscious and let it play itself out."

"Why?"

"Because, you must release the tension for the hurt to stop. Otherwise, some part of you is always carrying it around. You'll never be happy until you're free of the nightmares buried in your subconscious."

Peggy was overwhelmed. Max was concerned about her. In fact, he sounded like Charlie. Having a friend like this was a thrilling experience; having one so tuned in to her feelings was even better.

"Tell me what happened in school today, just as you've told Dog. Only this time, let yourself go and feel the emotions."

Without hesitation, Peggy began to speak to the board, to Max. From beginning to end, she told him about what happened and how it affected her. Soon she noticed tears streaming down her cheeks, staining her face and making the top of her pajamas wet. But she couldn't stop. She kept talking and crying.

When she was finished, she grabbed a Kleenex from a box on her nightstand and didn't try to stop the spasms in her body. These were sniffles and were good for the soul according to Max.

"Do you want revenge on those girls?"

"I guess."

"In what form?"

Peggy listened to the branches of trees scraping against her window and was suddenly uneasy. Maybe it was because Max had powers— he'd already proven this—and maybe it was because he would hurt those girls if Peggy gave her consent. "I don't really wanna hurt them. I just imagine doing it at times."

"Why?" Max asked.

"It makes me feel better."

"True. Just as talking to me a moment ago, while experiencing your inner anxieties, made you feel better. This is part of what I have been telling you."

"You mean—like therapy? Acting out my feelings without hurting anyone?"

"Right. And it worked, didn't it?"

"Yes, Max. I feel like a tremendous load has been taken away. Crying was wonderful. Max, you're wonderful."

"And so are you! And you have got to stop hiding everything, burying yourself alive. You're a thinking, feeling individual, not a robot. You must let yourself go without fear of having seizures."

"I've had so many in the past."

"You won't now. I'll protect you. You'll see."

Could Max stop her seizures? He was powerful in the sense he could see and hear what went on in her world, but did he have the power to stop her seizures as well?

"Just wait and see."

Turning away from the board, Peggy rubbed Dog's head, then kissed him. "And to think I was mad 'cause you wanted to play with the ouija board. I'm sorry, Dog."

"As you should be," the pointer spelled out, catching her attention. "I implanted the suggestion in Dog's head. It really wasn't his fault."

Peggy felt nervous again. Now Max was telling

her he had the power to dig into Dog's mind and make him react to commands. What else could Max do that she should know about?

"Why did you do it?" she asked.

"To make you play the game. How else could we get close and become friends?"

"I'm putting you away now, Max. I feel tired." She *was* tired, tired of being scared and happy at the same time. One minute she was thrilled with Max, then leery of his powers the next.

"Don't be afraid of me, Peggy."

"I'm not," she said, knowing it was a lie. Max must have known it as well.

"Maybe we'll meet in person some day," he said.

"Maybe. But not just yet."

She put the game back into its box and returned it to its hiding place in the closet. Her mind was filled with many things, mostly what she'd discussed with Max, and how she had a new friend, one who partly frightened her. "Maybe we'll meet in person some day," he'd told her.

Oh, I hope not, Peggy thought. She was disturbed by the idea of a game coming to life, of a spirit from a game materializing in front of her. Especially since she still lived with the memory of the man in the midst of the swirling breeze the day Nicky had fallen—the man who resembled an executioner.

She could still envision him in her mind. She could still see his powerful body rippling with muscles. He had been naked from the waist up, his head covered with a black hood. He reminded her of someone she'd seen in a movie about a French king once, a movie with a chopping block and a hooded executioner with an axe.

Max the axe man, she thought and almost fainted. "Dog! You listen to me from here on in," she said, wondering if Dog understood. "Don't listen to voices in your head."

Quickly closing the closet door behind her, she heard the wind howl outside of her room, heard the frenzied movements of the trees, and slid the slipper chair in front of the door so that the top of the chair caught under the knob. The door was jammed now; nothing could get out of that closet.

It was a silly thing to do, but she felt safer this way.

Nicky lay in her hospital bed and listened to the wind, paying no mind to the slime covering the walls; it wasn't real. Nor did she pay attention to the moving shadows near the foot of her bed and the closet door that kept opening and closing.

Picking up the phone, she decided to call Hank. She was supposed to have left the hospital this morning, but her nerves were shot, the doctor said, and he wouldn't release her. And yet, it wasn't her nerves that had gone bad; it was Max. He'd gone bad. He no longer loved or desired Nicky, so this left only Hank Brudhle.

She started to dial Hank's number when the lights in the room went out and the door leading to the hall slammed shut. She was frightened at first, but passed it off as more of Max's revenge. Max, it seemed, was determined to scare the hell out of her.

But she'd been through this before. Nicky had run the gamut of horror when chairs and other furniture at home turned themselves upside down. So this was nothing new, and if it weren't for the phone being dead, she might have laughed this off.

Clicking the button on the receiver, she pushed it about ten times and put the phone to her ear—nothing. Then the lights went on and the door leading to the hall opened.

At this point she recalled a conversation she'd had with Max not too long ago. She remembered holding the pointer in her hands while telling Max about the strange shit going on in her house. Max had said it was because of ghosts. Spirits of the dead were roaming Nicky's house, he claimed. Then he promised to protect Nicky and her family from the evil.

After that, Nicky had wondered more than once if Max had been lying, if Max himself had been the evil and the cause of all those strange happenings.

Of course the answer was yes. Max was the evil, and Max was all-powerful, Max was legion. Nicky had no one to protect her from Max. She wanted to cry at this point, but held back. Max was a bastard, the cruelest . . .

Lying on the bed daydreaming, Nicky had lost contact with the world of reality. She'd gone into her subconscious in search of answers to her predicament with Max and the search had left her less than alert, a dangerous thing when dealing with a spirit like Max. Hell, girl, you have to watch for it coming, for Max's revenge to manifest itself in whatever form Max chooses. But Nicky had gotten sloppy, and now she had a price to pay.

With the receiver of the phone still in her hand, she glared at the foot of her bed and saw a quivering mound of flesh with exposed nerves crawling towards her feet. Nicky glared at the tiny scalpel strapped to the side of its body and felt the hairs on the back of her neck rise with fear. It wanted her flesh, it seemed, the words of the creature resounding in her brain.

"Ridiculous," Nicky told it back. "I'm still wearing my flesh."

"No problem," the mound said.

Nicky laid the receiver down and thought about the button to summon the nurse, and yet she knew without trying that the button wouldn't work. The phone was dead so the button had to be just as dead. The door to the hall was closed again and probably jammed tight, and the mound wanted her flesh.

She could get up and run, only what place would she choose as a safe harbor from Max?

There was no such place . . . anywhere. Max was legion. So it was better to lie here and take her punishment rather than run her ass into the ground trying to escape when there was no escape.

Peggy was restless that night, and her dreams were a reflection of her mood. She couldn't stay with one for long it seemed and kept shifting to another like a movie changing scenes.

But when she woke up the following morning, things were suddenly different. There was a bright shaft of sunlight burning across her body; the wind had stopped and the trees were still. She wasn't as restless as she'd been last night and couldn't remember the content of her dreams.

The slipper chair was still in place, keeping the closet door from opening. She spotted it when she swung her legs over the side of the bed and laughed. She'd lost control last night. Playing with the ouija board had done strange things to her mind and had caused her to imagine a lot.

Max, indeed! The spirit in the board wanted to be called Max!

Jeez! Peggy always had quite an imagination, but last night was the best. Holding a full blown conversation with a game! Girl, you need help.

Dog was stretched out on the floor near the foot of her bed, his jowls dangling over one paw, his tail thumping the rug. Peggy looked at him and laughed again. Dog was the laziest creature she'd ever seen. And so was she. If not, then why hadn't she given the poor thing a proper name by this time?

"I gotta go pee, Dog. Then I'm going downstairs to get something to eat. And you know what that means?"

He cocked his head to one side, which made his ears seem awkwardly uneven. Dog was asking her why she was throwing him out. Why couldn't he stay in her room?

"You know the rules," she said. "You're not allowed in here alone."

After Peggy answered Dog, she began to wonder about this thing she was doing—speaking to a dumb animal. But Dog was her only friend.

"Great! Now I'm gonna sit here and feel sorry for myself," she said and rubbed Dog's neck when he came over and brushed up against her. "I'm also askin' myself why I keep talking to you." She also wondered why she'd had an ongoing conversation with a game last night when Max didn't even exist—not now, not ever. Max had been an illusion, something conjured up in her mind to escape her loneliness.

"Come on, Dog," Peggy said and opened her bedroom door. "Maybe Anita will let you back in when I finish breakfast. I'm home for a few days. She might let me keep you up here."

Dog, his head bowed, went into the hall to wait for Peggy, but the slipper chair had to be moved first. What if Anita came up here and made the bed while Peggy was eating? What if she saw the chair blocking the closet door? Of course, making the bed when Peggy had to spend the next few days there didn't make sense, but nothing Anita did ever made sense.

She then looked down at Dog, at his sad eyes and his floppy ears, and realized he was depressed. He was asking to stay in her bedroom where it was warm, where the rug was cozy and soft beneath his bones.

"After I eat, I'll come back up and let you out for a few minutes. Then you can come back up here with me, okay? See ya in a while," she said, giving him a final hug before leaving.

Dog watched the door close behind Peggy and waited. When she didn't come back, he trotted over to her bed and jumped up. After walking in circles, trying to find the right spot, Dog was about to lie down when a curious thing happened. The closet door opened by itself.

Dog froze. Maybe Mom was hiding in there. Maybe Mom had waited until Peggy was gone so she could raise hell with him. But from what Dog could see the closet was empty. So he just lay down and kind of stretched his legs as far as they'd go and was about to nibble at an annoying flea when he heard noises coming from the closet!

And they just weren't ordinary noises, the kind Dog was used to hearing. If they were, then Dog could have ignored them. But these noises were different. He swore there was a voice calling his name, a voice saying, "Here, Dog. Here, boy."

Dog sat up and cocked his head to one side to listen. There wasn't anybody in the closet. Who was calling his name?

After waiting a moment longer and not hearing anything, Dog rolled onto his side. He closed his eyes to take a nap and was almost gone when he heard it again. "Here, Dog. Here, boy." It was the damndest thing. What made it worse was that the closet door was closed now, so the voice sounded muffled.

"Here, Dog. Here, boy," the voice said again, persistently calling to him, not letting up this time.

And Dog, out of a natural, inner born curiosity—the same as most dogs had—jumped off the bed to sniff at the bottom of the door. If he picked up a scent and it was familiar, then he'd know who was inside calling his name. If the scent wasn't familiar, then he'd do the job he was partly here for. He'd bark good and loud.

Dog didn't recognize the scent. In fact, Dog didn't even like the scent. It was awful and almost took his breath away. He opened his jaws and was about to let loose with a good, loud bark when another curious thing happened. The closet door opened again—and again by itself.

Dog watched it swing wide and peered inside from a distance, but he didn't see anything. The closet was still empty. Someone was calling his name, but he couldn't see who that someone was.

Growing bored and disgusted with this game, Dog turned and headed for the door leading to the hall. He wanted out, and he wanted out now!

But since he couldn't open the door by himself, he intended to scratch and claw at the damned door until he got Peggy's attention. Or Mom's. Mom would let him out. And if scratching didn't work, he would just have to bark his throat raw.

Barking would bring Mom on the run. Oh yeah, she'd come running all right. She'd probably be real mad at him, too, and kick his behind outside. But Dog could take it. Anything was better than standing here listening to a bodiless voice. It was driving him crazy. Even the cold, damp ground in the yard seemed like heaven compared to playing stupid, maddening games.

Dog was halfway to the door when the voice called him back. "Don't go," it pleaded. "I'll let you see me now."

Dog didn't understand what the voice was saying, but something in the tone drew him back to the closet where he saw a tall man, husky, naked from the waist up and wearing a hood over his head. "Dog," the man said, "here, boy." He stuck out his hand as though he had a goodie for Dog.

Dog hesitated.

"Hurry," the man said, slapping his thigh.

Dog understood this time. If he wanted the treat, he had to be quick. After leaning back on his haunches for added momentum, Dog shot forward and took a running leap into the closet . . .

and couldn't stop when flames shot up from the floor and surrounded the man . . .

and couldn't stop when the odor of burning flesh scorched his sensitive nostrils . . .

and couldn't stop when the closet door slammed shut behind him . . .

and couldn't stop when the closet swallowed him whole.

CHAPTER TEN

Peggy was in the dining room when the sensation hit—something was dreadfully wrong. Although she was alone in the room, she felt the heat of another body close by. Standing still, she turned in all directions and thought she must be mad because there was no one that she could see or touch.

But the sensation lingered and grew. There was a hand pressing against her back. She whirled and saw no one. Then someone whispered to her, nothing she could hear and repeat, but the words scared her just the same. And the voice seemed composed of many, like several people speaking in unison. Was she going crazy?

Or was this another illusion like those that had

tormented her this past week?

Charlie and Anita were in the kitchen on the other side of the door. Her parents were so close, separated by a threshold, one she could cross so easily, but the whispered words were clearer now, warning her not to dare move, telling her that succumbing to the beast was her only choice.

What beast?

She felt a coldness wrapping itself around her like a blanket of death and knew that a force more deadly than anything she'd ever known wanted possession of her body, her soul, her flesh. This was the interpretation of the voices resounding in her skull. The voices were telling her these things, joined in unison in a macabre song of dementia.

"Succumb to the beast," they said.

Why me?

"Why not?" the voices whispered. "Why anyone else?"

"More coffee?" Anita asked beyond the threshold, and Charlie answered, "Yes," making her long to be with them, to be the recipient of Anita's coffee and subsequently her freedom.

Ignoring the voices, Peggy tried to move towards the kitchen, but the voices were magnetic, holding her back, luring her with the force of a siren's wail. Gripping the dining room table in front of her, she held on because there was something familiar about the sensation of heavily varnished wood against her flesh, the same flesh the voices promised to peel from her body.

"Be ours, Peggy," the voices sang. "Let us love you. Be one with us in death."

No! she screamed inside and tore her mind loose from the lure of this hypnotic insanity as she would tear herself loose from a seizure. This wasn't real. The voices weren't real, nor was the hand pressing itself against her back with an urgency now that she was breaking free. The hand wanted her to stay, the fingers softly kneading her flesh in an erotic way, letting her know they could do more, they could work her body with the passions of the lover she so longed for.

No, she screamed inwardly one more time, then steadied herself and headed towards the kitchen. This wouldn't be easy, facing Charlie and Anita while pretending that what happened in the dining room just now never happened at all. But if she were to recount her story to her parents, they'd swear she either had a seizure and didn't know, or she was completely insane.

Swallowing hard, she laid her hands against the kitchen door and forced it open to find Anita on her hands and knees in the bathroom back near the utility room. Charlie was at the table drinking coffee, staring into space. There was a folded newspaper on the table in front of him. Charlie and Anita must have been fighting, otherwise he'd be reading his paper instead of fuming to himself.

"Morning," Peggy said, her voice still shaky from the experience in the dining room. Then she held her nose against a terrible odor coming from the bathroom. She looked at Anita, still on her hands and knees, and wanted to ask what smelled. But her parents had been quarreling, and asking a simple question might start them off again.

Anita was the type who absolutely and positively couldn't stand a mess of any kind, and knowing her, she'd probably blamed the mess on Charlie. Somehow Charlie was to blame. But Peggy's curiosity got the better of her. Choosing her words, forcing her voice to sound sweet and innocent, she asked, "What smells?"

"The toilet," Anita said. "It's overflowed. Have you been flushing sanitary napkins again?"

"I never flush them."

"Then it's your father. He uses too much toilet paper."

"You want help?" Peggy asked, hoping she'd say no.

"Not really. Bad enough I'm sick to my stomach. I don't need you throwing up."

Peggy walked over to the bathroom door, looked in at Anita and felt her stomach flip. There was a steady flow of a thick, white substance oozing from the toilet; it resembled oatmeal. "God, it smells awful!"

"Tell me about it!" Anita was wearing shorts and a sleeveless top. From where Peggy was standing, Anita looked like a small child. She was so petite that Peggy envied her.

"How do we stop it from coming up?" Peggy asked. "It just keeps flowing."

Anita had been wiping up the messy stuff with a towel, then squeezing the wet towel over a bucket. When Peggy said what she did, Anita threw the towel at the toilet and sat back on her haunches. "I don't know."

"Let's call a plumber," Charlie said, for what Peggy imagined must have been the tenth time. "It takes a minute to dial a number."

"Go ahead," Anita murmured. "If we don't stop this soon, we'll be buried alive under this slime."

Peggy stared at the white substance, at the bubbles coating its surface, and wondered if it was alive. "I saw a movie once called 'The Blob'—"

"This is no movie," Anita said, getting wearily to her feet. "And you'd better eat before the plumber comes. We don't want to be in his way, now do we?"

"I'm not hungry, Mom," Peggy said. "I'll just have some juice." Her hands began to tremble when she poured orange juice into a tall glass. Anita wanted her out of here and fast. The plumber was coming. Mustn't be in his way.

"And don't forget to let the dog out before the plumber comes."

Peggy sipped her juice and tried not to choke. Anita was right. Dog had to be let out. The poor thing was probably holding his legs together by this time. Peggy had to run upstairs right now. Peggy had to cross the dining room again and again, first to get dressed, then to let Dog out. She had to put herself in the position of listening to those voices and to let the invisible hand molest her again. And all because of Anita. But no, it never happened—no voices, no hand. She had been hallucinating the whole time.

Besides, she told herself in an attempt to raise her spirits, Dog didn't have to stay in the yard, not if the plumber was coming. Dog was a large-boned animal—half Shepherd and half Doberman—and carried traits from both breeds. Repairmen were usually leery of him. So, Dog would have to be taken back up to Peggy's room. This way, Peggy wouldn't be alone.

Nicky Martin stared at the straps binding her hands and feet in the light of day and wondered why no one believed her. She did not slam the door so that it jammed. She did not rip the telephone wires from the wall, nor did she disconnect her nurse's button so that it wouldn't work. And she did not wreck her room.

Mainly, though, she hadn't taken strips of flesh from her own body. Hell no, she was stupid in a lot of ways, but she wasn't nuts.

It was Max, she tried telling the doctors and nurses. Max, the spirit from her ouija board, was responsible for sending the creature who needed her skin. Lying in bed while her body convulsed with pain, she tried to make them understand, but it was difficult, as though she weren't even speaking their language.

"And what did this creature look like?" her doctor wanted to know, while Nicky writhed in pain and asked for more Demerol.

"It was a mound of flesh," Nicky wailed, "with exposed nerves on his belly. So he needed my skin."

"Really!"

"Yes. And this creature was the one who jammed the door so you couldn't get in when he peeled my skin. He was the one who cut the phone wires and did all the rest of the damage."

"Really!"

"Yes, damnit! Now give me some Demerol. The pain is maddening."

Nicky got her Demerol and a whole lot more. Nicky got a new bed from the psychiatric wing with straps to hold her hands and feet. She also earned herself a new doctor—a shrink.

"Isn't someone going to do something about my wounds?" she'd asked the shrink, when he'd visited her room during the night.

"What would you like us to do?"

Nicky stared at the man in front of her, stared at the inquisitive face that sought answers, stared at his white doctor's jacket and at the pad he held in his hands, and she marveled that he was playing games when he should have been administering first aid.

"What would I like you to do?" she'd repeated. "Well, how about some ointment and bandages for starters? I'll also need skin grafts. I hope there won't be any scars. Please, do something about my wounds!"

"Would that calm you down? Would you stop screaming if we bandaged your wounds?"

"Of course," Nicky said, figuring by now that he was the one who needed help. The shrink needed a shrink. But then the nurse came and didn't know where to apply the ointment. She couldn't find Nicky's wounds.

"Doesn't anyone see the raw flesh where my skin has been peeled from my body?"

"No. You'll have to show it to us," the doctor said, letting her know it never really happened, that Max's pet hadn't stolen her flesh. It was all in her mind. Max was trying to drive her crazy.

At that point Nicky knew she'd been bound to her bed by the hospital staff to save her from her own self-destructive imagination.

And now, as she lay in bed and stared at a shaft of light moving across her body, she knew that morning had finally come. But this didn't mean she was safe from Max.

Max wasn't a vampire that had to hide from the sun, nor a flesh-eating ghoul that hid in the shadows of the night. Max could make himself human, and this made Max a dangerous—what? She'd almost used the word "man."

"I am, Nicole. I'm all man in *your* mind."

Nicky listened to his voice coming from somewhere around her and decided not to look. Max was using a veil of invisibility and would remain hidden until the mood suited him, but at least he was talking. She couldn't see him but she could hear him. At this point, any form of communication was better than nothing.

"Why are you messing with my head?" she asked, waiting for an answer and knowing she might be waiting a long time if Max was in one of his stubborn moods. The waiting didn't bother her, though. She wasn't going anywhere. She was strapped to the bed like a hog ready for slaughter, and she was drugged. What else did Nicky have but time?

The winged creature with the membranous appendages who'd wanted his turn with Nicky when she'd been having sex with Max was back, speaking to her in her mind like the rest. Nicky watched him approach her bed, his black body encrusted with heavy scales and tumors. His head was huge, the cranial portion of it jutting out over his eyes like a hood.

His tongue was the size of a small pipe and forked at the ends. Max had sent him, he told Nicky, to make sure she was cared for and her sexual cravings satisfied.

Nicky closed her eyes and dared not scream as tiny vignettes of psychotic pornography danced in her mind; the winged beast was using telepathy to signal his intentions.

But, oh God, it wasn't just sex he wanted; he wanted to devour her. And yet he wasn't after her flesh like the shapeless mound from last night. No. This beast wanted her organs, wanted to taste the sinewy muscles of her heart, her kidneys, her lungs.

"No!" she protested and opened her eyes as he flew over the bed and landed on her, his batlike wings spread wide, pinning her to the mattress. Covering her mouth with his own, Nicky felt his thick, forked tongue enter and thrust its way deep into her throat, choking her with its size, gagging her with the terrible acrid taste of his flesh.

Then her stomach began to wretch violently. She felt bile rising and tried to hold back because her mouth was blocked. Her heart began to pound heavily with the strain of not throwing up, of not being able to breathe. She listened to its constant thumping motions and feared it would explode in her chest.

Blackness was closing in; she was passing out. She was in pain and was passing out. But then, fainting would have been wonderful; to close her eyes and mind to this horror would have been a blessing. However, she had the feeling that this blackness, this overall numbness, was more than just a prelude to fainting.

Nicky felt she was about to die. The black, winged beast was sucking the life from her body, and she was about to die.

Peggy finished her juice and went upstairs, leaving Charlie and Anita to struggle with the mess oozing from the toilet. Dog had to be let out before the plumber arrived.

After crossing the dining room without incident, she climbed the steps to her room and
wondered why she smelled sulphur coming
from the upper floor of the house. The odor was
so strong it nearly covered the stench from the
white stuff pouring from the toilet. Charlie must
have been smoking up here in defiance of Anita's
ban.

"Way to go, Dad," she wanted to shout. Charlie had been whipped for such a long time it was
refreshing to think he'd rebelled, even though
his rebellion had taken on the simple form of
sneaking a cigarette in his own home.

But the odor grew stronger when she opened
the door to her room. It was sharp and acrid and
stabbed at her lungs. She saw whorls of white
steam rising in the air near her bed and wanted
to run back downstairs because this was no
ordinary cigarette smoke. It reminded her of the
colorful swirling breeze in the locker room at
school.

"Dog," she called, aware of the crack in her
voice. She was losing control. First the voices in
the dining room and now this. "Dog," she called
again, pretending the smoke wasn't real. "I gotta
go. Then I'll let you out in the yard, and Dog—"

She'd started to tell Dog about the plumber
coming and how he didn't have to stay outside,
but Dog wasn't in her room. He wasn't on the
bed or lying next to it. He wasn't even under it.
Where the hell was he, she wondered, until she

heard scratching noises coming from the inside of her closet.

Dog was in there, the dope.

"Come on, Dog," she said, opening the closet door. "Come on out," she coaxed.

And Dog came out, but not like he normally did. He wasn't prancing or bouncing on all fours. Instead, he was walking sort of lopsided as though his tail end was coming up to meet his chest, and his head was down. He smelled terrible, too, unless the odor from the downstairs toilet had climbed up here, and she was smelling that and not Dog.

No matter. "I really have to go," she said, heading for her bathroom with Dog following behind, kind of dragging his body like it was an effort to walk.

As she was washing her hands, she stopped to wonder if Dog was sick. Maybe this was why he had no life in him. In fact, the last time he looked this bad, Dog had caught the flu from her. Only Peggy wasn't sick now, and neither were Charlie or Anita. So if he caught something, it didn't come from them.

Peggy felt eyes burning through her now as she often sensed when Derek was nearby. But it was Dog who was staring this time and not Derek. Dog was standing just outside of the bathroom, looking cockeyed and crooked, his body twisted as if it had gone through a wringer.

His coat was mangy and wet. He really must

have been sick, she thought, sick enough for a visit to the vet. Yet, his eyes were bright and alert—bright and *hateful* and alert. Sparks of rage were practically shooting from his pupils.

"Are you all right, Dog?" she asked. Then she stared back into his eyes, saw two pools of rheumy, black death and felt her flesh turn clammy. She had been right about the expression on his face. She'd never seen it before, but it was there now, like a mad dog. And yet, it wasn't a crazy, foaming at the mouth kind of madness. What she saw was more in line with Dog being angry at her.

She heard a deep, soft growl rise from his throat and suddenly knew how repairmen felt when they came here and saw Dog. He was big. His teeth were big. God, she'd never noticed his teeth before. The only reason she'd taken notice now was because his lip was curled back as if he wanted her to see his teeth and be afraid.

Peggy held onto the sink and fought the aura she felt rising in her brain. Dog was about to attack; this was no time to give in and chance a blackout.

Concentrate, she told herself. Concentrate on the glitch in the computer and concentrate on finding a weapon. This wasn't Dog facing her; it was a mad, murderous beast.

There was a safety razor in the medicine cabinet over the sink. If only she could get to it before Dog got to her. She saw thick droplets of spittle dripping from his teeth and even thicker saliva coating his mouth. Rabies? Hell no, Dog had his shots.

He was in the middle of the bathroom now, forcing her back against the shower and tub. There was nowhere to go, nowhere to run to, nowhere to hide. She was trapped. Dog stood between her and the only way out.

Dividing her attention between the glitch in her brain and Dog, she stiffened her back when the only solution possible exploded inside of her head. She had no choice but to force herself to walk past Dog, and she had to do it in such a way as to throw him off guard.

Moving slowly, taking it one step at a time, Peggy began to walk towards Dog. He growled again when she moved, but she ignored him and the rawness of her nerves as well. She had to be strong. She couldn't afford to succumb to her fears and risk a seizure.

But it was hard. She'd never fought a seizure and a mean, hateful Dog all at the same time.

Still advancing towards him, she noticed he'd stopped in his tracks. For some unknown reason he seemed intimidated by her boldness. She watched his paws going backwards and knew he'd changed his mind about attacking her.

Great, she thought, but don't celebrate just yet. It's a long way to the bedroom door.

With her eyes still glued to his, she reached behind the bathroom door and took her robe from its resting place on a hook. The plumber was coming and she wasn't dressed, not that it mattered. Saving her life was more important. Only Anita would raise hell if she came downstairs in her pajamas in front of a stranger.

Peggy was in the bedroom by this time. Dog was still between her and the door, but Dog was backing up, retreating. She would win this one, but only if she kept her cool.

Slowly walking towards Dog, still concentrating on him and the glitch in her brain, she was at the halfway mark when something caught one of her feet and held fast, forcing her to look away from Dog for one moment.

It was Anita's stupid, rotten, pink bedspread. She'd snagged the toe of a slipper in one of the ruffles. She bent down to free her foot and felt Dog's hot breath on her neck, the stench of his madness searing her nostrils.

Dog had gotten brave again when Peggy stopped watching him.

Think, she told herself, think mean and cool. Look him in the face and don't show fear. But it was harder now because she was bending over. This took away the advantage of height and put her at Dog's level. "Get back!" she hissed and almost fainted when he growled, his lips barely touching hers.

If Dog attacked, her face was gone.

Rising slowly, Peggy stiffened her body to full height and watched him back away. She'd won. But would she keep on winning long enough to reach the door and safety? Somehow she longed for the warmth of the old Anita's embrace, the Anita she used to know.

Step by frightening step Peggy backed Dog up until his rump was against the door, until his body was blocking her only escape route. What now? Do I grab him and wrestle him out of my way, or do I stand here until either Charlie or Anita decide to come up and check on me?

Wrestling with him was out of the question. She'd wrestled him in the past, when they'd been friends, and always lost. He was strong as hell. And as far as her parents went, they wouldn't come up here until it was too late, until she was dead. The plumber was coming. Musn't leave the plumber alone.

"Get out of my way, you son of a bitch!" she hissed and waited. The words had escaped before she could stop them, but it seemed to be working. Dog was side-stepping the door, his mangy, wet and lopsided body moving at a crazy angle.

Once he was away from the door, she watched him and wondered if this was a trick. Was Dog drawing her into a false sense of security? Would he attack when her hand was on the knob? Or would he wait until she was halfway through the door and feeling safe?

"You'd better not even think of it, you bastard!" she said, trying to scare him again. Shouting at Dog had worked a moment ago and got him away from the door. Maybe shouting this time would stop him from attacking her. She reached out and fingered the knob while tiny streams of sweat ran down her body.

Dog growled again and staggered towards her. Closing her eyes for a moment to make a final repair in the glitch in her brain, Peggy pulled the door open in one furious movement and slammed it against the side of Dog's head. Dog lost his balance and fell over sideways, giving her time to get out and slam the door behind her as he was getting to his feet.

Standing in the hall outside, she both heard him and smelled him. He was close to her, with nothing more than a huge piece of wood separating her from Dog and his teeth, from Dog and the hatred she'd sensed in his eyes.

Now what? How do I come up here again without having to explain about Dog? How do I make Charlie come with me? Dog was sick. If she told the truth, Anita would turn him into the pound in no time.

"I love you, Dog," she whimpered, not wanting to give in to her fears and admit the dog had changed for the worst. "I love you," she repeated and felt her nerves dancing through her skin when he growled even louder than before. He was an insane beast, she told herself. He was shot, gone to hell.

Leaning against the door, she released the grip on her mind and cried, allowing her emotions to escape as Max had taught her to do. Max had told her that crying was good for the soul, and Max was right. Crying did make her feel better. Max was a good friend. In fact, he was her only friend now that Dog was sick.

What am I saying? Max didn't exist. He was nothing more than an illusion created out of loneliness. She'd already accepted the truth in her mind, so why dredge it up again?

Dog was sick, and Max was an illusion. There was nothing left—nothing, no one to lean on, no friends at all. Peggy never felt more lonely in her life than she did right now.

CHAPTER ELEVEN

Charlie's recliner wouldn't go back. He pushed the button on the side and waited for his feet to rise, but nothing happened. Then he took a crumpled tissue and wiped his eyes because this was the start of it.

At least if things went as they had years before, he knew that his chair wasn't smitten by something mechanical, just as the toilet in the bathroom hadn't been smitten by something a plumber could fix.

Of course it was only two small incidents—the toilet and his chair—nothing major. But everything started out small before it grew out of proportion. Those hauntings in his home years ago had begun as nothing, and before they had stopped, his family was all the better part of being crazy.

"Nothing I can do," the plumber had said earlier this morning when he saw the white mess oozing from the toilet. "Beats the hell outta me. I don't know what's causin' it. We probably gotta dig up the foundation."

And Charlie knew that this was the start of a haunting. Then he quickly questioned his own sanity for allowing Peggy to bring that damned, cursed, stinking ouija board into his house, because that damned game had caused this same thing years before.

But Charlie had this wimpish side of his personality. He let people walk on him and over and through him, and all he ever said was, "Thank you, thank you. Crap on my head all day if you like."

Clenching his fist in anger, he heard a noise on the stairs and saw Peggy. His first instinct was to slap her because she'd brought the game home. "Did the plumber come?" she asked, her eyes red like she'd been crying along with Charlie.

"Yeah, but he's gone. There's nothing he can do."

"And the mess? Daddy, what about that?"

"It stopped by itself. And before you ask, your mother's in the kitchen and she doesn't need help. She doesn't need us to get in her way, but then, isn't that the story of our lives." Charlie's voice trailed off then, leaving an awful silence between them.

Peggy came and sat in the chair next to him, Anita's chair, the one with the little, white doily covering the headrest. God, Charlie hated that friggin' doily. It was symbolic of Anita and the way she was—clean, sterile, rigid. Her whole life was wrapped inside that little, white doily.

"Did you have another fight with her?" Peggy asked.

Charlie couldn't answer, not right away. It was none of Peggy's business. In fact, she had one helluva nerve asking. But then he took a deep breath, let the wimp in him take over, and managed a broken smile. But there was still something tense in the way his lips curled back to reveal his teeth. "No."

"Good. I hate to see you two fight all the—"

"We're beyond fighting . . . Is the Ouija Board gone? Did you give it back?"

He stared at Peggy then, at her hair and the uneven curls framing her neck, at the flushed face, and waited for an answer. Her eyes avoided his. She was about to lie, maybe for the first time in her life. This was the impression she gave Charlie. And because of the lie, he'd have to tell Peggy the truth about his experience with the board whether Anita liked it or not. Besides, Anita wasn't here now to stop him.

"Did I give the ouija board back? Yeah, I did."

She'd taken too long to answer. Peggy *was* lying, something she didn't normally do. "That's good," he said, perpetuating the lie before slapping her with his past. "Day before yesterday I was in the middle of a story when your mother interrupted. It was about the ouija board, remember?"

"Yes. Four teenage boys, sitting around a card table in your room," she said.

"Anyway, seeing as how your mother is preoccupied, I'd like to finish that story." Sitting back in his chair, he pushed the button to raise his feet; this time it worked. He wasn't surprised. Taking his eyes off Peggy, he zeroed in on a spot on the steps and let himself go, knowing he couldn't tell this story and look at her at the same time. Peggy would probably be shocked, and the shock would force him to stop, and he couldn't stop, not now, not when the ouija board she had upstairs was fouling the air with its evil.

In his mind, Charlie took her back to the scene in his room, to the part where his occult nut of a friend was conjuring up the dead. Proceeding from there, he wondered if he should go ahead and tell Peggy the boy's name.

He wondered if he should tell Peggy how, after growing to adulthood, the boy had stayed here in town, as Charlie had. He wondered if he should tell Peggy that the boy had married and had fathered a son, and that the son had been given his father's name—Derek.

Then he decided against it. Peggy's Derek could have been someone else, not necessarily the son of the occult nut. True, Derek was an odd name, but why spoil his daughter's relationship until there was proof beyond a shadow of a doubt that his Derek and her Derek were related?

"This boy—I'll call him Edward. Anyway, there we were in my room with Edward summoning up the dead . . ."

Charlie saw it all. He saw three boys sitting around a card table in semidarkness, concentrating on a fourth while dying inside with fear. He saw a candle flickering on a dresser behind him, the light distorting the faces of the boys at the table. Then he saw the dark beyond the shadow of the candle, the dark surrounding them like some dreadful, ominous beast, and shuddered.

Then he listened to the words flowing from his lips.

"'Oh, spirit of the Ouija,' Edward had said, 'listen to us and answer our questions. We wish to summon forth the dead!' Then the pointer moved, asking who we had in mind. Three of us couldn't answer because there wasn't one dead person we wished to speak with. Edward, however, told the Ouija to use his imagination. We'd take what we could get."

Charlie broke then and pressed his head into the palms of his hands. He really didn't want to remember what happened, because sitting here telling this story to Peggy made it all seem so unreal and phony.

But it was real, and he had no choice but to

finish because his daughter here was fooling with a ouija board. Unless he could convince her to stop, they'd all pay the price in one way or another.

Going back to his past, Charlie continued.

"Would you like to meet this dead person?" the spirit from the Ouija asked next. "Would you like to speak to him face to face?"

Charlie stared at the boys around the table in muted shock and hoped they'd say no. He heard the wind whipping up outside of his room, saw the curtains at the windows dance straight out, and wondered why the candle was flickering as wildly as it was, as though driven by the breath of the damned.

"Sure," Edward said.

"What're you, nuts?" Charlie asked, knowing his parents would have a fit if someone dead, rotting and stinking showed up there.

"Pay him no mind, spirit," Edward said. "The rest of us are ready."

But they weren't, none of them. In fact, good old Edward wasn't even ready for what happened next.

"Nothing happened!" Anita shouted, her voice searing their nerves, almost sending Peggy into shock. "Not a damned thing. So why are you—"

"I'm gonna finish this!" Charlie said, his lips tight with anger. "I don't care whether you believe me or not. I'm gonna finish this. Now, your mother's right, Peggy. In a sense nothing happened. We waited and waited, scared half to death, but the dead didn't walk into my room that night."

"So the ouija board doesn't work, right, Daddy?"

"I didn't say that. We waited until ten and decided to break it up. After all, Edward had summoned the dead around eight. Two hours was enough to wait with our nerves at a high pitch."

"Don't do this!"

"Anita, be quiet."

Once he'd gotten control again—at least he hoped he had—Charlie went back into his mind once more and conjured up images of the past for Peggy. She saw Charlie in his room, sleeping. It was around three in the morning. The other boys had left hours ago.

Peggy looked into the room from Charlie's point of view and saw that, except for a slice of moonlight caressing the sill of his window, the room was bathed in darkness. And the curtains at the window were standing straight out, driven by winds completely foreign at that time of year.

Charlie was in the midst of a nightmare. He remembered dreaming about ouija boards and spirits and dead men with black stuff covering their lips, dead men who were after him. Charlie woke up when they caught him.

Sitting up in bed, he surveyed the darkness around him, blinked his eyes to accustom them to the dark, and sighed with relief to find that he was alone in his room. The dead had stayed behind in his dream.

Rising to go downstairs for a drink of water, Charlie recalled fumbling for his slippers and robe, making his way to the door, and running back to the nightstand next to his bed to snap on the light because the darkness was no longer still, and it frightened him.

Suddenly, as if by magic, there was movement in the shadows of his room, bodies swaying in time to a rhythm of dementia. And those bodies were everywhere. Some were standing in place, while others moved; some were hanging upside down from the ceiling, swinging from invisible bars; some were dancing, whirling and swirling in circles.

Charlie's hands were shaking badly when he snapped on the light and saw them disappear, but it didn't help. He couldn't see them, but he could still hear them. He could still hear their silent, almost nonexistent voices echoing in his head, mocking him, calling him fool, warning him of things to come. These were the dead ones Edward had called forth through the ouija board.

Or maybe they weren't the dead. Maybe these were creatures who had never lived, like the ones he'd read about in novels—creatures who thrived in darkness and fed on our fears, creatures who crawled the tunnels in a nether world running beneath our own, creatures who'd followed Charlie from his nightmare to the present tense of his room.

But Charlie couldn't swallow this, not at first. He snapped off the light and saw them again, surrounding him, leering at him, their voices promising torment. Oh, God! Then he snapped it on again and watched them disappear.

That was the beginning of the hauntings, for terrible things began to happen around his home after the creatures walked his room. Furniture in the house moved and flipped upside down as though guided by invisible hands. Revolting messes oozed from the toilets and from cooking pots on the stove. Radios blared on and off by themselves at all hours of the day and night.

And Charlie wasn't the only one who was suffering from the nightly walks of the dead—or undead. The other boys were suffering, too, especially Edward. But Charlie had no sympathy for him because he had caused it to happen. He was the one who'd called up the dead.

Since Edward didn't know how to stop the hauntings, the other boys nurtured a deep-seated hatred for him. Nobody should start something they can't finish or at least cure.

Charlie's parents almost went crazy. His father imagined they were beset by poltergeists and called in a priest. The priest studied the activity in the house for a while and decided to perform an exorcism when he had proof of the hauntings.

But the priest was old and forgetful and should have gotten help.

The night of the exorcism the creatures were still in full swing. Doors were slamming throughout the house; radios were blaring; someone had defecated in the middle of the dining room table. The priest, however, wasn't bothered by these displays of power from the forces of darkness. He went ahead with it, blessed the house, sprinkled holy water on the walls and prayed for God to help him. Only he kept forgetting the words, and he kept forgetting where he'd left his Bible. He'd put it down to sprinkle the water and then he'd walk away.

The creatures were laughing at him, their voices rising in unearthly howls of ridicule. Still, the priest continued. For hours he sprinkled water and prayed. Then his age caught up to him; he sat for a moment to catch his breath and fell asleep. The exorcism wasn't finished yet he fell asleep.

Peggy looked deeply into Charlie's story and saw the priest sleeping in an easy chair, saw the creatures moving about, and heard something huge and hideous land on the roof of the house. She saw the inner walls of the house vibrate, saw the floor move beneath everyone's feet, and heard a cry escape from above their heads, a cry of desired revenge being carried by the wind.

"Oh God," Charlie cried out, fearing they were in for it now. "Wake up, Father. Wake up." But the priest slept and they didn't know how to pray, not Charlie, nor his father, nor his mother. They were ignorant of the words of the church, and so they were forced to face this alone.

The thundering noises coming from the roof stopped at one point, and all was silent and still, and that silence disturbed them. At least when the creature had been moving about on the roof they knew where he was. At least when he'd been howling, they could track him down through his voice.

Peggy, still entranced by Charlie's story, saw the ground vibrate beneath their feet in a wild frenzy of motion. It had been vibrating before, but not like this.

The creature from the roof, the powerful one feared by the other beasts in the house, had left the roof to come hide under the floorboards. Peggy stared at her feet and almost died when something in her mind's eye came bursting through the floor. She saw splintered wood flying everywhere.

Then she saw a blackened claw that was scaly and covered with ulcerated tumors come up through the hole, and grab Charlie's father, peeling the skin from his arm—

"Your father burnt his arm at work!" Anita shrilled, the fear of the moment resounding in her voice. "This is bullshit!"

"No," Charlie shrieked, "it isn't bullshit. It was real. It happened. That story about him burning his arm at work was something he made up because he couldn't tell the truth!

People would have laughed at him, called him crazy."

Peggy listened to them fight and covered her chest with her hands to stop the pounding in her heart. Between what had taken place with Dog a while ago and Charlie's story, she feared a seizure. When an aura started to form, she knew she'd had enough. She concentrated on the glitch in the circuits of her mind and made repairs.

Then she rose and was about to go upstairs, because facing a crazy Dog couldn't be any worse than this, and yet she couldn't leave without asking the inevitable. "What happened, Daddy? Who stopped the creature?" She recalled that Charlie's father had died of natural causes, deformed arm and all. Someone had to have stopped the creature. "Who did it? Was it the priest?"

"No," Charlie fumed, turning away from Anita. "It was Edward, the occult nut. He showed up at the door just in time like the posse in old westerns. He'd found the secret of sending those creatures back to the tunnels of the damned where they belonged."

"Open the door, Peggy."

She heard the voice, traced it to her closet and wanted to die. This was exactly how Max would have sounded if Max were real.

Peggy had come up to her room moments ago to find Dog in the bathroom drinking water from the toilet. Of course, she hadn't come into her room right away, not before standing outside to listen at the door. When all had been silent inside, she took a chance and went on in.

And there was Dog, in the bathroom. Hell, she thought, if he was drinking water then he wasn't rabid. He was just nuts or overwrought. She ran to the bathroom and closed the door on Dog before he had a chance to attack.

Once Dog was locked inside and she was out of reach of those monstrous teeth of his, she sat on her bed to work this out in her mind.

Her parents were fighting. How the hell could she tell them about Dog? Especially Charlie. She'd wanted to say something when she found him alone in the living room, but Charlie had been so overtaken by his own misery—trying to tie the ouija board in with a simple plumbing problem—that she couldn't ask for his help.

Then she took a moment to think about what Charlie had said about his ouija board. It sure was strange. Peggy knew the damned things didn't work. She'd already accepted Max as an illusion, as the trees dancing in a frenzy outside of her window these past few days had been an illusion.

And now to hear her father recount a story from his past and swear it was the truth—

"Open the door, Peggy."

She heard the voice and automatically thought of Dog being locked in the bathroom. Dog was telling her to open the door, but dogs didn't talk. So this too was an illusion. And other

183

than Dog and herself, there wasn't anyone in the upper part of the house.

"You hear me? Open the door."

She heard the voice again and knew it wasn't Dog in the bathroom telling her to let him out. It was coming from the closet. But it was an illusion, so she ignored it.

"Come on now," the voice said gently. "I won't hurt you."

Peggy sighed heavily and covered her ears to stop the sounds that she knew were impossible. She couldn't be hearing this, not when she was practically alone and the only one in the room capable of speech.

"We're friends, aren't we?"

Friends? That alone told Peggy she was dreaming. She had no friends. Dog was crazy and Max was an illusion. Max! The ouija board? Was it possible?

"Let me out. We must talk."

Peggy opened the door and took the ouija board from its resting place on the top shelf of the closet because this was surely as Max would sound. Once it was spread before her on the bed, she sat down to talk to Max, but she couldn't. She needed two people to play, and Dog was sick. Yet Max was speaking aloud, not through the board, but in words she could understand?

"I'm legion," he said, the pointer moving by itself. "I know all and I can do all."

Staring at the pointer with eyes dulled by the mystery of this, Peggy read what Max was saying and wondered why he was no longer speaking aloud—*if* he'd been the one doing it.

"Why do you have to analyze everything that happens?" he asked. "You've already scolded yourself a thousand times for being so damned analytical. And yet here you are, analyzing Max."

"True."

"Now, let me tell you why I was so anxious to have this talk. Dog is sick, but it's not serious. The poor thing's had a breakdown."

"A breakdown? Dogs have those things?"

"Yes," Max answered, the pointer moving at a furious pace. "Because you were depressed, I went inside of Dog's head to find the problem."

Peggy read his words and knew this was the truth. Hadn't Max gotten into Dog's head to make him want to play with the Ouija just last night? Max had said he'd done this to get closer to Peggy, so they could become friends.

"What do I do about it? I don't think the vet can—"

"We don't need the vet. I can help Dog. But . . ."

Somehow Peggy knew there would be a but attached to his offer; nobody did something for nothing. Nobody!

"First," Max said, continuing on, "you must promise to accept me as a friend. I have wants and needs, too. I'm a thinking, feeling individual."

"That was it, Max? All you want is to be my friend?"

"Yes."

"No problem," she said. "Besides Dog, I don't have anybody else. I can always use a friend."

"Good, now leave me alone. Put the game back, wait five minutes, then open the bathroom door. Dog will be fine."

Doing as she was told, Peggy put the game back and felt partly elated about having another friend besides Dog. And yet for one moment there was a gnawing sensation in the pit of her stomach, something that couldn't be ignored. Max was a spirit. People didn't make friends with spirits, at least not if they were sane. Spirits could be dangerous. Hadn't she learned this over the years through reading books and watching TV?

Peggy heard Dog whine and came out of her reverie. Dog was locked inside of the bathroom, and Dog wanted out. The whining noises told her that Max had succeeded where her vet would have failed. Dog wasn't growling. Dog was all right.

Rushing to open the door, she stood back and stared down at Dog, at his half-crooked body, at his wobbly legs when he walked, and at that strange something she'd just seen flash in his eyes as if he were still angry. But Dog brushed against her legs and whined again. Dogs whined when they were okay, she repeated to herself. Bending to rub the top of his head, she found herself at eye level with Dog when the anger flashed again and was gone.

Slowly rising to her feet, she started to back away from Dog because the anger had frightened her. She'd seen two rheumy, black orbs of hatred and felt a need to get away, but Max's voice thundered through the air just then, cracking the stillness like a whip, making her stop.

"It's okay," Max said. "He needs time to get over his breakdown. Give him a day or two and he'll be just fine."

CHAPTER TWELVE

Nicky was sitting up in bed in her hospital room when her doctor walked in with a flat box under his arm. Staring in muted silence, with eyes swollen from crying, Nicky watched him drag a chair over and sit down, giving her a chance to see the box. It was a ouija board.

Nicky had her ouija board back. The doctor then went on to explain how he'd gotten it from Nicky's mother, who in turn had gotten it from Connie. But this didn't pacify Nicky; she couldn't be fooled by imitations. The board spread on the bed, ready for their questions, wasn't hers.

It was clean, smelled new and came encased

in clear, plastic wrapping. "This won't do," she told him when he insisted they place their hands on the pointer and begin. It seemed he was trying to convince her of the foolishness in thinking a spirit from a game had control over her life. "This won't do," she repeated.

"Why not?"

Because it's not *my* game. Max lives in *my* game."

"Well then," he said, his expression earnest and well-meaning, "perhaps we can ask the spirit in this board to send Max to us. This shouldn't be a problem, not if the alleged spirit has the powers you claim it does. Now, let's put our hands on the pointer."

"Listen, you," she spat, "I have been raped, skinned and almost choked to death by horrors you couldn't even begin to imagine in your worst dreams. Now you come here treating me like a moron—"

"Nicky," he said softly, his voice a whisper, soothing her, "none of it happened. It was all in your mind. I'm doing this to help you. Please cooperate."

She wanted to tell him to go to hell—enough was enough—but there was no fight left in her. The demons had taken it all. "I'll cooperate," she said dully, knowing she had no choice. Besides, the doctor was kind and gentle, nothing like the creatures she'd dealt with these past few days.

His skin wasn't scaly and his breath didn't smell like a sewer. What more could she ask for? Forcing herself to relax, she put her hands on the pointer and concentrated.

The Cave of the Marquis of Death was damp and reeked of rotted human flesh. The tortured cries of victims hovered like a blanket of madness. Max was in the cave and in control when the call came—someone wanted the spirit from the ouija board. Tired and overworked, he held two claws to his forehead to zero in on his victims and told himself that these two would pay heavily for the disruption in his life.

Scanning the darkness around him, Max's mind traveled many miles until his thoughts brought him to an abrupt halt. Nicky and a doctor were playing the game and wanted Max at once.

And since Max was the ever obedient spirit in the ouija board, he went without question, knowing that Nicky had asked for more problems than she'd ever be able to handle. As for the doctor, his mind was dead meat as well.

"Might I join you, Master?"

Max listened to the voice cutting the air like a rusty saw blade and knew it was De Sade, back from petitioning the prince of Acheron for new bodies to torture. Max considered taking him, but De Sade was too new at this.

"Just listen and observe for now," he said.

"Watch me twist some minds through the board."

"I see Nicky and a man in a white jacket," De Sade said, pointing towards the vision of the Ouija with two people seated on either side. "You're still having sport with Nicky?"

"Yes. And it's about to get better," Max answered, smiling. "You know, I've been toying with Peggy Rearden these past few days and I just had an idea. Nicky hates Peggy. Watch me stir up some problems in Peggy's life."

"Such as?"

"Just listen and observe," he repeated. "By the way. Nicky thinks this is a totally new board with a totally new spirit. Give me a name, De Sade. Something I can use to make her think she's right, that Max is lost to her."

"What is your name?" Nicky asked at one point. "I can't keep calling you Dr. Whatshisface."

Smiling, never taking his clear blue eyes off hers, the doctor touched the back of her hand and said, "Robert Miller, but you can call me Robert. My patients and I are usually on a first name basis."

"Okay, Robert, since you think I'm wrong about the board, let's do this."

But then Nicky's sudden enthusiasm died out; she sat before the board and waited. Somehow this setting was all wrong for a ouija board. It was midafternoon. Birds were singing outside, and lusty spring breezes were carrying the warmth of the sun in to caress her face. She'd never played this early before and wondered if they should wait until late tonight when darkness would settle over them. Max thrived in darkness.

But Robert was insistent, so how could she refuse? She'd never realized how young he was or how handsome until she'd spoken his name and felt the touch of his flesh against hers, awakening emotions deep inside of her, emotions she thought had been destroyed by the brutality of the demons.

Yes, the setting was all wrong. It was too light, and much too romantic for the likes of Max—

"Hey!" Robert said, disturbing her thoughts. "It's moving. It's answering my question."

"What question?" Nicky asked, because her mind hadn't been on the game when Robert spoke to the ouija board.

"I wanted to know if the spirit could get Max for us." Glancing down at the board and at the pointer moving furiously, Robert read the answer to Nicky. "Sorry. This is impossible. But I can do everything Max can."

"See, it's not working," Nicky shrilled at Robert, forgetting the touch of him and how good-looking he was. "I want my own Board back! I have to speak to Max. Otherwise you won't believe that I'm not crazy!"

"Wait," Robert said softly, "It's talking again."

"Your Ouija Board is in the care and control of a Peggy Rearden."

"What! How did that bitch get my board?"

"Connie and Hank gave it to her for safekeeping while you were in the hospital. When you wanted the board back, Connie had to buy a new one because Peggy wouldn't give it up."

"And why not?" Nicky asked, while Robert sat silently and watched the pointer, his face slack with disbelief. "Why won't she give it back?"

"Because Peggy Rearden knows how to control Max. She knows how to make Max do her bidding."

"Such as?"

"Such as tormenting you to get even for dropping her as a friend."

"That bitch!" Nicky said, rising to her feet to pace the room like a madwoman.

"It's only a game," Robert insisted. "I wanted you to play with me to prove it. Nicky, you're missing the point—"

"No! You're missing the point. That thing . . . that pointer told me something I never would have known. It named names. Connie and Hank are friends of mine. I know a Peggy Rearden."

Robert lifted his hand wearily and released the pointer. "Couldn't it be that subconsciously you were moving the pointer? I believe—"

"I don't care what you believe," Nicky spat, her boyish figure alluring even in a drab hospital gown, her blonde hair flowing wildly as her anger reached its peak. "This is a new game," she said, pointing at the board on her bed. "I didn't know what happened to the old one until the Ouija spirit told me just now. So how could I be supplying the answers?"

"Maybe you made them up."

"There's only one way to find out now, isn't there? Call Connie and ask her. Or better yet, let me call Connie." Nicky saw this as an opportunity to alert her friends, to tell them about Peggy Rearden and how she was trying to drive Nicky nuts. But Robert had other ideas.

"I'll call her," he said. "I'll ask the questions. And if Peggy Rearden doesn't have your board, will this prove there's nothing to the game?"

Nicky started to answer, but Robert wasn't paying attention. Robert was drawn back to the board, to the pointer, still moving at a furious pace although no one had asked a question.

"By the way," Robert read, trying to keep up with the almost maniacal movements of the pointer, "You can call me Matthew. You know, like in the first book of the New Testament. Just call anytime. I'll be here to help. This is what friends are for . . ."

"Peggy, I need your help."

Peggy couldn't stay in bed as Anita had ordered. Dog was recuperating from a breakdown, and Dog had already attacked her once today.

How could she just go to bed and otherwise act as though nothing were wrong when so many things were wrong?

Dog was still giving her those eyes now and then, those awful, hateful, gut-wrenching looks. This had her kind of scared. And then Max had spoken out loud, his voice coming through the door of her closet to pierce the air with kindness. Only she didn't sense kindness coming from Max, not deep inside where it mattered.

True, Max was her friend, but she had this queasy feeling about having a spirit as a friend. Then there were the voices in the dining room and the white slime in the toilet. Taking all of this together, how could she stay in bed and sleep? She wanted to be up and ready, just in case . . .

She was in the bathroom getting dressed when Max's voice reached her for the second time that day. She stopped and listened, her nerves dancing under the skin.

"I know you hear me, Peggy. Please answer."

"I'm losing it," she mumbled, walking from the bathroom to stand in front of the closet door, the slipper chair still where she'd placed it, holding fast under the knob, keeping guard. "What?" she asked aloud, feeling foolish.

"No need to feel foolish," Max said, probing her thoughts again. Max had this awful habit of reading her mind. "We're friends. You can relax and be comfortable with me."

"What'dya want, Max?" she asked, her voice old and resigned.

"I need your help. I want you to hide me."

"Hide you? Why?"

"Charlie is on his way up here. He knows you lied. He wants to find the board and destroy it."

"Charlie?" Peggy glanced over her shoulder and listened. There were footsteps on the bottom of the stairs. Max was right. Charlie was on his way up here. "Where should I hide you?" she asked, knowing this was going from bad to worse. She'd lied to Charlie a while back, something she didn't normally do, and now she was about to hide Max, further deceiving Charlie. "Oh, what a tangled web we weave, when first we practice to deceive—"

"What?"

"Sir Walter Scott. Where should I hide you?"

"Stick me on the window sill outside. It's the only place he won't look."

"Why are you afraid of Charlie? I thought you were legion."

She heard Max sigh heavily before answering. When he spoke, she sensed annoyance in his voice, the kindness gone. "If Charlie destroys the board, how will you call when you need me? Now hurry! He's getting closer."

Again Peggy listened, and again she heard Charlie on the steps. He must have been really angry. Normally the runners on the step muffled the sounds of his coming and going, but not now, not when he'd told an awful story about a ouija board and knew his daughter was lying about hers.

"Hurry!"

"Okay, Massa Max. Just don't beat me," she said sarcastically and quickly moved the slipper chair. Then she reached into the closet, grabbed the ouija board from its hiding place and ran to the window.

The sky beyond her room was royal blue and heavily layered with bold, pink slashes, she noticed, when she stuck the Ouija Board on the sill outside. Dark clouds were dotting it here and there, signaling the end of yet another day. It would be night soon. Dropping her gaze to the tree opposite her window, the one that danced and screeched and brushed against the panes when driven by spring breezes, she wondered if it would perform its ritual during the night, when the lights in her room were out and she was alone in the dark.

"Hurry and close the window before he looks out here!" Max commanded, and Peggy obeyed.

Then she went back to sit on her bed and wait for Charlie. Dog was back in the bathroom, lying on the floor facing her, his head draped over the door sill, his eyes narrowed on her face.

Peggy saw two orbs of hatred, saw his teeth— he was showing them again—and wondered if she should tell Charlie about Dog. He may have been recovering from his breakdown, but that didn't make him any less dangerous or frightening.

And yet, Dog was her friend. She couldn't squeal on a friend and risk losing him, now could she?

She heard the knob of the door turn, heard Charlie come in and saw Dog close his eyes. Then Dog covered his teeth with his upper lip.

Charlie explained his situation to Peggy while keeping his eyes fixed on a spot over her head; he couldn't stare her in the face and call her a liar at the same time. "I know how it goes with these things," Charlie was saying. "You get hooked on games at your age, and sometimes you're so mesmerized with a game, you can't see the dangers ahead."

"Games aren't dangerous, Daddy. At least not the kind you sit down and play with."

"This one is!" he insisted. "This one brought me no end of trouble when I was a kid. I just told you all about it."

"Why are you here now?" she asked, then looked beyond him at Dog, who still had his eyes closed while pretending to be asleep. Peggy knew Dog was pretending because she didn't hear the snoring noises he usually made when he was in his own little dream world.

Then, as if on cue, Dog opened his eyes and began to snore.

"I'm here because I feel you're hiding something," Charlie said softly, his voice coming from a distance away. Peggy was shocked by what Dog was doing, too shocked to really hear Charlie. "If you don't mind, I'd like to search your room to make sure the game is gone—but only if you don't object."

"Fine, Daddy," she mumbled, trying to keep up with the conversation. "Anything to make you happy."

This wasn't what she wanted to say, though. What she really wanted to do was to tell Charlie to turn and look at Dog lying there snoring with his eyes open. But then Charlie might figure something strange was going on with Dog because this wasn't normal, and Charlie might want Dog taken to the vet. And hell, Dog was just getting over a breakdown, thanks to Max. The vet might not understand. The vet might want Dog put to sleep. "Look anywhere you want," she said and watched Charlie turn towards Dog. Then she watched Dog close his eyes again.

Starting with her closet, Charlie searched for the ouija board, even going so far as to look through her dresser drawers, the cabinets in the bathroom, and in the toilet tank, while Peggy sat and drew small circles on the leg of her jeans with one hand. When he was finished, he apologized and left, leaving her with a snoring dog *with wide open eyes*.

At this point, Peggy made up her mind to lock Dog in the bathroom overnight. Max might have cured his breakdown, but Dog still had some meanness left in him, enough that she wasn't sure it was safe to close *her* eyes and sleep in the same room with him.

CHAPTER THIRTEEN

Dr. Robert Miller was sitting at his desk searching for a phone number, when the name Nicky had tagged on him—Dr. Whatshisface—came to mind. He'd had his share of labels pinned to his chest in the past, but this was the funniest. Of course not all of them were funny; some were downright degrading.

But then he expected no less of Nicky. She was a nice kid with a good sense of humor, lively and spirited—spirited? He thought about how spirited had been a normal part of his vocabulary until now, and wondered why it made him pause when it passed through his mind just now.

This nonsense with Nicky and the ouija board and spirits was getting out of hand. He didn't believe in spirits—not now, not ever. Not even when he was a kid and prone to have an active imagination did he believe in spirits and the supernatural. Spirits didn't exist except in fairy tales, in movies and on television.

"Would you bet your life on it?"

Robert heard the voice coming from somewhere in the room and smiled. Someone was playing a joke on him, one of his colleagues no doubt.

"Better guess again."

He felt a draft on his neck and got up to close the window, mindful that night was approaching, bringing cool, spring breezes to whistle and howl through the eaves of the hospital building. He shuddered. This was the worst part of the night shift—the dark, the eerie noises, something ominous lurking in the darkened halls—

"Thought you didn't believe in spirits?"

"I don't," he said without thinking. Then he realized he was answering a voice from out of nowhere, something nonexistent, part of a joke. "I know. Next you want to know what I'm afraid of it I don't believe in spirits."

As he spoke, he began to search the room. It wasn't much of a room to begin with, so it didn't take him long to realize he was alone. The storage closet and bathroom were both empty; no one was hiding in there. The hall outside was deserted when he opened the door. Then he wondered about hidden microphones or tapes and tore his desk apart. Finding nothing, he went to the stuffed chair opposite his desk and ran his hands up and down the legs and under the cushion looking for wires. Nothing.

At that point, he was starting to sweat. There was only one piece of furniture left in the room—a sofa—and searching it would be as useless as what he'd already done. He went back behind his desk and sat down, his mind dull with fear—

"What are you afraid of?" the voice asked.

The voice was holding a conversation with Robert, and Robert had barely spoken out loud. Most of his thoughts had remained in his head now as they had when he'd been standing in front of the window a while back, thinking about the night and how eerie it was at times. Someone was holding a conversation with him through his mind! And if he hadn't been so anxious to prove Nicky wrong—to prove there was no such thing as spirits—he would have realized that this strange sort of communication was going on, and he wouldn't have wasted his time searching for something he'd never find, that is, unless it wanted him to find it.

"You were thinking about the night and how eerie it was," the voice said. "Then I asked why you were afraid when you didn't believe in spirits."

"I know! I know!" Robert spat. His hands were shaking. He listened to the sound of his own voice and figured it must be coming from some-one else, someone whose words were laced with terror.

"No need to be afraid, Robert. I just want to be your friend."

"Like with Nicky. You want to be my friend so you can drive me nuts, right?"

"Honestly, Robert, you're acting hysterical. And for a doctor in your position—"

"Go away!"

"Not before you promise to at least try and like me. After all, I'm not so bad. Maybe if I showed myself—"

"It wouldn't help," Robert said, swallowing hard. His body was trembling now, his shirt drenched with the evidences of his own hysteria. The voice had been right. For a doctor, especial-ly a psychiatrist, he should have had a tighter rein over his emotions, but he didn't. He was losing control.

He hadn't believed Nicky and tried to prove she was suffering from an emotional distur-bance. Now he was hearing voices. Was he as disturbed as Nicky? Or was the voice real? Was Max real?

"Only one way to find out. Here I come!"

Robert sank back in his chair and waited, knowing he shouldn't. He should have gotten up, opened the door and taken off like his ass was on fire, but Robert realized that running was useless. Max was legion, and Max wanted to show himself—in the flesh. Robert would see

Max wherever he went, whether he liked it or not.

"Here I come!" Max said, dragging out the tension until Robert swore he'd go insane. "Look at me, Robert. This is what I am."

Robert saw a mist rise in front of his desk. Then he saw movement inside of the mist, saw someone in the core of the mist walking towards him, and, God, he didn't want to look, but he had to. Max wanted it this way, and Max was in control.

"See me as I really am," Max said, and Robert saw him as he really was.

Robert saw something inhuman, something with scaly flesh, large, bulbous lumps and festering sores. Robert saw something with a black hood covering its head and an axe in its hands. Then Robert saw bright lights and heard music.

Rising from his seat once more, he walked to the center of the room, past the inhuman creature near his desk, and listened for the sources of the sounds in his head. It seemed to be carousel music, and it was close by. The carnival was in town.

Oh, yes, he was going to the carnival. He was a child again, and his parents were taking him there, to a magical place where he could laugh, play games of chance, and eat cotton candy until his gut burst. He was going to the carnival where nothing bad ever happened and certainly not to him.

Robert had seen the demon, and now his

parents were helping him to escape. But then, somewhere deep inside, Robert knew there was no escape, not for him nor his mind, not now and not ever. Because in reality, Robert had seen more than a demon and a carnival. Robert had looked into the face of his future, and Robert had seen his own madness.

She was on the front porch with her body curled into a tightened ball of tension when she first thought about letting go and allowing herself to go crazy.

There was a chill in the night air, a chill she wasn't dressed for, but no matter. She was out here now—away from the mess in the toilet—and would maybe never go back inside again. Anita had had enough for one day, enough to last the rest of her life in fact.

She stopped thinking about the toilet then and about the white ooze that had spoken her name. She concentrated on the great outdoors that she never saw much of lately. New buds were springing up on her rose bushes, her azaleas and on her snow on the mount. Rising from the porch, Anita walked across the grass to examine the buds, wondering at this point if they knew her, too, wondering if they'd speak her name with as much fever and passion as had the white mess in the toilet.

But no, that didn't happen. She'd been dreaming. The white mess was dead waste, moving or not, and wasn't capable of speech.

She knelt beside a rose bush and felt grass, dampened by the kiss of dew, caressing her knees, and wanted to scream when two buds on the bush opened simultaneously, uncovering a pair of eyes. Black eyes in heavily slitted frames, like almonds, stared at her with amusement, stared at her curiously, stared and promised insanity.

She wasn't prepared for what happened next. She wasn't ready for two feet to hit the ground next to where she was kneeling. Nor was she ready for the beefy hands that fell across her shoulders, touching her bare skin with a familiar gentleness she found both demanding and annoying.

Charlie. It was Charlie. He'd come out here looking for her, wondering why she'd gone out into the damp night air clad only in shorts and a shirt. But then Charlie wasn't disturbed by a white mess that had spoken his name as clearly as though it were human.

And not once. No, once hadn't been enough. The white mess had spoken her name over and over until she swore she'd go insane. More maddening than this, the single voice coming from the white mess was composed of the combined voices of many creatures, their voices echoing in the stillness of the bathroom, assaulting her with a seasoned sense of what they were doing, echoing with a need to torment.

"You wanna come in and eat?" Charlie asked, looking at her and not at the bud eyes on the rose bush that were also looking at her. "I've taken the hair out of the stew. It was only a little bit."

Liar! she wanted to scream. She recalled lifting the lid on her simmering stew to stir it only to find the sauce layered with hair. But it wasn't her hair, nor Charlie's, nor Peggy's. The hair she found wasn't soft and curly. Rather it was thick and porous, each strand at least as thick as five human strands.

Then she thought of Dog, but he'd spent the day in Peggy's room. Besides, the hair was too long to be Dog's. So then whose hair was it? Who did that leave? No one. The hair was there in her stew, and she couldn't explain it away.

"Do you hear me, Anita? It's gone."

"Throw the stew away," she said, her voice dulled by the events of the day. "I won't eat it, and I won't let you or Peggy eat it either."

"The meat is too good to waste."

"Screw it." Having said enough, she reached out to grab at the eyes relentlessly pursuing her face and noticed they were gone; the buds had closed as if they had never been there to begin with.

"What?" Charlie asked.

"Nothing. Forget it." Anita couldn't share this with him, just like she hadn't told him about the white mess in the toilet speaking her name. Charlie had dredged up the past earlier in the evening, telling Peggy about his father and how his arm had been disfigured by a spirit from the ouija board. If she mentioned the eye buds on the rose bush or anything else that happened, Charlie would start with his stories again. It was better for Anita to store these things in the farthest reaches of her mind than to mention them to Charlie.

All she needed was for him to start again and she would go crazy for sure. Anita didn't believe in spirits with powers. Listening to Charlie talk about them was like having pins stuck under her fingernails. "I'll open a can of tuna," she said, rising to her feet. "It's not much of a meal, but at least there'll be no hair in it."

Peggy watched her parents from her bedroom window and wondered why they were attracted to the rose bushes and why they were outside whispering in the dark. She also wondered about dinner. She hadn't eaten all day and felt a gnawing sensation in the pit of her stomach. Glancing over at Dog lying beside her bed sound asleep—with his eyes open—she questioned the gnawing sensation in her stomach, wondering if it was hunger or fear.

Quickly crossing the room because she felt a sudden need to get out of there, Peggy listened to the swishing noises her jeans were making when her thighs rubbed together and realized they weren't as loud as they normally were. Her thighs were thinner; she was losing weight.

"You're so smart, Max," she said, speaking to a closed closet door. Max had told her to stop eating Twinkies and she'd lose weight. And yet Max's words were a reflection of Anita's. Her mother had told her the same thing, only long before Max entered the picture. Maybe Max wasn't as smart as Peggy imagined he was.

Reaching to grab the doorknob, Peggy felt something solid connect with her legs and knew it was Dog. The poor thing probably had to go real bad. He hadn't been out in the yard all day—

Dog growled then, letting Peggy know he was more interested in keeping her there than he was in getting out in the yard to pee.

"Listen, Dog, I'm going down to eat. I'll bring you something good if you behave." Maybe Dog didn't care to go out, but he must have been hungry by this time. After Peggy said what she did, Dog stepped aside, his body still moving at crooked angles, and let her leave.

Peggy saw a tuna sandwich on her plate, garnished with a few potato chips, but said nothing. Anita was eating the same, so Anita must have had her on a diet.

Sliding into the seat next to Charlie, she caught a whiff of the stew on his plate and thought she'd faint from wanting it so badly. Yet her clothes were getting big on her. Peggy had already felt what it was like to lose weight, and she wanted to lose more.

"You finish your homework?" Anita asked. Then she blinked her eyes, her mouth drawing back into what Peggy took for a smile. "Sorry. I forgot there's no school for a few days."

"That's okay, kid," Charlie mused. "We're all entitled to mistakes now and then."

"Not if you're perfect!" Anita shot back, pretending to be angry.

Peggy watched this and figured she was in the wrong house. Either that or she was asleep. It had been years now since Anita had kidded with anyone or even bothered to smile as she was smiling now.

"You're in a good mood," Charlie remarked, spooning more stew into his mouth.

"Yeah . . . well . . ." Anita began, but couldn't finish.

Peggy saw something flash across her face, saw her shudder and wondered what was going on. Anita wasn't really in a good mood. She was only pretending, acting now as Peggy had acted so many times in the past. Anita was covering some hurt inside by kidding around and flashing a smile. But the expression that had just passed over her face said it all. Anita was trying to forget something dreadful, something that just kept on pushing itself to the surface of her mind no matter what she did.

"Aren't you eating, Peggy?" Charlie wanted to know. He'd finished his stew and was mopping up the gravy with a huge wad of bread. He should have been dieting, too, Peggy thought to herself as she watched him. Charlie was always so concerned with his weight, and yet, here he was, gorging himself on stew and bread. "Well, if you don't want it—"

Peggy watched him make a playful grab for her plate and snatched it out of his way just in time. "I'm eating," she said and smiled, trying to keep an eye on him and Anita at the same time.

Except for Anita's nervousness, it was cozy there in the kitchen with its mixed scents of food and incense. Anita had burnt incense, she imagined, to kill the smell from the horrible mess in the bathroom a while back—and it worked. The odor was gone.

As Peggy ate her sandwich, she became aware of the curtains on the windows dancing softly, while more scents rushed in to mix with the scent of food. She could smell honeysuckle and roses riding on a crest of salt air, and she could smell freshly cut grass and house paint. Several families on the block were painting trim to welcome the change of seasons.

She could also smell gingerbread and knew that Mrs. Doyle from next door was baking.

Charlie took his napkin from his lap and dabbed at the corners of his mouth. Then he swept some crumbs from the wooden surface of the table onto his plate and rose to put his plate in the sink. "Can I get anyone anything while I'm up?" he asked.

Anita turned in her seat to stare at him, wide-eyed, her hand covering her chest. "You're kidding?"

"No, I'll get you anything you want."

"Tell me he's kidding, Peggy," Anita said, turning to smile at her daughter. "Charlie Rearden will get us anything we want. What do we want?"

"Pie à la mode," Peggy said, wondering if Anita would agree now that she had her on this diet.

"Make it jello with diet whipped cream and you've got a deal!"

"Sure, Mom. Say, Dad, two jellos, s'il vous plait?"

Charlie took a towel from a rack over the sink and draped it across his arm. "Coming right up," he said, swaying to a silent rhythm while he made his way over to the refrigerator.

It was a lovely evening, Peggy thought, the best she'd had in a long time. She was actually enjoying her parents company. They weren't fighting but were horsing around like they used to years ago. Oh God, it was more than anyone could ask for.

And maybe, just maybe it would last. Maybe it would never end. Maybe she'd have some place to run to for peace of mind after all, a haven from the everyday nightmares of her life.

"Say, girls," Charlie said, closing the refrigerator behind him, "how about we forget the jello and take a ride downtown for some ice cream, something fattening and gooey—"

"No way," Anita said, shaking her head. "We've consumed enough calories for one day . . ." Peggy heard her voice trail off, saw that awful expression on her face again, and knew it was over. This would be no haven in the stormy sea. "Is there anything wrong with the jello, Charlie?"

"No," he answered quickly and smiled.

But his answer was too quick, his smile too broad. Peggy watched his mouth twitch and knew he was lying. Anita knew it as well.

"Then why can't we have jello?"

"No reason. I just figured since we were having such a good time we should do something different for a change." Walking back to the counter, he slung his towel carelessly over the rack and turned to face them again. "Come on, girls, let's go and blow your diets—"

Before he could finish, Anita rushed from her seat to the refrigerator, as Peggy wondered just what was going on. Why was her father lying about a bowl of jello, and why was Anita so upset? What the hell was wrong with the jello?

"Anita, stop," Charlie bellowed, running to reach the refrigerator before she did. "Please, don't!"

But Anita ignored him. Grabbing the handle on the refrigerator door she opened it with a vengeance. Then she looked inside, slammed the door and leaned back, her face slack with shock. "Charlie, why are there maggots crawling around in my jello?" she mumbled, while Peggy stared at Charlie and waited for an answer.

CHAPTER FOURTEEN

After Charlie threw the maggot-laced jello into the garbage can outside, Peggy tried to shove the mystery to the farthest reaches of her mind and lock it away with the rest of life's nightmares. Anita wanted to know how the maggots had gotten there, as did Charlie. Peggy, however, didn't. Rushing upstairs to avoid Anita's hysteria, Peggy quickly undressed and crawled into bed.

Her pajamas, like her jeans, were getting loose around the waist. The double chin and pimples on her face were beginning to disappear. God, Max was so smart. Or was he? Max's advice about the Twinkies had been a reflection of Anita's, and Max could read minds.

"How little you think of me, Peggy."

Peggy lay in bed and allowed goose bumps to lump her flesh. It was a warm night, warmer than the past few. There were no breezes outside to chill the air or to drive the trees into a dancing frenzy. She listened to Max and let the words penetrate, then tried to turn her mind blank.

"It won't work. I can get inside of you. I can enter the farthest reaches of your subconscious and take what I want."

"Max, listen. I hate to be rude, but I'm really tired—"

"I thought we were friends."

"We are, but please, no games tonight. I just want to sleep."

"As you wish. But don't accuse me of using Anita's thoughts to make myself seem brilliant. I'm legion, remember? I know all! I knew you before I came here!"

Peggy was exasperated. "You just said a moment ago that you could get into the furthest reaches of my subcon—"

"I can, but I don't necessarily have to. Reading minds is a party game. I don't play games."

It was cold. His voice and the way he spoke chilled her and made her want to get another blanket for her bed. But Anita had hung Peggy's spare blankets over hangers and placed them on the rack in the closet—and Max was in the closet.

Peggy turned on her side, away from Max and

the closet, and started to curl into a fetal position for warmth. Then she noticed two orbs of raging anger reflected in the mirror over her dresser and knew it was Dog. He was still in the bathroom, still snoring with his eyes open, still watching her.

Rising from her bed and keeping her movements casual, Peggy went and closed the bathroom door, locking Dog inside, but not before listening to him growl, raising the small hairs on the back of her neck.

Standing by the door, she leaned with her back to the frame and studied the faint wedge of moonlight moving across the room towards her bed. Other than that the room was quiet and dark, reminding her of the room Charlie had slept in as a young boy and of the creatures roaming in the darkness of that room. Charlie had blamed the ouija board and his occult friend for his hauntings.

When Peggy had been listening to his story, she hadn't thought much of Charlie's explanation, how he'd blamed the ouija board for his problems. But now, standing there in the dark, she began to dwell on it.

"Charlie's house was haunted."

Peggy heard Max speak and wanted to scream. He was reading her mind again, delving into the farthest reaches. "Charlie said it was the ouija board's fault."

"No, it was Charlie's fault. Charlie should have asked the spirit in the board for help."

"Against those hauntings?"

"Yes. And if it happens here, I'll protect you. Now go to bed and dream sweet dreams."

Peggy did as she was told and fell into a deep, gentle sleep, but sometime during the night that old dream returned, the one where she was beaten and stomped to death by the kids at school. And, oh God, it wasn't fair. Those kids were supposed to hit her once in the mouth and give up.

Moaning softly, she released her knees from their fetal position and tried to roll onto her back, but Dog was in the way. Dog had been sleeping in her bed for years now, his soft, hairy body nestled against hers, his breath warm and soothing on her neck. She felt his paws dig into her flesh and swore she'd ask Charlie to cut his nails.

"Come on, Dog. Roll over!" she mumbled, but Dog never moved. Hell, he was the most obedient dog anyone could ask for, so this sudden stubborn streak was puzzling. Since he'd been sick these past few days, Peggy had to be patient.

She felt his nails dig deeper into her back, felt his breath grow warmer still as he began to breathe harder—small gasping noises escaping from his mouth—and wondered why she hadn't locked him in the bathroom—

Peggy shot up out of bed and reached for the light. She'd been groggy when she first woke up, but not now. Dog *was* locked in the bathroom, and if he was out here sleeping in her bed, then someone must have opened the door for him. When the lights went on, Dog was gone. He wasn't in her bed or lying next to it. He wasn't even under it.

Rushing to the bathroom, Peggy opened the door and stood back. Dog was on his feet, his body still leaning at crazy angles. Dog had been sleeping standing up. His head had been bowed until she snapped on the light. But when he raised his head to stare at her, Peggy saw those familiar orbs of rheumy, black hatred and slammed the door before he had a chance to attack.

Dog hadn't been in her bed just now, but she'd felt him up against her. If it hadn't been Dog, then who was it?

"Max," she called, but Max didn't answer. This was bullshit. Max was supposed to be her benefactor, her guardian. Max was supposed to supply the answers, and Peggy needed an answer now. Peggy had to know who had been in her bed.

She walked to the closet, then stood still and waited. The slipper chair wasn't in front of the door; she must have forgotten to put it there. She wondered if that was a mistake, or maybe it had been there and someone had moved the damned thing. Reaching for the chair, she called to Max again and waited.

The top of the chair was under the knob when

she called once more. Again she waited, her attention drifting to the sounds being carried on cool night breezes, those that had suddenly arisen as if driven by some mysterious force. She heard a branch scrape against her window and imagined it dancing in a frenzy, while throwing dark, moving shadows across the lawn.

"Max! Answer me, damnit!"

Peggy grabbed onto the slipper chair and swore she'd faint when animal claws sunk into the soft flesh of her back. She could feel hot breath that carried a putrid stench on her neck. Dog! It felt like Dog, but the breath wasn't his, nor was the raspy breathing pattern. Besides, Dog was locked in the bathroom.

"Peggy," it hissed, making her name sound like a profanity. It knew her name, but still, she couldn't answer. Her throat was constricted with fear. "Peggy, look at me," it ordered, "Turn and look at the face of your future."

With the nails of the creature digging into the soft flesh of her shoulders, Peggy turned and sank into the slipper chair, her head falling down against the cushioned armrest. She didn't want to look, but curiosity compelled her to. Surely this wasn't real. Surely she had to be dreaming.

Looking up, Peggy felt her chest tighten in one fast, heavy movement as she sucked in her breath to scream. She saw a black-skinned beast covered with ulcerated scales; she saw a flat, square head and wings that rose in hairy tips above its body, then ran down to drag the floor like a bridal train.

"I am the face of your future," it repeated, its tongue a forked pipe that swayed with the hideous motions of its mouth. "When you pass over to the other side, when you die, I'll be waiting."

Peggy allowed her upper body to collapse against her knees as a wail of terror passed through her lips into the still night air.

"I'm coming," Charlie screamed from his bedroom down the hall while Peggy wondered if he should. The beast was an illusion that would turn to dust and vanish as soon as Charlie snapped on the overhead lights. Only an illusion! She'd been having a lot of those lately.

Nicky opened the door to her hospital room and looked out. It was late at night; the hall was in semidarkness. After looking both ways to be sure she wouldn't be seen, she left her room and headed for Robert's office. She had to know if Robert had called Connie and if that Peggy bitch was holding her board hostage. The suspense was driving her crazy.

After making a stop at the nurse's station, she searched the directory and found that Robert's office was on the same floor as her room. When she found it, she stood outside for a moment and wondered just how she'd go about this. Robert was evasive at times, especially when he felt it was in her best interest to keep the truth a secret. This wouldn't be easy.

She knocked and waited. Robert didn't answer at first, but after a few moments he told her to come in. Before Robert had spoken, Nicky heard weird noises coming from inside, someone giggling incessantly.

"Come on in, damnit," Robert bellowed, making her wonder if she should. Robert was normally calm. The voice she heard urging her inside sounded nasty. She heard the giggling again, then the door opened and Robert was suddenly in front of her. "I told you to come in. What's your problem? You don't know how to open a door?"

Nicky wanted to run. This didn't sound like the Robert she knew. It looked like him, but there was something different in his eyes— anger and impatience. "I'm sorry," she said. "I shouldn't be here."

"It's all right, Nicky," he answered, taking her by the arm and pulling her inside. "You wanted to know about Connie and Peggy and the board, didn't you?"

"You called?"

"Yes."

"And?"

"That Peggy bitch has your board, and she's holding it hostage. I warned Connie about Peggy and how she's trying to drive you crazy."

Nicky heard his words and was afraid of him. It was so uncanny for Robert to be using the same expressions that had been in her thoughts as she walked here to his office. It was almost like having Max back. Max read her mind a lot, but Robert wasn't Max.

"You wanna bet?"

As he closed the door behind her, Nicky saw him push in the lock and knew she was trapped. She was alone in this room with a man who had somehow lost it, and there was no way out. "Robert?" she said, backing away from him until his desk came in contact with the back of her legs. "What's wrong?" she asked.

"Nothing really."

Nicky watched him moving closer, watched his lips move to form the crazy giggling noises she'd heard outside, and watched the color of his eyes change from blue to raging black. This was so eerie. People's eyes didn't change colors like this. It was almost as if . . . But no, this wasn't Max. This was Robert, she kept telling herself over and over until she could no longer believe it, until she knew this was Max.

"In the flesh," he said.

But in whose flesh? Certainly not his own.

"Watch me!"

And Nicky watched him go through a transformation because she was too terrified to do otherwise. She saw Robert's smooth young face turn into something hideous. She saw large festering sores form on his body. She saw an axe in his hands. And suddenly he was there before her. Max was there with his axe.

"Dr. Miller," someone shouted while pounding on the door. It was a female voice, probably a nurse.

"Yes?" Max answered, doing his best imitation of Robert. "What's wrong?"

"Nicole Martin is missing from her room. She's left the hospital."

"No need to worry. She came here to speak to me. I'll call the desk when we're through."

Nicky heard footsteps moving away from the door and had a sudden urge to scream for help. But Max was legion. Max could do anything, such as causing the vocal cords in her throat to constrict to prevent her from calling out. He'd done it to her only a few days ago. Max was in charge here.

"What do you want?" she asked, knowing she didn't really care to hear his answer.

"You said you'd do anything. First do me, then Robert through me, then maybe some of my friends."

Nicky had a vision then. She saw his friends, those faceless, shapeless, foul-smelling creatures that had haunted her nightmares this past week and knew if they touched her, she'd die. Or worse yet, she'd go the same route as Robert. Her mind would belong to Max.

"By the way," Max said, "I got you pregnant."

Nicky's mouth opened wide as his words passed through her mind. Pregnant? In a week? How could Max know . . . ? But the answer was simple. Max knew everything. Max could read your mind, get inside your body and brain. Nothing was hidden from him. She had a macabre mental image then of something small and scaly growing inside of her, maybe something with wings like the black demon Max had sent to quell her passion.

"Not to worry," Max said, reading her mind, "I performed an abortion on you." Then he held out a tiny plastic bag containing a bloody embryo. Nicky watched in fascinated horror as the miniature, shapeless horror wriggled its body like a snake, its mouth thrust open while its lips formed sucking movements.

Then she threw back her head and screamed, but no sound came out. Max had control over her vocal cords, as he had control over her life at this point. Oh God, don't touch me, she screamed inside when he drew closer. Don't touch me! I can't take anymore!

Somehow Peggy got back to sleep, but only after Charlie sat next to her bed for a while and talked about how black beasts with wings didn't exist. "The beast," he said, "was something you fabricated in your mind. The room was dark and you were scared, so your mind made up the image of the beast. And the voice you heard? Well, that was the rustling noise made by the wind moving through the trees outside."

The only problem was that Charlie didn't sound completely convinced himself. His voice was calm and low, but the calmness had a made-up quality to it, as though Charlie was forcing himself to act cool. Once in a while, though, his nervousness came through, especially when he held her hand and she felt him quiver.

It was eerie.

Charlie was usually the sane one in the family, not subject to the same fears and phobias as Peggy and her mother. She wondered why was he so nervous when his explanations about the beast and its voice were so damned plausible? However, she had no intention of dwelling on Charlie's insecurities when she had a mystery to clear up. Where the hell was Max earlier when she needed him, when someone resembling Dog had been sleeping in her bed?

And where was he when she needed someone to explain about the beast and how it really wasn't there? Max was evidently a bullshit artist who only meant half of what he said. How many times had Max said he'd be there to protect her? And now, the first time she needed protecting, it was poor Charlie who came to the rescue. Damn that Max anyway!

Now, as she sat in her room in the light of day, the incidents from last night didn't seem as crazy and frightening as they had at the time. Nothing seemed frightening once it was over, once you reflected back on what happened, especially not when your feet were bathed in morning sunlight.

Taking her mind off Charlie and Max and the

black beast who wasn't there, Peggy watched a stream of sunlight make its way up across her ankles and begin to climb the length of her body. Dog was still locked in the bathroom; she heard him whining through the door and thought about letting him out.

Then she remembered how angry he seemed most of the time and decided to wait until after breakfast. Maybe if she brought him some table scraps mixed in with his food, he'd be a bit more reasonable.

Her hand was trembling, when she placed it on the oak railing on her way downstairs. Peggy hadn't taken her seizure medicine yet. When she was late she usually got the shakes, but it wasn't the lack of medicine that was making her tremble.

Even if she didn't have epilepsy she'd be shaking now. Look at what was going on around her. The nightmare of Dog being sick with his breakdown and now Charlie losing his temper all the time. Charlie was normally the calmest person she knew.

Walking downstairs, she thought of the many mysteries in her life of late. But then she found herself in the middle of the living room, listening to Anita cry, and wanted to run back up to her room, to the haven she'd once found there. She wanted Dog to be normal again so she could tell him about this awful sight she was faced with and how it made her feel inside.

There was no furniture scattered around the

living room. Peggy saw it stacked near the book shelves, stacked in a neat column that rose like the swirl of a cyclone to meet the ceiling overhead. Oh God, whoever did this must have been awfully strong!

Another mystery had been added!

CHAPTER FIFTEEN

Peggy sat in her usual seat on the school bus and tried to think of nothing but going back to school. She hadn't planned on returning this early, but too many things were wrong at home. Peggy decided the nightmare of school was easier to face, and right now, the nightmare of school was hitting her full force. Peggy had to face those very same students here on the bus who'd caused her last seizure—Connie and Tracy, the two redheaded bitches who were sitting in back whispering.

At one point, the bus stopped at Anderson Avenue and Hank Brudhle got on amid screams of "All right!" and "We're gonna see some action now!" Peggy turned to look out of the side window as Hank passed her by, but not before stopping to welcome Peggy back.

"Ya don't know how glad we are to see ya," he said. "And I got a message from Nicky. She's grateful yer holdin' her ouija board and takin' real good care of . . . Max? I think she said it was Max."

Peggy wondered what he meant but wasted no energy trying to figure it out. They were a bunch of moronic pigs. When the bus came to a stop in front of Philmore High, Peggy waited until it was completely empty before getting off. She'd been tripped and roughed up so much by the other students, she'd long ago found it better to wait.

Derek, she noticed, was inside of the high school near the main entrance, peering out through a set of double doors. She stared into his eyes and found nothing to prompt her to smile at him, and that was painful. She recalled her last conversation with Derek and how he'd said they should stick together, yet here he was ignoring her. Ignoring him back, Peggy got off the bus, turned away from Derek and walked into a hard chest covered by a Philmore High football jacket—Hank Brudhle.

"We wanna speak to ya out back," he said, his face up against hers, his features distorted in her confusion.

"Why?"

"Don't ask, bitch! Just come along and don't

make no noise."

As Hank held her roughly under one arm, Peggy looked at the double doors near the main entrance but didn't see Derek. Oh God, at least if he were still there he could have gone for help, and right now Peggy sensed that she needed help. If Hank and the rest of Nicky's gang wanted to speak to her out back, Peggy saw trouble headed her way.

Following along reluctantly, Peggy recalled the nightmare she'd had these past few weeks. She saw herself beaten to death at the hands of a jeering crowd of classmates in the yard of Philmore High with no teachers around to stop them. Was the nightmare to become a reality? The teachers inside of the building were covering their home classes. Unless one of them happened to be near a window . . . Then Peggy wondered about the rest of the adults who eked out a living in Philmore—the secretaries, the kitchen staff. Would one of them notice and stop this?

"Why're ya so scared?" Hank asked and laughed. "Ya done somethin' wrong?"

Oh no, she thought, she didn't do anything wrong, but then nobody had to do anything wrong to set off this bunch of crazies. Peggy was thrown forward when Tracy hit her back. Falling to the ground, Peggy felt the flesh of one knee burst open and hoped the knee wasn't broken.

"Get up, ya fat bitch!" Hank spat, grabbing her

hair near the tender nape of her neck. "Can't friggin' walk?"

"No," Connie said, "but she can sure use that ouija board to drive Nicky nuts!"

"What?" Peggy said and flinched when a hand shot out of nowhere and struck the side of her face.

"Shut up, fat bitch. You just listen!"

It was Tracy. Peggy stumbled to her feet with Hank's help and knew that dreams sometimes come true.

"Max is hurtin' Nicky 'cause of you!" Connie spat.

Max! Up until now Peggy hadn't given Max a second thought, not even when his name had been spoken by Hank on the bus. Now she wondered if Max was really her benefactor as he'd claimed to be? Could Max come and help her now when there was no one else?

Silently, Peggy stumbled towards the back of the school building while fighting a seizure and while at the same time calling Max inside of her head. She told Max how Nicky's friends wanted to beat her, to stomp her to death. Then she told Max how there was no one left to help. Then she waited, confident he'd be out back to stop this lynch mob from killing her.

But when Peggy arrived out back with Hank and Tracy and Connie, she saw a crowd of teenagers, but no Max.

As Hank whirled her around, she saw his fist coming and ducked. Unlike the dream, she'd managed to move out of his way. But for how long? Could she duck the next blow? After all, this wasn't going to be one of those hit her once in the mouth deals, not if it followed her nightmare.

Hank growled and brought his fist up again, connecting with her eye. Peggy hadn't ducked in time. And like the nightmare, Hank had gone for her mouth first, then one of her eyes.

Peggy held both hands over her face to protect herself and to sort of quell the throbbing sensation from Hank's blow. Staggering backwards, she tried to regain her balance while fighting the blossoming aura in front of her.

When Hank raised a steel-tipped work boot to kick her in the leg, Peggy thought back to the nightmare, as though it had been a script of things to come.

And, oh God, it was all too real this time.

Stepping out of the way, she avoided the boot and the steel tip and wondered again if she could keep doing this. When the boot was raised again, Peggy screamed. Hank was about to shatter one of her shins. She knew that after he kicked her she'd look down and see a sliver of white jutting from her leg below the knee.

Knowing she couldn't move out of the way this time because Hank had placed himself directly in front of her, Peggy closed her eyes and waited for the boot to connect—but it didn't. She heard Hank's muffled scream, heard his body hitting hard against the pavement and knew that help had come. Max had heard her pleas for help and had come to the rescue.

"Oh, Max," she said and opened her eyes to find Derek standing over Hank, the muscles in his body as tight and taut as a fiddle string. Derek was enraged.

"Touch her again and you're dead meat, you bastard," Derek hissed. Then he faced the rest of the crowd and asked for a challenger, someone to protest what he was doing. No one answered.

Derek was supporting Peggy's body with his, leading her towards the locker rooms to clean up when she noticed how gentle his grip was. "How did you know?" she asked. "You walked away. You never saw them drag me out back."

"I know because they're stupid. It was all over school. Those morons started making plans to beat you yesterday because of that wasted bitch, Nicky, and some wacky nonsense about how it was your fault she was crazy. You had her ouija board?"

"Yes. I have it—"

"Great! Just friggin' great! What's it gonna take for you to smarten up? Them bastard things are dangerous." Derek stopped talking then and pulled her around to face him.

Peggy saw the dark hair, the blue eyes, the sudden softness of his features and felt depressed. Derek still had the ability to turn her on, an emotion she'd tried to forget long ago. What the hell would Derek want with her when he could have his pick of Philmore High beauties?

"I'm sorry," he said. "I didn't mean to yell at you. This isn't the time. By the way, you'd better tighten your belt, your jeans are loose."

Peggy felt her jeans bag in the crotch and knew he was right. "I'm losing weight," she said, a sudden glimmer of hope in her expression. If Derek noticed, he might like her a bit more, but Derek remained silent, his eyes zeroed in on hers. "My face is clearing up, too."

"I've been standing near the main entrance for days now," he said, "waiting for you to come back. I heard what happened with Tracy and Connie in Home Economics. I wanted to kill those two bitches."

"You've been waiting for me?"

"Yeah. And not just to protect you from Hank and his mob. I really missed you, Peggy."

"Why?"

"Because we're a lot alike. We're both outcasts, outsiders."

"You don't have to be, Derek. You're not a freak."

"And neither are you. Peggy. You've been put down for so long you just can't see your worth. You're a damned attractive girl."

"That's not so." Peggy knew what she was; she looked in the mirror every morning.

"If someone is blind in this world, they can't be good-looking," Derek said, staring her down. "The same holds with a mute. If you're deaf and can't talk, then you have to be ugly. Very few people look beyond a handicap to see what's really there. Well, when I look at you I see big, brown eyes laced with innocence, the gentle cut of your features, a full, sensuous mouth. Like I said, you've been put down for so long about your epilepsy that you believe every word they say."

Peggy couldn't speak. She wanted to, but the words wouldn't pass through her throat or form on her lips. Derek said he missed her. Then he said she was damned attractive. Peggy figured she was dreaming. She'd never awakened this morning; the incident with the furniture never happened. "Thank you," she said, knowing it didn't hurt to play along even if she was dreaming.

"Now, getting back to the board," he said, moving away from her. Derek's expression changed then. No longer a man making eyes at her, he was now calm and cool. "Why did you keep it after I warned you not to? If you'd given it back, those crazies in the yard wouldn't have pinned Nicky's so-called breakdown on you."

"Breakdown. Then they weren't kidding?"

"No, they weren't."

"How? I mean what happened to her?"

"She claims you did it. You conned her friends into giving you the board, then you turned Max, her spirit, against her. By the way, when I saved your neck out there, didn't I hear you say something like 'Oh, Max?'"

Peggy didn't answer. Derek continued to match her eyes with his, only now he was cutting her with his thoughts. Peggy was fooling with the board the same as Nicky had.

"You'll never believe me until it's too late," he said.

"But, Derek—"

"Go and wash up. Then we'll call your parents to come and take you home."

"But, wait. You're angry at me and I don't know why. You never told me what's so dangerous about the ouija—"

"Ask your father, Peggy. He should have some of those answers for you."

Peggy lay in bed with a beefsteak over one eye to stop the telltale marks of a shiner from discoloring her face. Dog was still locked in the bathroom. Strangely enough, neither Charlie nor Anita had come up here to chain him out in the yard, but then her parents had spent quite a few hours attempting to get the furniture down and reorganized.

Charlie finally had to call someone in to help. He and Anita could reach the ceiling on ladders, but the furniture was just too heavy to move.

Peggy glanced towards the window and the tree outside and tried to forget about the furniture, how it had gotten piled up so high, and who put it there. It must have been someone awfully strong.

"Your house is haunted."

Peggy heard Max speak through a closed closet door and thought about ignoring him the same way he'd ignored her hours ago. Where were you when I called for help? she wanted to scream, but didn't. Max was into reading her thoughts.

"I was about to step in and stop the beating when that handsome young boy intervened."

Sure, she thought.

"That's right," Max said, a hint of hurt in his voice. "Give all the credit to Derek. But then you love Derek."

No.

"Don't lie to me. I can read your mind and your feelings as well. Up front you're thinking it's no, but in your subconscious, it's yes. You do love Derek."

Let's go back to the haunting. After running those words through her brain, she was still amazed to be having a conversation without speaking aloud.

"This isn't what you really wish to ask, is it, Peggy? You're using the haunting as a cover up for the real important questions."

Such as?

"First of all, you want to know what happened to Nicky and why it was blamed on you. Secondly you want to know if your nightmare was a premonition of things to come since the beating today followed the same pattern. Finally, you want to know if you stand a chance with Derek."

Max was right on target. Those were her

questions. Maybe not in the same order—she wanted to know about Derek first—but Max had been close.

"Forget Derek!" Max said. "I can supply your needs. I can fulfill your sexual desires."

Peggy laughed and felt the small hairs on the back of her neck bristle when hideous growling noises came from Dog behind the bathroom door. "I didn't mean to laugh," she said, speaking aloud for the first time. "I imagine you can do everything you say you can. Only it would be more fun with Derek."

"You never know until you try. I don't always live in this board. I can materialize—"

"Like you didn't today, right? Like you stayed invisible and let them beat me when I called for help!"

"Peggy, I told you—"

"Right! Derek was there so you didn't interfere!"

"Peggy," he said, only softly this time. Gone was the hurt and indignation. "What really has you upset is not who saved you from a beating, but why you were beaten. Isn't that so?"

"I guess."

"That's no answer. Listen, remember when we first met and I made you face the reality of the rat in the cooking pot incident, and how those girls, Connie and Tracy, caused a seizure? Well, it's the same thing now. Here you are, trying to think about Derek, laughing at me for wanting to be the man in your life, and the whole time you're avoiding the issue. You lied to Charlie and Anita about how you got hurt, and now you're trying to lie to me about how the hurt isn't worse inside."

Max was right on target again. Peggy felt tears misting her eyes. It was an awful feeling to be hated, especially by so many different people. "Tell me about Nicky and why those creeps think it's my fault."

"Connie bought Nicky another ouija board, only this one was inhabited by a vicious spirit. When Nicky had a breakdown due to the stress of her everyday life, this spirit told her it was because of you. The spirit told her that you had control over me and I was the one causing her mental breakdown. Can you imagine such lies?"

"No, Max, I can't. But then lying has never come easy to me. What do we do about this mess? How can I ever go back to school if everyone hates me?"

"I can even the score if you want."

Peggy stared at the sky outside her window, saw light blue streaked with reddish pink and began to trace small circles on her bedspread with one hand. What did Max mean? This was the second time he'd offered to avenge a wrong against Peggy.

"I mean I can hurt them . . . or scare them. It's your choice. Either way, they'll leave you alone."

The choice was tempting. For once in her life Peggy had the power—through Max—to give those bastards the same as they'd given her. But somewhere back in her mind there was a phrase that wouldn't or couldn't be ignored. "Vengeance is mine sayeth the Lord."

"I'll leave them to God, Max, if you don't mind." After she spoke, Dog growled again and Max sort of hissed. "Did you hear me, Max?" she asked, hating the trembling in her voice.

"As you wish! Call if you need me!"

Max left the board then, but didn't go back to his cave. He was upset with Peggy because the bitch didn't want revenge, and revenge was part of his existence, not that he cared about Peggy or about her getting hurt. It was just that Max loved to dole out pain, and Peggy wasn't about to rob him of the opportunity.

Floating in his ethereal state, Max drifted over the town of Floyd Acres until his mind locked in on his intended victim—Chester Quigley. Quigley was at home, alone in bed as usual, dreaming sweet dreams of his native England and the doe-eyed maiden he'd left behind, the one he'd marry during summer break.

Too bad, Max thought, knowing the dream running through the teacher's head would never become reality, knowing that Quigley's bodily functions would stop for good when Max entered his body and caused a brain hemorrhage. Then he wondered if Quigley would enjoy death, the ultimate fantasy in Quigley's quest for a higher level of suspended animation.

Because killing Quigley's brain and making use of his body the following morning was a means of destroying most of the bastards Max was after.

Max would be in charge in science class.

Anita brought Peggy dinner in bed. Her big, overgrown daughter had fallen in school and banged up her knee. What was worse, Peggy struck her face on the pavement, giving her a black eye.

At this point, Anita figured Peggy had had a seizure or was outright lying. Maybe someone hit her. But Anita never argued with Peggy's explanations, not without getting into a good one with Charlie. And considering what had been happening these past few days, Anita didn't look for arguments unless she had no choice.

"Do you want me to let Dog out?" she asked before closing the door to go downstairs.

"No thanks, Mom. I'd better take him out. You rest."

"But your knee?" she argued, knowing it was wrong. Charlie might hear.

"I'll be okay."

Anita went back down to the kitchen. Her movements were cautious. If the furniture was upside down in any room in the house, Anita wanted to see it at her own pace. No use rushing into a disaster, she told herself, ignoring the footsteps on the stairs behind her.

She was getting better at this.

It was not like the first time she'd heard footsteps walking the hall upstairs, opening a door and entering Peggy's room, or the footsteps she'd heard coming up behind her when she was alone in the kitchen. Both times there was nobody in the house except her. Both times she'd checked it out and had found nothing.

Since then, she'd learned to live with those footsteps.

Charlie was still at the table where she'd left him looking dazed and depressed. Charlie wanted to sell the house and move. Charlie said he'd never go through a haunting again.

"More coffee?" Anita asked, pouring herself a cup when he refused.

"All that damned coffee's making a nervous wreck outta you!" he said.

"What's your excuse? What's making you so nervous?"

"Oh, nothing. Just finding furniture turned upside down and piled up to the ceiling. But then it happens to everyone."

Anita ignored Charlie, but then she had to. Too many things were happening here, things she couldn't explain. Sitting opposite him, she studied the curtains dancing at the windows, which reminded her of those in the basement that needed changing. Funny, she thought, how she could never completely enjoy something as insignificant as curtains being driven by warm, spring breezes without thinking of work that had to be done. Even the scent of the breezes themselves—honeysuckle and roses—reminded her to buy more room deodorizer.

"Can I say something?" Charlie asked.

"Sure. But for once, let's not talk about selling the house or hauntings."

"Then I have nothing to say!"

"Please don't do this. I've heard enough about haunted houses and ouija boards today to write a novel. Selling this house would be a foolish move. If we waited until Peggy was in college—"

"We'd be dead for sure."

Anita sighed heavily. She stared at Charlie, at the receding hairline, the tightened mouth and the protruding abdomen. She also took notice of the puppy dog eyes she'd fallen in love with years before, and she wanted to hold and comfort him. Charlie was falling apart in front of her, wanting to sell the house and move, and he kept giving her the craziest excuses ever—haunted houses and spirits.

Then again, she had no explanation for the strange events that had taken place this past week. Even knowing this, she couldn't accept his idea of spirits and ouija boards. For some reason, these things only happened either in the movies or to people staring at you from the front pages of those tabloids found near supermarket checkout lines. These things did not happen in real life.

"Would you at least consider it?" he asked and she said she would. "Now I'll have that cup of coffee."

Anita watched him get up and amble over to the stove while she brought her cup to her lips. Charlie wasn't so bad when she gave him half a chance. Anita knew that most of his anger stemmed from her and her eternal fetish for cleaning.

Something in the coffee had wiggled itself out of the cup and into her mouth while she'd been taking inventory of her relationship with Charlie; it was something big with the bodily consistency of taffy. At least it felt like taffy, but it wiggled like a snake. She felt it side winding its way across her tongue to the entrance to her throat and knew it would choke her to death if it wasn't stopped. But how? She couldn't let Charlie know what was wrong, and if not, then Charlie couldn't save her.

The only choice left was for her to bite down on the bastard thing and kill it before it killed her. But then what if it was slimy inside? What if its blood tasted terrible and oozed down her throat, choking her with its acrid taste? Oh God, she had no choice.

Opening her mouth slightly, she ignored Charlie when he wanted to know what was wrong and bit down . . . on nothing, her teeth clamping together in one fierce motion that threatened to snap her jaw.

"Anita?" Charlie said, bending in front of her.

"Anita, my ass!" she screamed. "I was choking on something—"

"Baby, are you all right?"

"Of course, I'm all right. I tried to kill the fucker in my mouth because it was alive—"

"Alive? What the hell?"

"It came from my coffee. It crawled into my mouth. I bit it to keep it from choking me, but, oh Charlie, when I bit down it was gone."

"The hauntings!"

"No!" she shouted. "Oh God, it won't stop!" Pulling away from him, Anita grabbed his cup from his hand and hers from the table and smashed them in the sink. The coffee pot was next. Then she upturned the kitchen table, screaming that it was her turn now to do a job on her furniture. "Those fucking spirits aren't going to have all the fun, not if I can help it."

Charlie moved back away from her and watched her vent her anger on the furniture in the kitchen, the pots, the pans and the dishes before allowing the upper part of her body to crumble across the sink like something dead.

"You all right, babes?" he asked. "Anita?" The way he was staring at her, you would think she was possessed.

"I'm fine, honey, just fine. And you know what? My whole kitchen looks like a tornado blew through it and I don't give a damn. I couldn't care less." Anita knew at this point that something dreadful was happening here; she was finally ready to accept Charlie's explanation about spirits from ouija boards and what they could do.

"Charlie, I've seen so much. That slime in the

toilet spoke to me. The rose bushes outside have eyes. That thing in my mouth just now was too big to be part of my imagination. Something's happening here, something bad. Christ, I need a cigarette. Let's go in the living room and have a smoke."

"Are you kidding?"

"Hell no! I need a smoke and I'm gonna have it here, inside this house, because this is my fucking house. If anyone destroys my fucking house with cigarette smoke and garbage like upturned furniture, honey, it's gonna be me!"

"Mom, Dad?"

Anita saw a frightened Peggy framing the doorway and wanted to cry. Anita was supposed to be a parent, one who would protect, and now she'd probably scared the kid into an oncoming seizure with her tantrum. She saw Peggy's gaze narrowed on Charlie, realized how she, herself, was slung over the sink and managed to laugh. To someone who had just walked in it would appear as though Charlie had beaten her. "It's okay, honey," Anita said. "I lost my temper and trashed the kitchen."

"Holy shit!" Peggy muttered. "Sorry I didn't mean to curse."

"No problem. I just invited your father to join me in the living room for a cigarette. You smoke?"

"No . . . Geez, for a first timer, Mom, you did a great job," Peggy said, studying the kitchen. "This is perfect."

CHAPTER SIXTEEN

Peggy rose early the following morning and got ready for school. Although the decision to go back wasn't easy, not after what happened yesterday, Max had held a long conversation with her last night and swore on the ouija board that he'd protect her, that he'd be with her all day. He also said he'd do a better job than Derek because Derek wasn't always around and he was, so Peggy believed him. Actually, she had no choice. She'd missed so much time from school as it was that staying home for yet another few days would mean she'd fail most of her courses and be left back. Then her enemies would have more ammunition to throw at her.

After taking a pair of jeans from a dresser

drawer, she remembered the load of dress slacks in her closet; she didn't know why, but suddenly the jeans looked too shabby for school. Moving the slipper chair away from the door, Peggy went into the closet and chose a pair of grey slacks with a blue and gray print blouse.

Then she brushed her hair until it could shine no more, dabbed some blush on her cheeks and sprayed perfume behind her ears. Anita had given her the perfume last Christmas, but Peggy hadn't tried it until now. When she was finished, she surveyed herself in the bathroom mirror and almost saw the girl Derek had been speaking about, the one he'd referred to as damned attractive.

After gathering her books for school, she tried pulling Dog by his collar to lead him downstairs but let go when he snarled and growled. She didn't know where he was relieving himself since he hadn't been in the yard in a week, but her room didn't carry the odor of urine. She'd never seen dog excrement lying around, so she rang this up with the other mysteries in her life of late.

She was still limping badly when she entered the kitchen downstairs and found it clean. Charlie and Anita had fixed it up last night after enjoying a cigarette in the living room. Another mystery. First, Anita had wrecked the kitchen, then she smoked in the house with Charlie. Peggy had never seen her mother smoke before.

There was a note on the table telling Peggy to have some dry cereal for breakfast. Her parents were sleeping in, which confused her even more; they never slept late. There were so many changes going on around her in so short a time that Peggy was worried, especially when it came to Anita.

Anita was almost human again, but it happened too fast. Considering how unstable she was, Peggy feared Anita would wake up one day, see the sudden changes in her personality and crash, like an addict going cold turkey.

Peggy was sitting in the kitchen and down to her last spoonful of cereal when she heard footsteps crossing the dining room. Either Charlie or Anita had woken up, but then she noticed something about those footsteps that disturbed her. They sounded too lively, too awake, not at all like the footsteps of someone who'd just woken up.

When the door to the kitchen opened slowly at first and then swung wide and no one was there, Peggy felt her heart pounding heavily in her chest. Then the door closed and those same footsteps continued across the floor to where she was sitting, making her want to get up and run for the safety of her parents bedroom.

Her hands were trembling when she finally found the courage to rise. Backing slowly, never taking her eyes off the direction the sounds were coming from, Peggy moved towards the door leading to the yard outside. But then the footsteps doubled around in front of her and blocked that escape route as well.

"Don't be afraid," a voice said. She was right; she wasn't alone in the kitchen. "Don't you know me?" the voice asked.

"No, and I don't want to," she answered while visions of the executioner and the black, winged beast shot through her head. Both had to be illusions. "Please don't let me see you," she begged, backing into the kitchen table.

"You're acting hysterical. And hell, we're old friends."

Friends? She had no friends. Dog was nuts and Max—

"Is your only friend," the voice said, "and if you think otherwise, you're wrong."

Oh God, it was Max. She should have recognized the voice. "Max, I . . ." she began but couldn't go on. The horror of the moment had just now struck her full force. Max was here. Max had left the board. Max was no bull artist; he did have powers after all.

"Would you like to see me in the flesh?"

"Not really." And that was true. Hearing him was enough. She was scared beyond reason at the moment. "What's this all about, Max?"

"I promised to protect you in school. How can I protect you if I stay in the ouija board?"

True, she thought. But when Max first promised protection, she'd never dreamed of anything like this.

"I'll go on ahead, Peggy. I'll meet you in science class. This should be a day you'll never forget."

Then he was gone, leaving Peggy alone in the kitchen to wonder if she'd made the right decision in allowing Max to protect her. There was something awful about Max at times. There was also something awful about his voice when he'd promised her a day she'd never forget.

"Hey, kid, you look good!"

Peggy heard Charlie's voice and turned to see her parents, still in their pajamas, coming into the kitchen. She'd never even heard them on the stairs or crossing the dining room. Max had taken her total attention.

"Yes, for a change she does," Anita agreed. "She's finally wearing those dress slacks I bought last year, but I don't know why. Peggy, where are you going?"

"To school," Peggy answered, trying to keep up with the conversation though her mind was on Max and how he'd gone on ahead to protect her. "I've missed so much time."

"What about your knee?" Anita asked. "And that shiner!"

Peggy had noticed the black eye when she'd been brushing her hair earlier. At first, she felt sick inside and wanted to go back to bed and hide for the rest of her life, but Max had promised to protect her.

And now Max was keeping his promise.

"It's okay, Mom. Those kids in school have bruises and shiners all the time. Gotta go. Bye."

Peggy thought about Max while waiting for the bus to pick her up. How would Max protect her? If someone hit her, would Max materialize and shield her body with his? And just what did Max look like?

She was startled then when an arm wound itself around her shoulders and someone tall and muscular stood by her side. Turning, she saw Derek, as handsome as ever, with a smile turning up the corners of his mouth. "I figured you'd go to school today. You can be one stubborn female. Anyway, I came just in case they decided to start their crap on the bus."

Derek had come to play bodyguard. And oh, what a body he had to be guarding hers with. His arm was still around her neck, holding her close. Peggy could smell the strong, masculine odor of his cologne, could see the blue brightness of his eyes, could feel his warm breath on her face. Derek was acting as though he was stuck on her, too, but then she dismissed those thoughts and figured he was just being friendly. "I appreciate this," she said, returning his smile.

"No problem." Derek brushed her face with his fingertips. "You look very pretty today. Even the shiner looks good."

This was a magic moment in her life. She was

waiting for the bus with one of the biggest hunks in school. Then, for one instant, Peggy went back over what she'd told herself yesterday when Derek had saved her from Hank. She remembered thinking about how she must have been asleep and dreaming when Derek showed an interest in her. Now she felt the same, like she was still dreaming.

Peggy rode halfway to school with Derek before either of them spoke. Up until then, they were so intent on watching the other students reactions to seeing them together they'd remained silent. Hank, for instance, got on and started for Peggy when he spotted Derek next to her. Then Hank's face turned crimson, and he walked to the back of the bus without saying anything.

"This is too good for words," Derek said at last.

"Yes. The guys are bad enough, but did you see the girls cutting their eyes at me?"

"Why would they cut their eyes at you?"

"Because I'm sitting here with you and they're jealous."

Derek had been staring straight ahead, but Peggy's last phrase made him turn and look at her. "I guess they'd better get used to it. They'll be seeing a lot more of this from here on in—if you have no objections."

Peggy felt herself go berserk inside. She felt hot and cold and crazy all at the same time. "Oh no," she insisted, "I don't object."

"In fact, if your parents don't mind, I can drive you to school tomorrow in my car. I would have today, but I wasn't sure how they'd react."

"It'll be fine with them."

Then she said no more. Derek had left her speechless.

But then Derek, after keeping quiet for a long time, asked her a question.

"Did you ask your father about his experiences with the ouija board like I told you to do yesterday?" he asked.

"No, I didn't speak to him."

"Why not?"

"Daddy told me a week ago about the board and what happened when he was a kid."

"Did you think he was making it up? I mean, is this why you kept Nicky's board?"

"How come you know so much about my father and what he went through?"

Derek studied the front of the bus again. "Did he tell you about his friends? Did he mention this real weird guy who was into ouija boards and seances?"

"Yes," she said, frowning. "He said his name was Edward."

"He lied."

"But—"

"I don't know why, but he did. Actually his friend's name was Derek Westmore, Sr., and I'm—"

Oh, God! Peggy knew the answer before he spoke. He was Derek Westmore, Jr., the son of the occult nut. She was speechless again.

"I've studied the occult ever since I can first remember," he said. "My father taught me all he knew, but the one thing he never counted on was me turning against him. Somehow, and don't ask me why, I knew that using things like spirits and demons to gain power and wealth was wrong. Ever since I found out about those boys he tainted with his nonsense, who incidentally are men now with families of their own, I've tried to help."

"Is this why you'll be hanging around me from here on in? To help undo the damage your father did?" Peggy didn't want to believe this was true. She wanted to hear Derek say that he really liked her. "Because if that's so, your father stopped the hauntings soon after they started."

Peggy remembered Charlie telling her about the exorcism gone awry because the priest was so old, and how "Edward" showed up to help his family when a demon burst through the floor.

"You're kidding. So everything's cool, huh?"

"Yes. So I guess that means we can't be friends."

"Not necessarily. I'll just have to find another reason for staying in your life, such as getting you to leave the ouija board alone. You know, Peggy, Nicky's breakdown had a lot to do with the board. Even when she got hurt and landed in the hospital, it was connected. In fact, whether you believe me or not, I saw a man inside of a colorful swirling mist coming after you the day she fell from the locker."

Peggy heard what he said, remembered Derek standing outside pounding at the door to the locker room in a frenzy and wanted to die of shame. She'd been so afraid of Derek at the time that she was willing to face the monster inside of the swirling mist and all Derek wanted to do was help. "Uh . . . To be absolutely honest, Derek, my family and I . . . A couple of things did happen over the past few days, and we can't explain them. But I just know it had nothing to do with my board." After saying it, she watched his eyes go cold on her again.

Derek remained quiet until the bus stopped outside of Philmore High. Taking her by the arm he helped her off, then led her towards Quigley's science class. "We need to talk some more about that damned ouija board," he said. "But we'll have to wait until after this class."

"I know what's going on," Derek said. "When you do your Fantasy of the Mind experiments on your own, when you stop your heart and travel in space or wherever else you go, this is known as an OBE—out of body experience. If you're going to teach this to the class, you'd better warn them about the silver cord running from the physical body to the astral one."

Derek, his body taut and shaking, was arguing with Mr. Quigley. Peggy had never seen Derek's face go red with rage before. In fact, Derek hadn't been this angry when class started. He began to lose control only after Quigley announced he was going to teach the class how to stop their hearts and suspend their bodies in limbo—and he intended to do it now, today.

"It's not a Fantasy of the Mind game," Derek argued, continuing on. "This is a dangerous thing you're doing."

"But then it's my decision, isn't it?" Quigley answered, his voice strangely calm, his face a mask of indifference. Quigley was bored.

"And I hope you can live with it if one of these students snaps the cord and dies," Derek spat.

"What the hell are you talkin' about?" one of the students wanted to know.

Derek stared at the student, at his purple/pink streaked hair, his leather and brass-studded clothing, and turned back to Quigley. "Are you gonna tell them?"

"Why not?" Quigley asked, fingering a piece of chalk.

As Quigley approached the board up front, Peggy watched him sketch a rough figure of a person lying down. Then he sketched another figure, suspended in midair over the first. Then he traced a thin line from the first figure's forehead to the back of the suspended figure's head. "This is me lying down," he said dryly.

"Overhead you can see my spirit, or soul as some call it, leaving my body. There's a silver cord running from the forehead of my physical body which is attached to my astral one. The cord is only visible during an actual OBE experience."

"What'dya need this cord for?" someone asked.

"It's like an umbilical cord. If it breaks, your astral being will not be able to reenter your physical body." Quigley was still bored, still indifferent.

"And you'll die!" Derek said, with as much emotion as when he'd warned Peggy about the ouija board.

"Only your physical body," Quigley added. "Your astral being will survive."

Peggy saw the thin body and handsome face, heard the British accent, but couldn't believe this was Quigley speaking to the class. Quigley had acted bored a lot in the past, but now she sensed more than boredom. Quigley was acting as though he didn't care about his students, whether they died or not.

His face was chalk white, too, as if he were dead but not buried.

"If your physical body dies," Derek said, softly this time, "your spirit will be left to wander for an eternity in a strange outer world."

"Stranger than this we live in now?" Quigley asked. The students laughed, and Derek sat down, knowing he'd lost. He was trying to save

their lives, to stop them from involving themselves in a dangerous experiment, but he was
playing to a feeble-minded audience with an
"oh, well" attitude, so Derek accepted his defeat
in silence.

"To begin," Quigley said, "we must first enter
a state of complete relaxation, which is difficult
in a noisy school building, so first we lock the
door. I hope those other students show up
before we start." As Quigley crossed to the door,
several things happened so fast that Peggy had
trouble keeping up.

Derek threw a crumpled piece of paper in her
direction. It landed on the other side of her desk
near the window. Peggy stared at him, then
picked it up at his urging. It was a note warning
her not to participate in the experiment, to just
pretend she was caught up in this madness.

Peggy nodded and promised she'd listen to
him, but then she heard voices coming from up
front. Taking her attention away from Derek she
saw Quigley talking to three students who had
just now entered the room. Peggy saw Connie,
Tracy and Hank and turned back to Derek. He
shrugged. Derek was as confused as Peggy.

"Class," Quigley said, his voice full of an eerie
enthusiasm, "three students from my seventh
period session will join us for this very special
experiment." Amid catcalls and jeers, Quigley
continued on. "The students in seventh period
aren't as advanced as this group; however, there

are exceptions. Therefore, Hank, Connie and Tracy have been allowed to participate."

There were two empty seats near Derek. He rose and motioned the three to his area of the room, then he walked to the seat next to Peggy and sat down, his face rigid and red with rage. "This is crazy. Those three are the stupidest bastards I know," he whispered and turned back to Quigley, who was in the process of locking the door. Then he turned off the overhead lights.

"Now," Quigley said, sitting behind his desk up front, "to begin with, we must make ourselves as comfortable as we can. Let's loosen our clothing and jewelry." More catcalls. "This is important!" he bellowed, and the students settled down. "Relax your mind and body . . . let yourself go. You are puppets on a string with no muscular control."

Peggy slid down in her seat and felt Derek's hand touch hers. She clutched his outstretched hand to let him know she was only pretending to be going along with this.

"Close your eyes and breath softly," Quigley said, his voice low and strange. "Try to establish a rhythm. Keep your mouth slightly open. Once you reach the state where you're not asleep, but not quite awake, begin to focus on your heart."

Quigley waited for a few minutes until he heard soft, rhythmic breathing fill the air, then he continued on. "Try to match the beat of your heart with the rhythm of your breathing. One, two, in, out. One, two, in, out. Keep the beat constant. Now, try to slow down your breathing and in turn your heart. One, hold, two, hold, in, hold, out, hold. Do this for a minute or two, then move on to one, hold, hold, two, hold, hold and so on.''

Peggy held Derek's hand and listened to the shallow breathing around them. She had her eyes closed, but because everyone was so constant and in time, she imagined at one point that the class had fused and become one. She was sitting there listening to one huge body trying to stop its heart and experience what Quigley had termed the ultimate experiment.

"The longer you are able to hold back the beats in your heart and to slow your breathing to the same rate, the faster you will achieve a state of limbo.''

Peggy had never imagined herself as intelligent as Derek—there were few in this school who were—but right now she could see what Derek had. She could see the dangers involved in this experiment. Not counting Connie, Tracy and Hank, these kids were a bunch of happy-go-lucky punk rockers who didn't do their science homework half the time, let alone become involved in this.

She wanted to scream as Derek had, to warn them to stop, but Quigley had graduated from teacher to cult leader and Quigley was in charge. He had the students mesmerized and hypnotized—just like Max would have.

Funny how she should think of Quigley and Max all in the same breath. Funny, too, how much Quigley reminded her of Max at this very minute.

"Stop your heart," Quigley said, his voice droning on, dragging out the words. "Stop it and concentrate on a point above your body, about three feet above will do. Try and imagine how wonderful it would be to float up to that point and let go, allow your spirit to drift—"

Peggy heard choking noises and opened her eyes. Derek's hand clamped down on hers so tightly she feared he'd snap her bones. "Are you awake?" he mumbled. Peggy squeezed back and followed the noises to that part of the room where Derek had been sitting.

She saw Connie, Tracy and Hank, their heads thrown back against the seats behind them, their bodies as limp as rag dolls. Connie's chest was making slight convulsive movements, something you wouldn't notice if you didn't really look. Faint choking noises were coming from Tracy.

Peggy hated them, but she didn't want them to die as they were doing now. She dug her nails into the tender flesh on the back of Derek's hands and tried to get up, but she couldn't. Her legs were not able to support her weight. She tried to scream, but her throat was slightly constricted.

She glared at Derek, wanting him to help, but Derek released her hand and clutched his throat area. He was trying to scream but couldn't. Derek was as helpless as Peggy.

Oh, God! She'd looked to Derek for help and he couldn't. That left Max. She had to get Max. This teacher was killing them and only Max could stop this. Max! she screamed in her mind, but received no answer.

Max! Do something! You promised you'd be here!

Peggy saw a small aura forming in front of her and knew this was no time to have a seizure. She glared at Connie, at Tracy and at Hank and saw them convulsing heavily, their bodies moving like hers during a seizure. Then she glanced at the other students and saw some of them imitating her three enemies by convulsing as well.

The aura was beginning to grow as Peggy was left with the knowledge that half the class was dying and she couldn't do anything about it. Closing her eyes, she concentrated on the gulleys of her mind and stopped the conditions that would lead to a seizure. Once this was accomplished she opened her eyes and stared at the ceiling to avoid the throes of death around her.

Then she tried to raise her hands to cover her ears because there were many death rattles, but her hands were frozen to her sides. Max, please, she pleaded inside. You promised. Where are you? But Max, wherever he was, remained silent —and so did Connie, Tracy and Hank. The choking noises and death rattles had stopped. They were dead.

Quigley remained silent, too. Either he was in limbo in outer space, or he was dead along with the rest.

Peggy felt stinging sensations in her arms and legs, in her hands and feet, as though her extremities had fallen asleep and were now coming to. Trembling, she placed her hands on the desk in front of her and got to her feet. Derek was able to do the same.

First she stared at Derek and almost fainted when she saw the shock written on his face, forcing her to acknowledge that this was real and not a dream. Then she glanced up front and almost fainted again when she saw Quigley with his head lying across folded arms on his desk. He was neither moving, nor breathing. Quigley was dead, too.

And, oh God, there was someone near the door. Peggy saw the faint outline of a body and had to hold onto Derek to keep from passing out. Then she went back into her brain to make repairs in the gulleys before having another seizure. Peggy was staring at an ethereal figure, the executioner she'd seen in the midst of the swirling cyclone in the locker room. She saw two eyes full of raging hatred staring back from the holes in the hood covering his head. Then he was gone in a puff of smoke!

"Let's get out of here," Derek said. "We can walk to my place; it's close by. I wanna get my car and drive you home."

CHAPTER SEVENTEEN

Max did more than cause convulsions and stop hearts. Max talked those who'd survived his limbo lesson into severing their silver cords, dooming them to an endless existence in a world of no substance, a world running parallel to their own, a nether world.

Max had returned to his cave and was near the entrance when an old friend approached him. Gingerly sliding across the moors surrounding him because he moved on exposed nerves, the mound of unrecognizable flesh clutched at Max's legs and begged for new skin.

"Master," he wailed, "my outer crust grows older and rots more each day. Please, master, some new flesh to heal my wounds."

"Soon, old one," Max said fondly, adding, "I know you want Nicky's flesh, but she's still alive. Therefore, you'll have to settle for what you get." Then he rubbed the crest of the mound with a claw before walking into the cave where the Marquis de Sade greeted him warmly.

"Excellent," said the Marquis. "Those you've killed are young, their flesh firm. When may we expect them?"

"I've presented my petitions to the Black Master, his most holy lord Satan. I await his word."

"Why the petitions? They're ours. You killed them."

"But not through the board," Max reminded him. "Therefore I can only wait and hope."

"Hope is for lovers," the Marquis spat in outrage. "We need the flesh."

Max studied the Marquis and marveled again at his position here in the cave. By rights, the Marquis should have been damned and tortured, but there were some so evil they captured the admiration of Satan and his council of demons. The Marquis was sent here to Max to do what he did best in his earthly life. "We must be patient."

"By the way," the Marquis said, the flesh of his body in various stages of decay, his nobleman's clothing torn and tattered, "I congratulate you once more." Max was puzzled. "When you entered Nicky's board and pretended to be someone else," the Marquis explained, "it was a wonderful job of manipulation against that Peggy Rearden."

"It was nothing. My efforts were merely enhanced by Nicky's stupidity. Soon you will be in active training for the board; then you will know how easy it is to manipulate those fools who quest for answers they're not entitled to."

As Max spoke, many voices hovered above him, piercing the air with their pleas for mercy. He walked towards the entrance to the Cave of the Deranged while motioning for the Marquis to follow. "They're here," he said. "Hank Brudhle, Connie, Tracy, and the others. My petition has been granted."

"Should I bring my peeling knife?"

"Yes," Max said, "and Marquis, the old one who guards my cave has been promised new flesh for eons now. See that he goes first."

Derek's house was a lot like Peggy's, only more elegant. Peggy saw a two-story house done in white brick with custom-cut, stone tiles laid in a mosaic print lining the walkway as she followed Derek inside. She was still limping badly from a skinned knee, but once she entered behind Derek, she soon forgot about her wound.

The foyer, she noticed, was layered in white marble. The living room off to one side was a costly blur of expensive carpeting and furnishings, all done in black and white. There was so much to see Peggy couldn't absorb it all, but she tried. "Geez, what does your old man do for a living?"

"He was a stockbroker," Derek said, his voice gone dull.

"Was?"

"He's dead now. My mother, too."

Peggy leaned back against the wall and wanted to cry. Derek had no one, and here she'd been feeling sorry for herself because she had no friends. At least she still had parents. She couldn't begin to imagine the loneliness. "I'm really sorry," she said.

"Don't be." He forced a smile. "I've managed on my own. They left me well off. I can more than hold out till I finish college."

"Who lives here with you now?"

"Nobody."

Peggy followed his lead into the living room and sat on a wonderful white couch that threatened to swallow her whole. She wasn't sure, but she'd read once about how it was against the law for a minor to live alone. Derek wasn't much older than she. "Don't you have any relatives?"

"When my parents first died, there was an aunt on my mother's side. She was given charge over me in court, but the house spooked her and she left. And before you ask, she wanted me to leave with her but I couldn't. This is the only home I've ever known."

He sat opposite her and stared at his feet, making Peggy feel awkward. Derek had lost everything a child holds sacred, and she couldn't react. She didn't know how. "I should have minded my own business, huh?"

"It's all right," he said, a smile still frozen in place. "You would have found out sooner or later. Anyway, I didn't always agree with my father's life style, but I loved him. As for my mother, she was gentle and soft-hearted with a personality that was the complete opposite of his. How the marriage survived with no fights I'll never know."

Peggy thought about her own parents and their constant struggle for the upper hand. All they did was fight, and yet she was glad to have them and not be an orphan like Derek.

"How about some lunch?" he asked. "Or maybe brunch because it's so early?"

Peggy glanced at an elegant wall clock with golden, gilded edges and saw that it was eleven. Where the last two hours had gone was a mystery to her. She remembered the orgy of death in science class, and she remembered fleeing from the building with Derek, and she remembered wandering around in shock until Derek convinced her to come here.

But she couldn't remember what Hank looked like, or Connie, or Tracy. She imagined herself still in shock.

"Peggy, are you hungry?"

"No."

"How about a Coke?"

"Sure," she said, the small hairs on the back of

275

her neck rising when the front door outside opened and closed. She looked at Derek and tried to be calm. He had said he lived alone. Who just came in?

Then, as if he could read her thoughts, Derek spoke, giving her reason to side with his aunt. "It's eleven. My parents usually take their walk at this time of day. They just left."

Peggy heard what he said and figured she'd better leave. The dead don't walk, so either Derek had lied to her or she'd just imagined the sounds a door makes when it opens and closes.

"They died in this house. I'm not sure they were ready to accept death, so they sort of hung around. Now you know why my aunt couldn't stay. I'll get you that Coke," he said, getting to his feet.

"I'm going with you!"

"Peggy, they won't hurt you. Besides, they're not in the house. They've gone for a walk."

Everything wonderful has its drawbacks, she thought. Here she was, stuck on Derek, and it seemed now that he felt the same. But he had these dead parents who were still hanging around. Why is it that nothing can ever be perfect?

Sitting alone, waiting for Derek to return, Peggy studied the room around her. She saw white, brocade drapes, black, onyx end tables with glass tops, a white, marble fireplace that was huge, and she wondered how Anita would feel about living here. Anita, for all her flare, preferred the plain and simple to the lavish.

Then she noticed that everything was spanking clean. There was no dust anywhere, nothing to show a passage of time or neglect. Either Derek was a good housekeeper—or his mother was.

"Here," Derek said, carrying two Cokes into the room. "I'm heating some roast beef in the oven for us. I like warm food for lunch, not like the cold, stale food we get in school."

Why not let Mommy do it? Mommy does everything else, she thought. But she said nothing, smiled and watched him sit next to her instead of in the chair opposite.

"You have to be home any special time?" he asked.

"Well . . . as long as I'm there by three. I usually get home at three. If I get home any later . . ." She paused then, not wanting to go on with this. She'd started to say that if she got home any later, she'd have to explain why, and that would mean relating what happened in science class and why she'd gone to Derek's house.

"Tell your parents you cut science," Derek said, reading into her thoughts again. "I know it'll be hard to tell what happened—"

"What did happen, Derek? Did Quigley freak out?" She recalled the figure of the executioner standing in the mist by the door, but if Derek hadn't seen it, how could she explain it to him? At this point, she knew Quigley wasn't to blame since he'd died along with the rest.

"Peggy, I saw the man in the mist again," he said, looking away. "I doubt it was Quigley who killed them. I mean, if this man in the mist had the ability to transcend his ethereal state and to chase you and hurt Nicky, then he had the ability to take over Quigley's body." After he spoke, he turned and faced her as if to measure her reaction.

"I saw him, too. I was just wondering how I'd tell about him. I'm glad we're both tuned into the same wave length. I'm also glad I listened to you and stayed out of the experiment. Derek, do you think those kids are really dead?"

She could still see Hank and Connie and Tracy—not their faces, that was lost to her—with their bodies quivering violently in the throes of death. She closed her eyes to erase it, but could not. Then she felt the cushion next to her sink with someone's weight and hoped it was Derek.

She felt his warm breath on her face and wanted to scream because she loved him so. When she felt his mouth cover hers, she moaned. Derek was kissing her, but not with a strong need for fulfillment. Peggy sensed that he wanted to be comforted as much as she. This kiss was his way of reaching out, of asking her to erase the memory from his mind as well as from hers.

"Peggy," he whispered, once the kiss was over and she was locked in his embrace, "we have to stick together. Our lives may depend on it."

Once spoken, she opened her eyes, then analyzed his words, something she'd been criticized by Max for—being too analytical—then she realized what Derek was saying. The creature in the mist hadn't tried to stop them from leaving class today. Maybe he'd come back. And the creature had powers, there was no arguing with that. He probably was the cause of the paralysis that had kept them both in their seats and that had kept them from screaming for help.

"Can you do anything about him?" she asked. "You've studied the occult."

"Only if I see him coming. If he gets us by surprise . . ." He stopped there and kissed her again, as though he didn't want her to have time to think about what he'd said.

This time, however, the kiss was more demanding. Using his hands to roam her body to signal his desire, he gently forced her mouth open. Moaning heavily, Peggy allowed him to slowly lower her into a prone position on the couch, knowing she was about to experience the thrill of his love for her.

She didn't fight when the full weight of Derek's body came down on her. Instead she continued to kiss him and to let herself go with the flow of his lovemaking.

But then the front door opened and closed, and Derek stopped. Peggy glanced towards the foyer outside, anticipation giving her the shivers, but saw nothing. "Damnit!" he cursed and buried his head against her chest. "They're back, and I know they're watching. But then," he said, looking up, "maybe it's just as well. I really care for you, Peggy. This isn't the way to show it, not with someone as innocent and naive as you. Please forgive me. I was out of line, letting my passion rule over my better sense."

Peggy smiled, and he kissed her again. "Ready for that lunch I promised you? I know I am. I'm starved." Derek's line about lunch was his way of getting over his embarrassment.

"Let's eat," she said.

Derek got up and helped her to her feet as a thousand things raced through her mind. She was disappointed because she'd been ready for someone she cared for to make love to her. She wanted Derek more than anything. And yet, Charlie had always said that being in love was a commitment, and Peggy felt that maybe Charlie was right. A commitment was the same as making a vow, and Peggy was too young to vow she'd love Derek forever.

But then how long was forever? If the creature in the mist came back, there might not be a forever for either of them. Ten minutes or an hour from now may be all that was left.

Following him out to the kitchen, she hesitated in the foyer when something cold and airy brushed against her flesh. Which one, she wondered, touched her? Was it Mommy or Daddy?

Charlie was pacing the floor in the living room

when Peggy arrived home around one with Derek.

Derek had driven her there in his car, a late model Ford resembling a family car and not something a teenager usually would drive. Derek said his choice of cars was his way of being cautious. He had a junior driver's license, which meant he couldn't drive alone, only with an adult driver. If he had a souped-up sports car the cops would be after him every chance they got, but cops never bothered you when you were driving something sensible.

"Once I'm eighteen," he explained, "I can drive whatever I want to—"

"It's about time!" Charlie hissed once they were inside. "And who's this?"

"Derek—"

"Derek who? You got a last name, pal?"

Peggy had never seen Charlie this angry. She was hurt and confused. She was also embarrassed in front of Derek. "Daddy, what's wrong?"

"What's wrong? There's a class full of dead kids in Philmore, a class my kid was supposed to be in. Only she wasn't in that class. In fact, she wasn't even in school when her mother and I ran over there like two maniacs. Where the hell were you?"

"At Derek's."

"Oh, excuse me," Charlie raged, "if I'd only known." He turned back to Derek again as Anita came barging into the room, her face ashen.

"This is what she did to her mother," he shouted at Derek. "Her mother swore she was dead. Now she tells me she spent the day at your house. Doing what?"

"We had lunch," Derek said politely. "And as for my last name, I think you already know. It's Westmore."

"Son of a bitch!" Charlie roared, moving quickly towards Derek while Anita tried to stop him. "Your old man screwed me. Now you're screwing my daughter. Ain't no way history's repeating itself in this house, not while I'm alive."

Anita had him around the neck, but Charlie kept walking and dragging her behind like a rag doll. Peggy figured the whole scene would have been funny if it weren't so tragic.

"Stop it, Charlie!"

As soon as Anita spoke he stopped in his tracks, barely five feet from where Derek stood.

"Maybe I'd better leave," Derek said, heading for the door. But Peggy had other ideas.

"No, you stay right here. You saved my life. You can't leave."

"Let him go!" Charlie spat.

"Daddy, you've got to listen. He's not like his father was. He's spent his entire life trying to undo the damage his father caused. You can't throw him out because he's got the same name."

"This is my house. I can do what I want!"

"Bye, Peggy," Derek said.

"Just a minute!" Anita shouted, stopping him.

"I trust Peggy. If she says you're all right and that you saved her life, you stay right where you are. Charlie can deal with his past in his own way. Guests do not get thrown out of my house. Now, let's all sit down and have a cold drink to cool off."

"Who is this man in the mist?" Charlie asked suspiciously after Derek explained what happened in school.

Derek had wanted Peggy to lie about being in science class so neither of them would have to explain what happened, but when Derek saw her parents and how supportive they were, he told them himself. "We don't know, sir. But after he killed the others, we were allowed to leave unharmed. I took Peggy to my house."

"Why?"

"Daddy!"

"It's all right, Peggy. I wanted to get my car to drive her home. There's no early morning bus."

They were seated in the living room, Charlie in his recliner, Anita in her chair with the doily covering the headrest. Peggy and Derek shared the loveseat. Anita had brought them tall, cool drinks of iced tea, with whole wheat crackers and cheese to snack on.

As Peggy sipped her iced tea, she marveled that this was the first time she'd ever eaten or drunk anything in any room but the kitchen. Anita was changing for the better. She seemed relaxed and caring.

"This man—this executioner—you say he's the one who hurt Nicky?"

"Yes, sir."

"Please, I'm Charlie. I'm nobody's sir. Now, could it be that Nicky's ouija board had something to do with this executioner putting in an appearance at school?"

"Yes," Derek said. "Nicky called him Max by the way."

Peggy heard Charlie's question, Derek's answer and felt enraged. Max and the executioner were nothing alike. Max wanted to help; the executioner wanted to destroy.

"Peggy brought Nicky's ouija board here," Charlie said bitterly. "And I—"

"Let her!" Anita said, finishing the sentence for him. "But that was weeks ago. The board's gone now, isn't it, Peggy?"

Peggy swallowed hard and nodded. Now she was lying to her mother as well as Charlie. Derek stared at her, and she saw outrage in his features. Derek knew the truth.

"I think you both have been through a helluva lot," Charlie said. "Maybe it's best if there's no school for a few days. This way we can talk and get it out before you crack."

"I was thinking along those lines," Derek said, the old hardness underlining his voice.

"And, Derek, I'm truly sorry about your parents," Charlie mumbled. "I didn't know your mother. And what the hell, if you can understand how wrong your father was in his dealings with black magic and the occult, I was thinking . . . why not stay here? No use going back to an empty house."

Peggy began to make small, circular movements on her leg with one hand. Derek's house wasn't empty, if Charlie only knew the truth. "Yes, why don't you stay?"

Derek stiffened his jaw and refused. "I don't wanna impose."

"We don't feel imposed upon," Anita said, smiling. "I'll make us a nice dinner. There's no spare bedroom, but the couch opens up. Come on, kid. Stay."

"Okay."

"Good," Anita said, getting to her feet. "Now you three just sit and talk while I fix dinner. And Charlie, don't forget to make that call."

"Uh, yeah, I won't forget."

Once Anita had left the room and they were alone, Charlie explained how he wanted to go on half time at work because of the strange happenings in his life this past week. "My commission structure is such that I can afford it. Besides, even if I couldn't, my wife and daughter come first. I'm kinda nervous about leaving them alone in this house."

"I thought the hauntings had stopped."

Charlie eyed Derek with surprise. "Didn't Peggy tell you? This is something new, nothing to do with what took place years ago. First of all . . ."

Derek's body became tight and tense as Charlie explained the recent hauntings. "Sounds like you need my help," Derek said when he was through.

"Your help? What can you do?"

"Well, sir—"

"Charlie. It's Charlie."

"Well, Charlie, I studied under my father."

"Really? Then how do I know it's not you doing this?" Charlie gripped the armrests of the recliner, and Peggy saw his knuckles turn white with anger. This was turning sour again. Charlie had gone from open trust to feeling that Derek was responsible.

"I studied only to stop my father. I was a good student, but I didn't graduate."

"What's that supposed to mean?" Charlie had moved forward in his seat. Peggy wondered about running out to the kitchen to get Anita. "You didn't graduate?"

Derek, however, watched Charlie and kept his cool. "The lessons ended when I told my father how wrong he was and how I wanted to stop him. From there on I had an awful time with him."

"That's terrible—" Charlie began, but never got the chance to finish. Anita screamed, her tortured and tormented voice echoing from the kitchen.

Anita hadn't meant to scream. In fact, when she first began to make dinner there wasn't anything to scream about. She wanted to make braised beef over rice, so she took onions and rice from a cabinet and placed them on the table. Then she went to the refrigerator for the carrots, celery and meat.

On her way to the refrigerator, she noticed her curtains dancing at the windows and tried to enjoy the sight without being reminded of work to be done in the house, of curtains that needed changing. It was wonderful to be having company for dinner. It seemed years since they'd had anyone over.

She was singing when she opened the refrigerator door, but stopped when she realized the meat was gone. Anita remembered taking the meat from the freezer hours ago and placing it on the bottom shelf to defrost.

She was still trying to puzzle this out when the scent of fresh spring flowers drifted in on a breeze and made her forget the meat for a moment. Anita had once been a romantic, so many years ago she couldn't begin to count them. Fresh flowers in spring, mingled with sea breezes, were those very same aromas that had made her flesh tingle when she was younger and made her yearn to be riding in an open convertible with Charlie by her side.

Going back into her past, she tried to recapture the thrill, to grasp that old feeling of being in love with Charlie and somehow carry it back to the present. Charlie loved her. Hell, it wasn't fair for her to be this way.

And yet things had turned sour when they got

married and took on responsibility. Things turned worse when Peggy was born. There were no more convertible rides to the beach, no more lying in Charlie's arms on the sand at the edge of the surf, making love while whitecaps broke over their bodies. Somehow, along the way, she fell out of love with Charlie.

Oh God, let me love him again, Anita prayed, then stopped at the sound of footsteps behind her. She was afraid at first, but only because she'd been hearing so many of those cursed footsteps lately, only to turn and find no one there. And yet this was different. She wasn't alone in the house this time. There were three people sitting in the living room. One of them must have walked out to the kitchen to join her. Charlie! It had to be Charlie.

Anita turned and wanted to faint.

Someone *had* joined her in the kitchen, but it was someone she didn't know.

It was a tall man with a huge, muscular body—and a hood over his head. She saw the naked chest, the axe in his hands, and felt she was about to die. It was the man in the mist Derek had spoken about—the executioner.

"I took the meat from the refrigerator," he said in a calm voice that surprised her. She'd expected his voice to be as gravelly as sandpaper being rubbed over her eardrums. "But I have my axe. I can get more. In fact, you can have my arm."

While Anita watched in horror, he placed his

arm fully across the kitchen table and came down with the axe. When it connected, blood flew up and covered her face like a wave in an ocean. She stared at a bloody stump with bones jutting out and tried to figure her next move. After all, what if his arm wasn't enough? What if he used the axe on her as well? What if her body became part of the braised beef she'd planned for dinner?

With this in mind, Anita threw her head back and screamed.

CHAPTER EIGHTEEN

Anita screamed. There was blood everywhere —on the counters, on the stove, all over her.

She looked down and saw tiny bats with rust-colored bodies, wings and sharp teeth consuming the blood, sucking it from her skin. But it wasn't her blood. It belonged to the man with the hood, the man with no shirt and one arm. The blood was his.

Slapping at the bats in a useless effort to stop the nightmare, she suddenly found herself begging the executioner to help, but he was busy slicing his arm into chunks to duplicate the stew meat he'd stolen from her refrigerator.

"Almost done," he said and smiled, his voice sweet and melodic, overpowering Charlie who was screaming for Anita to let him into the kitchen; the door was jammed.

Then she heard Peggy, then Derek, and yet she couldn't let them in, couldn't move. The bats were heavy, dragging her body to the cool tile floor beneath her, but Anita knew she musn't allow them to get her down. As long as she was still on her feet, she felt strong, felt she had a chance to fight.

"Sius, Acarius, Volanum! Demon of evil be gone!"

Anita heard the voice and knew it was Derek. The boy had been trained by the best, if she could take Charlie at his word.

She gazed at the executioner, his head cocked to one side, his attention drawn to the door beyond him. Black fluid covered his lips, then streamed across his teeth when he smiled. "The boy will play games with me," he said with some amount of satisfaction in his tone. "Someone challenging, at last."

"Nebus, Repellum, Mindalius. Demons of the dark underworld of Satan. We beseech you to gather your brethren and depart!"

"The boy's good," the executioner said, his axe bloody, small scraps of flesh coating the blade. "I will be gone, but not for good."

Anita watched him disappear in a puff of smoke, hoping he'd remember to take the bats. Feeling a release of weight, she looked again and began to cry. The bats were gone, thank God.

* * *

Peggy saw the blood and made repairs in the gulleys of her mind while Charlie and Derek searched for wounds. Anita had to be bleeding badly, otherwise where did the blood come from?

But Anita was no help. All she did was mumble and rant about the executioner and how he gave up his arm for dinner. Then she mentioned rust-colored bats and how they'd licked most of the blood from her body. Peggy knew about the executioner, but he lived in Philmore High, not here at her house—and there were no bats. Oh God, Anita was losing control. Peggy had feared this right along.

"Mom, please," she said, scanning the kitchen, fearing too that there might be a hint of truth to what Anita said. After all, Charlie could find no wounds on Anita. Besides, if the blood covering the walls and floor and cabinets belonged to Anita, she'd be dead by now.

Charlie took a trembling Anita past Peggy while Derek ran water into a bucket from under the sink. Derek wanted to clean up, but Peggy didn't—or couldn't. If Anita was right, and this was demon blood, Peggy didn't want to touch it. Yet Derek insisted, so Peggy cleaned and wiped and disinfected until there was nearly as much blood on her hands as there'd been on Anita's.

Afterwards, she sat in the living room with Derek and spoke of dinner. She wasn't hungry, but he probably was. Charlie had to be starving by now, too. "What should I cook?" she asked, knowing it wouldn't be meat. "I could make pancakes or something like that."

"It's all right, baby," Derek said, taking out his wallet. "I got some bucks. We can pick up hamburgers—"

"No! No meat! Derek, the blood . . ."

"All right. Fish then. Fish and chips."

"It's on me," Charlie added, suddenly standing at the bottom of the stairs with a shaken Anita by his side.

Peggy marveled at how wonderful Anita looked despite what she'd been through; she was radiant and glamorous, everything Peggy wasn't. Anita looked down at her hands and shuddered. "I got it off," she said. "The blood's gone. Are we having fish, or should I cook?"

"Fish," Charlie said, helping her over to her chair.

"I'm not hungry," she said, "but Charlie will pay. Derek should hold onto his money."

"It's okay. I gave myself an allowance now that I control my own trust fund."

"I won't hear of it," Charlie said, digging through his pockets for cash. "You're a guest here. Although I don't think you'll wanna stay now."

"What happened gives me more reason to stay."

"What did happen?" Anita asked, her brow

furrowed with confusion. "I was making dinner, but the meat was gone. And that man . . . Charlie, where's the arm?"

"It's gone," he said, squatting down beside her.

"The son of a bitch lied. He took my meat and then he lied—"

"Anita, stop it."

"No, Charlie. I hate liars . . . I . . ." But she didn't finish. She buried her face against the nape of his neck and cried. "It's my own fault," she said, her voice quivering. "Those kids died in Peggy's class and I didn't mourn them. I tried to go on with my life, but God punished me."

"Babes," Charlie said softly, "what happened here had nothing to do with God or His punishing you. This was the work of that bastard from the ouija board. He did this!"

Peggy heard what Charlie said and didn't want to believe it. Max wasn't dangerous. Max had promised to protect her. But then something struck her with the velocity of a bolt of lightning. Before Max came on the scene, there weren't any problems to need protecting from other than her epilepsy and the kids at school, but those were normal problems.

She glared at Anita, saw the shock, remembered what Derek and Charlie had said about the ouija board and knew she'd been wrong about Max. Hadn't things started right after she'd first spoken to him? Hadn't that mess oozed from the toilet the very next morning? If not, then it was shortly after.

Then there was the incident with the furniture turned upside down, something else that never happened before she played games with Max.

And as for Max and his promises of protection, the bastard was never around when she needed him, like when he promised to protect her and she was almost beaten to death at school. No, he was never around when she needed him. Or maybe he *was* around and didn't help because every tragedy this past week had been his doing!

Then she remembered he'd helped once. Max had brought Dog back from his breakdown, only Dog was worse now. He was nastier than ever and he didn't listen.

Breakdown!

A key word. Dog had a breakdown and so did Nicky! Why so many breakdowns these days? Even poor Anita was on the verge. "Come on, Derek," she said, getting to her feet. "Let's get the fish and hurry back. I have something to take care of. Something important."

Something like burning that damned, stinking, cursed ouija board, she thought, but kept it to herself.

Anita was sleeping on the couch. Charlie watched her sleeping form from his recliner and wondered about taking her upstairs. He hated to wake her, but she wasn't safe alone. She had to

have someone around to guard her from the
executioner. Leaning forward in his chair, he
saw Derek consume two large pieces of filet and
enough french fries and cole slaw to fill any
portion of his stomach that might still be empty.

Peggy, like Charlie, only picked at her food.

He wondered that Derek was almost unaf-
fected by the nightmare in the kitchen until he
recalled the boy's training. But instead of training, Charlie preferred to think of it as brainwash-
ing. The boy had been brainwashed since he'd
spoken his first word. Christ, what kind of parents were they? True, his father was a bit shaky
mentally, but his mother should have interfered.

"Can you help us?" he asked Derek, hating the
fear in his own voice.

"Yes, but there's one thing I have to stress . . ."
Derek stopped there and made the wait between
his thoughts a tortuous thing.

"Look, sir . . . uh, Charlie. I can't guarantee
results."

Charlie gasped and quickly covered his
mouth. Then he glanced at Peggy, saw how pale
she was and wanted to kick his own butt for
adding to her fears. But the idea of this going on
forever, of this haunting being a never ending
process was beyond him. Charlie believed in
miracles. Derek evidently didn't.

"I'm sorry," Derek said, "but when it comes
to anything dealing with dark supernatural
forces, there is no positive factor. They're tricky

devils, if you'll excuse the pun, and they have the ability to come back after they've been exorcised."

"Like the executioner," Charlie said, clutching the armrests until his knuckles turned white. "You beat the bastard and saved Anita—"

"But not for good. He'll be back."

Charlie was on his feet now, pacing the floor, his fingers working at his mouth. They had to move, get out, let the bastards have this house.

"I know what you're probably thinking," Derek said, looking up to let Charlie know he was sincere. "Moving won't help. They'll follow you."

"Then what will help?" Charlie bellowed, forgetting the sleeping Anita. She stirred, turned over and went off again. "How?" he whispered.

"I'm not sure. I know a lot about ouija boards and what they can do, the messes they cause, but I've never dealt with an exorcism of a creature from a board before. And no two exorcisms are alike because you're facing different forces with different strengths."

"I don't understand."

"The exorcism you would use on a poltergeist may not work on another dark force, simply because there are many levels of strength among these creatures. The stronger the force, the more difficult it becomes. Sometimes we can't gauge that strength until the exorcism is actually being performed. Do you happen to remember what technique my father used when he exorcized your house?"

Charlie stood and stared and tried to go back in his mind, but he couldn't. "Your father took the ouija board out into the backyard, but he was alone. He told us to stay in the house."

"Well," Derek said, sighing heavily, "at least it's a start. Tomorrow I'll go home, get my father's journals and bring them back here. Meanwhile, I think we should all turn in early. We'll need our rest for what's ahead."

"Good idea," Charlie said, bending to lift Anita into his arms.

"Where will Derek sleep?" Peggy asked. "Certainly not down here."

"I'm as safe here as I'll be anywhere else in the house."

After he'd spoken, Peggy found herself wishing he hadn't. He basically was saying the house was tainted, all of it. "I'll get you some pillows and sheets," she said numbly, going upstairs to the linen closet.

Opening the door, she saw rats climbing the shelves and fought an aura. They never had rats before. This was part of the haunting, something meant to terrorize her. Stiffening, she erased the memory of the dead rat in the cooking pot at school and reached in for the linen. One of them, a large black one with heavily slitted, blood-red eyes made a grab for her hand with its huge teeth.

She pulled her hand back and hissed, "Get the hell away!" She snatched the linen and closed the door before any of them had a chance to attack.

"By the way," Charlie said, coming up behind her with a sleeping Anita in his arms. "How do we justify the deaths of those kids at school?"

Peggy thought she must be dreaming. Charlie felt they were responsible for the orgy of death in science class? "We don't. Daddy, it wasn't our fault."

"Then whose?" he wanted to know. "You said it wasn't Quigley teaching the class, and you said you saw the executioner, the same executioner who threatened your mother in the kitchen. Somehow it's connected to us."

"I can't hack this, Daddy. Could we discuss this tomorrow after a good nights sleep?"

Peggy closed the door to her bedroom and leaned back against the frame, savoring the memory of Derek's lips. Derek had kissed her good night only moments ago, stirring up the same yearning Peggy had experienced in his house earlier in the day before Derek's mother and father had come home from their walk.

Shuddering, she dug the box of stick matches from the pocket of her slacks and waited. She wanted to burn the ouija board to destroy Max and the hold he had on this house, the hold he had on her, but Max could materialize. Max was legion. What if he materialized while she was burning the board?

Then again, Max had already proven what a lazy, boastful bastard he was. Max was forever bragging about lots of things he could do, things he'd never done. Maybe he was too lazy to even leave the board to save himself.

"Wanna bet?"

Peggy heard his voice and shriveled against the door frame. How stupid to forget that Max could read her mind.

"Look, Max, I'm really tired—"

"Liar! You weren't too tired when you were down there smooching with Derek a while ago. The only time you're tired it seems is when it comes to me!"

A jealous lover! This is the impression she got from Max. Some nerve!

Moving towards the closet, Peggy fingered the matches and fought to keep her mind a blank. No use tipping her hand, forcing Max to leave the board. After all, Max would never sit still for his own cremation.

"Put the matches down, Peggy."

"Matches? What matches?"

"Those in your hand. Put them down! Don't even dream of torching me. Besides, it's hotter than hell where I come from, if you'll excuse the pun."

Peggy heard what he said and died inside. Max not only read her thoughts, but somehow he was able to foresee her actions. How?

"By watching every move you make."

"Is this how you knew about me smooching with Derek? Is this how you seem to know everything that goes on in my life, even when I'm not here?"

"Yes, I've already told you—"

"I know. You're legion!"

"Fine. Then you're aware of my powers. Put the matches down!"

Peggy listened but didn't heed the warning in his voice. Opening the door, she took the ouija board from its hiding place and moved quickly to the bathroom, where she placed it in the tub, almost tripping over Dog in the process.

"Don't make me kill you, Peggy!"

"Yeah, yeah. You really hate to hurt people, don't you, Max?"

Rushing back to her dresser, Peggy tore a batch of paper from her spiral notebook and wadded it into a ball. Then she went back to the bathroom, placed the paper on top of the ouija board and lit a match. The paper would get the fire going faster than if she just torched the cardboard.

Standing back, she watched the paper burn and tried to feel happy. If she was right in her thinking, Max was the tormentor responsible for the hauntings in her home and the murders in school. Yet Max used to be a good friend, at least this is what he'd led her to believe.

Now, with Max on his way out and Dog

half-crazy, Peggy had no one to confide in, no one to tell about the thrill of having Derek in her life. It really was sad.

"Don't shed any tears for me, kid. You're the one who's in trouble. Burning the board won't break the spell. Anyway, I'm not letting you do it."

Peggy was aware then of cool night breezes raising the curtains on the bathroom window and making them stand straight out. Ignoring Max, she breathed heavily of the scent of flowers and the ocean and wanted nothing more than to be in Derek's arms right now.

But the breezes stirring her desires to a pitch were tricky like Max, and like Max they couldn't be trusted. What had started out as a soothing rush of sweet-smelling wind had suddenly become stronger, strong enough to lift her hair and blow it back away from her face, strong enough to cause Peggy to grab the towel rack and hold on for balance, strong enough to extinguish the flames in the bathtub.

"Son of a bitch," she cursed and tried to close the window, but it was stuck. Grabbing a hand towel she forced it over the top of the frame and pulled it down over the sill in an attempt to stifle the wind, but it didn't help. The wind was too strong.

Frustrated, Peggy ran past Dog in the doorway and got more paper and matches. If she slid the plexiglass enclosures across on the tub and the tub was completely encased, maybe she could block the wind. Maybe the fire would hold long enough to burn Max's ass and send him back to his world of darkness. Max wasn't the smartest person—

"Wanna bet?"

"Yes!" she fumed. "I wanna bet."

Peggy was sliding the plexiglass enclosures in place when she noticed that Dog was near the window, and the doorway he'd been lying in up until now was engulfed in flames.

Then she listened to the window slam so hard she half-expected glass to fly in all directions, and she fought the tiny aura forming in her mind.

"I fight fire with fire," Max said and laughed while Peggy went into her brain to repair the glitch in the computer. Only it wasn't as easy as she thought. Smoke was filling her lungs, causing her to cough and choke; fire snapped at her and made her want to run and forget the repairs.

Now Dog was snarling and hissing, his anger rising to assault her senses and disturb her concentration. But she had to stop this. If she had a seizure there was no way she could save herself from a fiery death.

Think! Shut everything out and think! Find the glitch and fix it. You're trapped between a snarling dog and a fire. Think and save your life.

Peggy screamed and watched the aura grow when Dog's teeth closed in on the tender flesh of her ankle. Dog had his teeth deep in. She glanced down and watched him twisting his head, ripping her flesh until the agony shot to her brain and she could no longer concentrate on her seizure.

Watching him through a brightly lit haze, she sunk to the floor and screamed when fire singed the back of her hand. The fire was moving fast, and it struck her as being odd that the fire was eating its way through the tile floor as though it were wood.

But then this was no ordinary fire; this was a demon inferno. And Dog still had her by the ankle. She felt her body begin to vibrate and knew the seizure was upon her. Lashing out with what little strength she had left, Peggy raised a fist and punched Dog square in the face. He let go, backed away and shook his head as though he were in shock.

Leaning her head against the cool tub, she made one last attempt to repair the glitch, but she couldn't find it at first. Her brain was fuzzy and hazed over from the aura and the smoke from the fire as well. Oh God, please help me, she prayed—and she found the glitch.

She was about to repair it when Dog attacked again. Peggy had a choice of either succumbing to the pain from Dog's teeth or doing the repairs in her brain. She chose the latter, but it wasn't easy. Searing hot pain racked her body as the animal tore at her flesh again. Fire licked at her face.

And yet she did it; she fixed the error in her brain and came back to reality. Raising her fist she punched at Dog again. Dog stopped, only he didn't back away as he had a moment ago. Instead, he eyed her face and opened his mouth full, revealing long, jagged teeth laced with spittle.

Peggy punched him again and felt his teeth slice across the flesh of her knuckles, but she stopped him again. Pulling herself to her feet, she realized that half of the bathroom was gone. Smoke hovered in the air like a blanket of death, filling her lungs and searing them with foul, acrid sulphur.

She remembered the window and thought about how she was on the second floor and would probably break something if she jumped. Still, it was better than this, but Dog was between her and the window.

Pulling back the sliding plexiglass doors, Peggy climbed numbly into the shower and ran cold water over her body. She'd seen this done in a movie and hoped it would work as well in real life. Once her body and hair were drenched, Peggy stepped out of the shower, entered the flames and couldn't fight back when another aura, a stronger one this time, surrounded her body and closed in.

Peggy woke up on the couch. Through a haze, she saw Charlie and Derek, but not Anita. Oh

God, her mother was upstairs alone!

Raising her head, she spotted Anita on the loveseat. Charlie must have dragged her back downstairs again when he rescued Peggy. The absurdity of Anita's sleeping form being carried from one end of the house to another, while she continued to sleep, reminded Peggy of a comedy sketch, except there was nothing funny about this.

"What happened?"

She heard Charlie and didn't know how to answer. Like Charlie carrying Anita all over the house, her story was absurd.

"I'm gonna ask once more," he said. "I wanna know what prompted Dog to bite you."

"The fire—"

"What fire?" Derek asked with as much panic and anger in his voice as Charlie's.

Propping herself on one elbow, Peggy told what happened in the bathroom, even knowing Charlie would kill her for lying about the ouija board. When she was through, Charlie continued to watch her, his face blank, his mouth tight, as if she'd left out a lot.

"There was no fire—and no ouija board," Derek said quietly, taking her attention away from Charlie. "The fire was an illusion. And Max—"

"Took the ouija board!"

"Yes." Derek's face was blank. Derek was as mad as Charlie. "Why don't you go ahead and tell your father everything."

"I can't!"

"You have to. He has a right to know the connection between the executioner at school and what's happening here."

Taking her eyes off Derek, Peggy zeroed in on a spot over Charlie's head and told him the story from the beginning, leaving nothing out. Doing this was reminiscent of the happier times she'd spent in her room talking to Dog. Unfortunately Charlie wasn't Dog, and Dog was insane.

Charlie smiled when she was through, but it was awful. "Those bastards in school were beating you and you never trusted me enough to tell me? And yet you told this demon, Max, and he killed them. That was your answer?"

"Daddy, no," she whimpered, tears streaking her face. "I told Max not to hurt them. I told Max to leave them to God."

"I hope you realize Max is also responsible for Dog and for what happened to your mother."

"Yes."

"Where do you think Max hid the board?"

"I don't know, Daddy."

Charlie sighed heavily and got to his feet. "Where's Dog's leash?"

"Why? What're you gonna do?" She looked to Derek for an answer, but Derek was staring down at his feet. This was none of his business.

"The fire wasn't real, Peggy, but Dog did attack you. Look at your leg."

For the first time since coming to, Peggy felt searing, hot pain in her ankle and knew Charlie was telling the truth. "But he's not acting right. Max did this to him."

"Yes, Peggy," Charlie hissed, "but we've got enough problems now trying to conquer Max without worrying about Dog, too. I'm taking him to the pound."

Peggy buried her hands in her face and cried. "Maybe the vet—"

"No!" Charlie bellowed, rushing upstairs to get Dog. When he came back down Peggy saw the leash on Dog and felt dead inside. Then she saw that Charlie had put a towel through Dog's jaws and had pulled it back and tied it behind his head. Dog must have attacked Charlie, and Charlie was using the towel in place of a muzzle.

Knowing this, she couldn't interfere. She watched Charlie, his face a mask of determination, take Dog outside. Then she reached for Derek and began to cry again when the sound of the engine in Charlie's car started up. Dog was going to the pound to be put to sleep.

And Max was the enemy. He'd proven it in more ways than one in such a few short hours. Now Peggy had no one left to confide in, neither Dog nor Max. She felt alone and defeated until Derek rose and sat down beside her. Wrapping her in his arms, he covered her lips with his and tried to muffle the hurt.

Suddenly, though, their kiss was interrupted

when Charlie came back inside looking sheepish. "I was so angry that I forgot about your ankle, Peggy. It's really bad. I have to take you to the hospital. Meanwhile, Derek can stay here and guard your mother."

CHAPTER NINETEEN

The treatment room in the hospital was cold, sterile and impersonal, reminding Peggy of how her house was kept before Max entered her life and caused such a profound change in Anita.

Waiting for the doctor, Peggy started to think about Dog, about the sadness in his eyes when Charlie took him into the pound before bringing her here to the hospital. Dog had changed again. He was just like he used to be, friendly and lovable.

Peggy pointed out the sudden change, thinking Charlie might not want him destroyed after all, but Charlie wasn't impressed. Charlie said

Max was playing head games, and so Charlie went ahead with the execution plans. Dog would be put to sleep.

Feeling herself overcome by grief, Peggy forced Dog from her mind and hoped the doctor wouldn't take long. Charlie was out in the waiting room alone.

Now the injection the ER nurse had given her moments ago, against her will, was starting to work. Peggy had argued against the pain killer, but her hospital record from previous visits had *Epileptic* written across the top in glaring red letters. The doctor felt she needed something before they treated her for the open wound on her ankle. Then she found herself hoping they'd give her another doctor. This Dr. Robert Miller she'd drawn in the Emergency Room shuffle was a nut case. He giggled a lot and made Peggy nervous.

She also wondered why a psychiatrist would be willing to treat an ankle wound until Dr. Miller explained that the hospital was short-handed so he'd been assigned to the Emergency Room. "Besides," he'd said in defense of himself, "a psychiatrist has to be a medical doctor first, then he studies psychiatry. I am a doctor, you know!"

Lying there on a hospital bed, Peggy listened to the sound of footsteps coming down the hall and hoped it was Dr. Miller with a nurse by his side. No matter what Dr. Miller had told her, she was still leery of being alone in the same room with him.

When the door opened, Peggy watched it swing wide, saw Dr. Miller come in—but, oh God, that wasn't a nurse behind him. Peggy saw a deranged Nicky Martin, who was so disheveled and dirty that she bore no resemblance to the Nicky she knew. Nicky's eyes were heavily bagged and glazed with insanity, her hair dirty and clumped in snarls, her hands curved into claws.

Peggy stared at Nicky and wanted to run, but she couldn't. The drug was taking effect. Then Peggy watched Dr. Martin lock the door and give Nicky a scalpel. "There she is, Nicky—Peggy Rearden. She's the one who took your board and turned Max against you. This is your chance to get even!"

Charlie was in the waiting room when he heard Peggy scream. Then he heard her call him and followed the sound of her voice knowing she was either in a lot of pain or scared to death. Either way she'd have a seizure, and Charlie had to be there to help.

But there was this huge male nurse guarding the desk near the treatment rooms. He told Charlie to go back outside and wait, that Peggy would be just fine. Only Charlie wouldn't go back. Instead, he tried explaining about Peggy and her epilepsy and the biofeedback lessons, while Peggy's screams tore at his heart. But the guy wouldn't listen.

"I don't care, pal. You wait outside—doctor's orders. If you wanna argue, you gotta get past me."

Charlie glared at the heavily muscled shoulders, the oversized forearms, the chest that was at eye level, heard Peggy scream again and shot out with a right hook to the guy's abdomen. Nothing happened.

"Oh, shit!" Charlie mumbled and braced himself for a good walloping, but the guy only smiled because Charlie was small and out of shape. In short, Charlie was a joke. Knowing this was behind the smile, Charlie shot out with the same right hook, connected with the guy's chin and watched him go down.

"Sorry about the glass jaw," he said and stepped over the bruiser's body to follow the sound of Peggy's screaming.

At first, Nicky chose only to stalk Peggy like a crazed hunter after helpless game. Walking with her back hunched and spittle dotting her lips, she encircled the hospital bed, her body so close that Peggy could almost feel the heat of her hatred.

But Nicky soon grew bored with this and approached Peggy from the side. Reaching down to clutch at Peggy's slacks, Nicky took the scalpel and sliced one leg up to the thigh. Nicky's once blue eyes were black with madness; foam laced the sides of her mouth when she smiled. "Your heart," she cooed, "I'm gonna dig it out!"

Her breath, laced with narcotics, stung at Peggy's nostrils while Peggy lay still and marveled that there was no aura, no oncoming seizure. But Peggy prayed for an aura; at least if she had a seizure, she wouldn't feel the pain of that scalpel.

Nicky lurched then, swinging the scalpel like a wild woman when someone pounded the door and shouted Peggy's name. Peggy heard her father's voice and knew he'd come to help, but the door was locked and so heavy that breaking it down would be next to impossible. Charlie could never do it alone.

Staring up at a smiling, deranged face, Peggy watched the scalpel slice the buttons off her blouse, watched it slice through her bra and knew that Nicky was clearing the way to her heart. But Nicky wanted to play with her victim before cutting her heart out. Sliding the scalpel flat side down across the flesh of Peggy's breast, Nicky ran the blade up and down several times until Peggy swore she'd go insane.

Charlie was still at the door and pounding furiously. "Daddy," she cried. "It's Nicky—" The words caught in her throat when Nicky flipped the blade around and sliced into her flesh. Peggy saw her breast open, saw an open cavity filled with raw meat and marveled that it didn't hurt more. She'd heard once that real sharp blades could cut and leave no pain, but she hadn't believed it until now.

Concentrating on the glitch in her brain and the aura that was now forming, Peggy heard another voice coming from the hall outside. Someone was arguing with Charlie. Then she heard two bodies hitting against the door and heard the frame give.

She started to lose consciousness, but fought it when so many things happened at once. The door crashed open and hung on its frame. Dr. Miller disappeared in a puff of smoke, but Nicky was still there. Nicky was still holding the scalpel when a huge, male nurse grabbed her and dragged her from the room.

Charlie was there, too, holding Peggy's hand, promising to stay with her until a doctor treated her wounds. Peggy closed her eyes then and prayed for a second time that it wouldn't be Dr. Miller. True, he'd disappeared into thin air, but what if he came back?

Peggy lay in bed the following morning and listened to the sound of birds outside of her bedroom. She heard robins and blue jays and even welcomed the crows with their outrageous squawking.

Rolling onto her back, she half-opened her eyes and flinched when the pain in her ankle shot to her hip. A large surgical bandage covered her ankle where Dog had bitten her; another covered her left breast where Nicky had sliced into it with the scalpel. Peggy hoped there wouldn't be scars, at least not huge or hideous ones. She wanted her body to be perfect when Derek made love to her.

A shaft of sunlight had wedged itself across the room to her bed. Closing her eyes, she reveled in the warmth of the sun, wanting its healing powers to erase the wounds on her body and the scars on her psyche. But something moved next to her bed, forcing her to slowly open her eyes again and turn.

It was Dog! He'd escaped from the pound, and from his expression he was angry. He must still be under Max's spell, only that was ridiculous. Dog had been his old self last night when Charlie took him to the pound, so it had to be that Dog was pissed at her. He was blaming her for his predicament, for winding up on death row. She gazed into a pair of rheumy, black eyes laced with hatred and started to tell Dog it wasn't her idea when a knock came at the door.

It was Anita who wanted to speak to her.

Peggy tried to call out, to tell Anita that Dog was here and Dog was dangerous, but the words were stuck in her throat. Dog cocked his head to one side, then swayed across the room to the closet with the same lopsided gate he'd had since his breakdown.

When the closet door opened, stirred into action by invisible hands, Dog walked in and waited, giving Peggy a chance to see the ouija board lying on the second shelf on top of the movie magazines. Apparently Max had put it there. Then Peggy saw the closet door close on Dog just as Anita opened the door to her bedroom and came on in.

"Most girls turn to their mothers," Anita was saying, her voice shaky and weak, "but I closed the door on you years ago."

"Mom, no."

"Yes, it's true. I shut you out, and it's time you knew why." Anita had been standing by the window, facing out, her small, shapely body looking good in jeans and a pullover. With a toss of her ash blonde head, she turned and walked over to Peggy's bed.

"Because of what's happened, the turmoil in our lives, I sort of snapped to and took a look at myself. I've been acting like a real shrew!"

Peggy sat up higher in bed and attempted to digest Anita's words. Her mother a shrew? Well, maybe. "But you didn't mean it," she said. "You probably had a lot on your mind."

"That's no excuse," Anita said, sitting on the bed and placing her hand over Peggy's. "Charlie told me how you tried to burn that ouija board last night, how you did it by yourself and how Dog almost killed you."

Dog! Peggy remembered him going into her closet moments ago and knew she'd have to tell Anita. No more lies, no more hiding the truth. But first, Anita had to be allowed to finish.

"You poor, helpless kid. Doing something so

318

dangerous because I made you afraid to share the truth with me. I turned you away. Only now I know why, and I have to explain it. Do you remember how when you were younger I used to come into your room at night and just stare at you? How I never spoke?" Peggy nodded. "Doing that and my fetish for cleaning were all part of my frustration.

"Peggy, before you were born, I was a normal, all-together person. I cooked, I cleaned, and I loved your father. I was in charge of my life and happy with the way it was going. You see, some women get this idea that they're super beings, able to plan their lives and make the impossible possible. I was going to have the most perfect marriage, the most perfect life, the most perfect children. But when you were born with epilepsy, I felt I had lost control. You were sick and so I blamed myself—"

"Mom, don't do this."

"Let me finish," she said, her eyes misting with tears. "I couldn't erase your sickness, couldn't make it go away. Planning my life wasn't enough. Things still went wrong. Then one day I discovered the one thing I could control—this house! My fetish for cleaning was a way of putting the perfection back in my life, but there were times I'd remember you and how sick you were.

"Those were the times I'd come into your bedroom at night and just stare at you and try to find a solution. Somehow I had to make you perfect again. I couldn't accept defeat. Out of frustration, I became callous and bitter. I closed the door on you, then I closed it on your father. I locked myself in a world where everything went as I wanted it to. The house was always clean. It never turned on me. Oh, Peggy, I'm sorry. The wounds on your body and all the hurt are my fault!"

After she spoke, she collapsed in Peggy's arms and cried as Peggy imagined she hadn't in years. And that crying was infectious for Peggy soon found tears flowing as well. The old Anita, the one with the warm, inviting arms was back, never to leave again. Something good had come from the tragedies they'd suffered these past few weeks.

"Mom," Peggy said when she was able to speak. "Can you go downstairs and get Daddy and Derek."

"Why, baby?" Anita asked, wiping her tears with the palms of her hands.

"Because we need help. Dog's in my closet, and the ouija board's back!"

Anita's mouth dropped open with shock. Quickly glancing at the closet, she pulled Peggy from the bed and helped her to her feet. "I'm not leaving you here. I don't know how they got back, but I just want you out before Dog attacks again!" Her hand was on the knob of the door by this time, but it wouldn't open. It was jammed tight. Letting go of Peggy, Anita pulled as hard as she could, twisting the knob every which way, but still it wouldn't open.

Another door opened, though. They heard the closet door squeaking on its hinges and dared not look. Dog was in that closet.

"Charrrlieee!" Anita screamed, pounding on the door in a panic.

Peggy heard footsteps coming up behind them and wanted to shrink into the carpet because those footsteps weren't normal, not even for a wobbly lopsided dog. She heard a one-two rhythm and knew this being walked on two legs. Max said he could materialize!

Leaning back against the door frame, Peggy fought an aura with everything in her, but Anita had turned to look at the creature from the closet. Anita was calling him a liar, demanding the meat he'd promised her. The executioner was behind them, and Anita had lost control.

"Max," he said. "You can call me Max!"

Peggy listened and felt her insides collapse in a wave of shock. Max was the executioner! Max was the enemy! If she hadn't realized it before with all that had taken place, she knew it now. Max, the man she'd befriended, the man who was to be her protector . . .

But no, he wasn't a man. He was a beast from the inner sanctum of insanity.

Zeroing in on the glitch in the computer of her mind, Peggy fought to make repairs before Max attacked, only something was wrong. Someone was hiding in the dark recesses in the folds of her brain, someone with a black hood over his head and an axe in his hands. Someone with awful skin and open sores everywhere was blocking her way.

"Get past me and the glitch is yours!" was all he said, but it was enough. Peggy would have to get past this monster she'd once called a friend to save herself from a seizure, but he had this axe—and he had help.

Peggy saw moving shadows near his feet in the semidarkness of her brain and didn't know at first what those shadows were. Were they creatures or figments of her imagination? But then Max waved his hand and more light appeared, and Peggy saw the creatures for what they were —faceless, shapeless blobs of flesh that crawled and slithered.

She heard them talking to her, calling her by name, but Anita's voice was there too, overpowering the voices of the beasts surrounding Max.

"Peggy," she screamed. "Fight it, Peggy. I've got your hands. You can do it."

No, I can't! Peggy wanted to scream back. Anita wasn't aware of the menace inside Peggy's head. Anita thought this would be so simple, this thing called biofeedback, and yet it couldn't be when creatures from a black nether world were forcing Peggy back, away from the glitch.

"Peggy, listen," Anita crooned, "Max is gone. I don't know where he's disappeared to, but we're safe. You can do it. Find the glitch."

Peggy listened to Anita, listened to Charlie and Derek hollering at the door and mumbled, "He's in my mind, Mom, blocking my path."

"Not my child, you bastard!" Anita raged and began to mimic Derek's chants from the night before. Peggy didn't know if Anita was saying the proper words, but it was her effort that counted. Anita did love her, enough to try anything to save her from Max.

"Sus, Acarus, Vol . . . Oh God, the words are all wrong. Derek, I know you can't get in here. If you'll just shout the words through the door!"

"Sius, Acarious, Volanum. Astaroth, Kali, Ishtar. Demons from the world of blackness, we summon your assistance against this foe."

Peggy listened to Derek's muffled voice and remembered Max's phrase about using fire to fight fire when he conjured up the phony scene in the bathroom the night before. Derek was obviously using the same technique, using demons to fight a demon. If it would only work.

But then her brain reeled. A hideous, frightening darkness such as Peggy had never known was closing in, robbing her of the consciousness she so badly needed. She was passing out.

Hours later as Derek scanned his father's journals, Charlie sat by his side in the living room and tried to help. This was totally new and confusing to Charlie. Most of the stuff was written in Latin. When he came across a few pages written in English, he concentrated, searching for an answer to end the hauntings.

Looking up now and then to check on Peggy lying on the sofa, Charlie thanked God that although she'd passed out, the seizure had stopped by itself. Otherwise, they would have been in one helluva fix what with Max inside her brain along with a score of creatures.

At one point Charlie stopped reading and marveled at Derek's knowledge and how he'd stopped Max more than once. Derek had said his chanting worked but only on a temporary basis. What they needed was something to send Max back to hell or wherever vicious demons went when they . . .

Charlie had almost ended his thoughts with the word "died," but from what Derek said, demons didn't die. Demons were banished, but not for long. Sooner or later Max would come back to torment some other poor fool foolish enough to play games with the ouija board.

"Penny for your thoughts, guys," Anita said, laying a tray heaped with sandwiches and Cokes on the coffee table near them.

"They're more than thoughts and worth more than a penny," Charlie said, smiling. Anita had changed so much these past few days he hardly recognized her. It was as if she'd gone into their past, had found that part of herself he'd loved so dearly and had brought the old Anita back with her.

The house was different, too. It wasn't sterile and neat with those nauseating cleaning odors hovering in the air. Also Anita wasn't so hyper about finding errors, about things being out of place like the magazines on the coffee table, for instance. Derek had wanted to use the kitchen table to spread out his journals, but Anita wouldn't hear of it. As Charlie watched in horror, Anita had swept her neatly stacked monthlies onto the floor while an "I don't give a damn" kind of expression crossed her face. "Use this table," she'd said. "Lay them out here and don't worry about the mess."

Don't worry about the mess? Charlie had waited eons to hear her say that.

"Yo, Derek," Anita said. "Fill your empty stomach, then worry about solutions. I mean, we got us a chant to get rid of old Max if he shows up. Temporary or not, it's better than nothing. Now eat!"

"Does that go for me, Mom?" Peggy said dazedly, rising to a sitting position.

"Sure does, sweetheart. Tell me what you want. I've got salami and provolone as well as ham and swiss."

Peggy chose the ham and swiss and tried to get it down. Charlie knew she hadn't eaten since the night before, but then, as he went back over it in his mind, Peggy hadn't eaten dinner either. Like him, she'd barely picked at her food.

In fact, he'd noticed a slump in her appetite lately, and although she could afford to lose a few pounds, Charlie didn't want her getting sick from lack of nourishment. "After we eat, what say we take some time off and go for a ride," he said. "Just to get out of the house?" A ride would do them all some good.

But Derek didn't agree. Charlie studied his dark eyes and listened when he mentioned a solution. Derek had found the answer.

"It was in this last paragraph. Oddly enough it's something taken from an ancient text called the Key of Solomon, the key being the answer to the complete control of dark, supernatural forces."

"Who was Solomon?" Charlie asked. "We're not talking about the king, are we?"

"Yes," Derek said in between bites of his sandwich. "Solomon strayed from his religion when he married the daughter of the Pharaoh. He did this to effect an alliance between their nations and to strengthen his kingdom as well. Then, as if once wasn't enough, he married several other princesses from heathen cultures for the same reason. Because of these marriages and the influence of his brides, Solomon became heavily involved in black magic. He wrote this text on spells and incantations for summoning demons."

"But how could he write about a ouija board?" Charlie wanted to know. "How old are those things?"

"They go back before Solomon's time. Not in the form we know them today, but Ouija Boards in one form or another have been mentioned in too many texts not to have been in existence in ancient Egypt and Persia. There was even a reference to a board for summoning spirits in a research book that went back to the Twelfth Century B.C., about a hundred years before Solomon's time."

Charlie whistled. "Man, I didn't know Max was that old!"

Anita sat nearby and nibbled thoughtfully on her lunch. Charlie saw lines crossing her brow; she was still upset about Max and what he had tried to do to Peggy. He marveled that she was no longer afraid for herself. She had Peggy to consider, and she seemed stronger because of it.

"Okay," he said, narrowing his attention on Derek again. "How do we get rid of Max for good?"

Derek rose and paced the floor as suddenly as if he'd been jabbed with a hot poker. He was nervous, his slim, muscular body tight and taut. "You know, I've been sitting here acting like this is nothing, like we were just searching for an answer. But there's danger involved. Charlie, this won't be easy. We have to bury the Ouija—"

"Like hell you will!"

Derek heard Max's voice and went into shock along with the rest. He'd forgotten about how Max was legion. Max knew all. Max heard all. "Let's get the hell outta here," he said. "Go to my place. Any plans we make will have to be done elsewhere, otherwise Max will stop us before we start—and he can!"

"What about the ouija board?" Charlie asked.

"What if he hides it again? Shouldn't we take it with us?"

"No. Max is arrogant enough to leave it in Peggy's closet," Derek said quickly, as though anxious to leave. "He won't hide it again. He's daring us to stop him."

"Besides," Peggy said dully, "Max lives in the board. If we take it, we'll be bringing him along."

Charlie stared at Derek and then back at Peggy. She was right. Taking the board would have been a terrible mistake.

CHAPTER TWENTY

Peggy held onto Anita for support while Charlie paid for a motel room in the middle of Floyd Acres, not far from Philmore High. Derek had wanted to pay since this was his idea, presuming Max would follow them to Derek's house. Coming here to the motel would throw Max off the track.

But Charlie wouldn't listen. "Bad enough you're involved in our mess without taking money outta your pocket, too."

"It would have been my pleasure," Derek said, taking Peggy's other arm to lead her to their room.

My pleasure, Derek said, causing a knot in Peggy's stomach to twist even tighter. My pleasure! At one time Peggy had felt that playing with the ouija board had been a pleasure, as was making friends with Max. But, like the old saying about all good things coming to an end, the pleasure of Max soon became a nightmare.

Their motel room was larger than expected with two double beds, two dressers, and a comfortable looking, stuffed chair which Charlie sat in. Anita and Peggy sat on one bed while Derek very properly chose the other.

"Before we start," Anita said, "is anyone hungry? We didn't finish lunch."

Always the hostess, Peggy thought and smiled, or perhaps the mommy who felt compelled to baby her brood. "I'm not hungry, but I could sure use something cold to drink."

Anita picked up the phone and ordered room service, which meant the manager would send a maid to the diner next door for Cokes. Then she sat back and waited for someone to bring up the subject of Max and the Key of Solomon.

"Before we were interrupted at home," Charlie began, speaking to Derek, "you mentioned burying the board."

"Yes. Burying it underground is the only solution."

"Why? I thought it would be better to burn the damned thing and reduce it to ashes."

"Peggy tried that," Derek said, "and she was almost killed. You see, Max comes from a world of fire and brimstone. Fire is nothing to him, but by being buried alive with a crucifix covering the board, Max would have no escape. He'd be trapped in the board until someone removed the cross and freed him.''

"Damned if it'll be me!" Peggy said, sounding like her old self again. "I had enough of Max."

Derek smiled, but then just as quickly hung his head and grew serious. "There's more to it. I mean, I intend to use a ceremony from the Key of Solomon text to conjure up creatures that wouldn't be found in your worst nightmares. If I do it incorrectly, those creatures will tear me to pieces and carry my flesh back to Acheron."

Peggy felt cold. She glanced down and saw the trembling in her hands and drew the covers from the bed up over her. The thought of losing Derek now that they'd finally become more than just friends was too awful to imagine. "Then the hell with it!" she said. "I'll throw the board away and let it become someone else's problem."

"It won't work, love." Derek's voice was so low she barely heard him. "Max has already made you and your family victims of his cruelty. He won't stop until you're either as crazy as Nicky Martin or dead."

"All right," Charlie said, "then it has to be buried. But tell me, Derek, just what the hell is this *I* stuff. We're all in this together. No way are you doing this alone."

Derek sighed heavily and faced Charlie as Peggy fought the urge to run to him and hold him in her arms. She'd started this, and now she felt she had to protect Derek because of it. "I've been trained since childhood. I know how to handle the beasts I'll be conjuring up. Listen, Charlie, I know your intentions are good, but one mistake and they'll kill you—and it won't be pretty or quick. They'll rip off your head and, pardon the expression, shit in your neck."

It was Charlie's turn to sigh now. He was silent for a long time, along with everyone else. Peggy saw him shudder and knew he was trying to fathom the danger in what Derek had just said. "What the hell do we need them for? You're conjuring up these evil bastards, and for what?"

"Charlie, what makes you think Max will sit still and let us bury the board and place a crucifix on top knowing he'll be trapped? Max is gonna hit us with everything he's got, and Max's got some good stuff to use against us. We need those creatures to get Max inside of the board and to get Max to stay there."

Peggy listened to Derek and knew he was making sense. None of them had considered Max's reaction to being buried for centuries to come, but Derek had dealt with this before, and now his experience was showing. Peggy moved closer to Anita and placed a trembling hand on top of Anita's trembling hand. They both squeezed at the same time for comfort.

"Derek," Anita said, her voice low and strained, "if these creatures come from the same place as Max, how will you get them to help us? They're not about to turn against one of their own!"

"They will if the ceremony is done correctly. The idea of summoning these creatures is to get them to grant favors, to get them under the spell of your incantation, to gain control of their strengths. If done properly, the creatures, although they will hate me and will long to destroy me, will also be compelled to do my bidding."

"And if they get the upper hand," Charlie said, "you're dead meat!" Derek nodded silently. "Then there's no question we're all in this togeth—"

When a knock came at the door, Peggy's throat began to close until she remembered Max never knocked. Max was legion. Doors didn't stop him. Charlie opened the door and was handed a paper bag with four Cokes inside. Reaching into his pocket, he gave the skinny, blonde maid a tip, then closed and locked the door behind her, sliding a metal bolt into place.

"After we drink these Cokes, I think we should try and get some rest. We're gonna need all the strength we can muster. Peggy and Anita will take that bed, and Derek, if you don't mind, we can share this one."

"Fine," Derek said. Opening his Coke, he started to drink it, then hesitated as though something had been left unsaid. Charlie sat back down in the chair and studied his expression while Peggy and Anita worked at getting the tabs back on their drinks.

"Look, kid," Charlie said, his voice breathless with anticipation, "if there's more, just let it out. We've heard so much already that we're beyond shock."

Derek stared back at Charlie. Peggy saw the workings of Derek's jaw and knew he wanted to drop the subject, but he couldn't. Charlie was right; they were entitled to hear it all. "Peggy," Derek said, turning to face her, his eyes showing torment, "do you know why Max was forever using the expression *legion*? Do you know what that means?"

"No."

"Well, I'll tell you. Legion means a large group of soldiers, an army, a multitude. In other words, Max knew all and could be everywhere at once because Max's body is composed of more than one. This is how he knew what happened while you were away from home, how he knew every conversation that took place between you and someone else, how he knew every move you made. Max is legion. Max is a multiple of demons."

"The black skinned demon in my room with the wings," Peggy said, "was Max? He was part of Max's body?"

"We'll probably see a lot of those creatures

from here on in," Derek answered. "This is why it's so important that when we do the ceremony and put him underground, we must be certain they are joined as one in his body."

"Some chore, huh, kid?"

Peggy heard the voice as did Charlie, Anita and Derek and wanted to die. The voice belonged to Max. He'd found them. They wondered how much of their conversation Max had heard, and if Max would be ready for them when the time came.

"Let's finish our Cokes and get the hell outta here," Charlie said. "Now that Max has found us, we might as well go home!"

"Good idea," Max said, but they ignored him.

Anita was the first to enter the house. Peggy saw her fall back against Charlie and cover her face with her hands. Small sobbing sounds escaped from her, and they all knew something was wrong.

"Take her for me, will you, Derek? I gotta see for myself." The door was only halfway open, blocking Peggy's view, but because of Anita's reaction Peggy didn't care. Whatever Anita had seen, it was bad.

"Son of a bitch!" Charlie raged. "I'll kill that bastard, Max!"

"Don't challenge him," Derek shouted. "No matter what he does, leave it be."

After Derek had spoken, Charlie forced the

door open enough so that Derek and Peggy could see for themselves. Peggy gasped and grabbed Derek's arm for support. The living room furniture was stacked and piled ceiling high again; mounds of excrement laced with hair were seen everywhere; a white foamy substance, resembling the ooze that had flowed from the toilet a week back, covered the walls. The stench was terrible.

"And you say don't challenge him!" Charlie spat.

But Derek never lost his temper. "Okay, so it's not my house, but these demons thrive on our tempers. If you threaten Max, we've lost before we've begun. I mean, you're forcing his hand to prove himself, and he'll do more, much worse than this."

"How could it get any worse?" Charlie asked, his mouth twisted with anger.

"It can and it will. Even in your worst nightmare you couldn't begin to imagine what Max and his helpers are capable of doing. Charlie, look, arguing is getting us nowhere. Maybe we should send Peggy and Anita back to the motel and clean this mess ourselves—"

"No!" Anita fumed, recovering from the shock. "This is my house! If anyone cleans my house it'll be me!"

"Can we help, sweetie?" Charlie asked. Charlie's temper defused when Anita lost hers. Only one of them could be mad at a time, an odd quirk Peggy had noticed over the years.

"I can use a hand if that's what you mean."

Going on inside, they tried not to gag at the stench or gasp at the sight of similar messes in other rooms. Max had been busy in their absence, Peggy noted, not allowing the growth of the small aura that pushed itself in front of her now and then. She would not succumb to a seizure and worry her parents and Derek. Having a seizure also meant giving Max the satisfaction of feeling he'd won another victory over them.

Knowing this, Peggy held on and cleaned along with Anita, Charlie and Derek.

After several hours, most of the furniture was back in place, and the piles of waste removed. They still had the walls to scrub when Charlie called it quits for the day. Charlie was beaten. At one point, Peggy had seen him glancing down the stairs off to one side of the utility room in the kitchen, had heard him groan and wondered why. Now that he was calling it quits she had a chance to look for herself and wished she hadn't. Their finished basement was filled with a myriad of disgusting things—animal waste, white slime and bones.

But that mess was nothing compared to the real horror. Peggy saw a skeletal hand with a Philmore High ring similar to the one Hank Brudhle used to wear floating on top of the slime. She had hated Hank at one time, but she never wanted him to end up like this—bones in her basement.

Turning away, she crossed the kitchen, saw movement in the yard outside as she passed the window, stopped and saw Dog out there. As Peggy watched, Dog turned sideways. His body was still lopsided and wobbly, but Dog managed to lift a hind leg and let go with a stream of urine directed her way. Dog still hated her.

It was late at night before everyone finally settled in the living room. Peggy had showered with Anita standing guard. Then Anita had taken her turn. Charlie and Derek did the same, feeling that somehow there was safety in numbers.

Awkward as the arrangements were, they were refreshed and sleepy.

"Anita," Charlie said, taking charge again, "you're small, so you can sleep on the loveseat. I'll take my recliner. Peggy take the couch and Derek . . . I think we're short one place."

"It's all right. I'll use Anita's chair. One of us has to stand guard and—"

"I'll do it," Charlie said. "You take the recliner."

"No, because I know the words for stopping them. You don't," Derek said stubbornly.

"Write 'em down," Charlie insisted. "Then we can take turns." But Derek never consented. "Look, you're as tired as me. You'll never make the night."

"Okay, I'll write it down. And while I'm at it, I might as well list the things I'll need tomorrow night for the ceremony. There'll be a full moon then. I don't know," he said, running a hand through his hair in a helpless gesture, "but maybe the moon will help. My father used to talk about the awesome powers of a full moon. He put so much stock in it that I got to thinking he might have a point."

"Then tomorrow night it is," Charlie said with determination.

"Wanna bet?" Max said, his voice booming in the air over their heads, but they chose to ignore him. Instead they gathered around Derek while he made a list—an unused pad of parchment paper, a quill pen, ink, candles, incense, a salt shaker, both a knife and a cleaver with wooden handles, and a branch from a dogwood tree.

"We'll get on it first thing in the morning," Charlie said. "Everyone of us will take a part of the list and find what we need!"

Peggy drifted off to sleep soon after with her eyes glued to Derek, hoping her dreams would be full of him and wonderful. She longed for a happy ending to the nightmare she'd created. But instead of the pleasant dreams she desired, her mind was ablaze with creatures chasing her throughout the curvatures and hidden crevices of her brain.

When at last she could take no more, she woke up and found herself eye to eye with a breathing, blackened mass of flesh kneeling on the floor beside the sofa. With her body limp and lucid, Peggy stared at the crisp skin that was oozing fluid and was tightly stretched across its body and knew she should scream. If she wasn't awake, screaming would do the job.

As she stared, the creature leaned in closer as if it had a secret to whisper in her ear, but it just made rasping noises, the sound coming from lips coated with white, fluid-filled blisters while its hot, putrid breath stung her nostrils, choking her and making her long for air.

And while it was closing in, Peggy kept telling herself that she wasn't alone in the room with this horror from Hades. Her parents were there; Derek was there. She couldn't see them, but they were there. Why didn't somebody stop this? Why didn't Derek chant and send it away? He was supposed to be on guard.

While the creature's hot breath washed over her face, Peggy tried to reach the pad on the coffee table with Derek's instructions. Using Derek's incantation, she could have sent the beast away, but her arm was too short. She could have searched her memory for the words, but her mind was racing by this time. She couldn't concentrate on anything but the glitch in the computer circuits of her mind.

"I need your flesh," it rasped while black fluid flowed from the sides of its mouth and streamed across its blistered lips. "I was as human as you once, but I was punished in the fires of Hell. The pain has driven me crazy. I'm insane and want your flesh.''

Peggy heard what it said, stared at a pair of eyes that were almost fused into one and thought about screaming, but the scream died in her. This thing wanted to peel the flesh from her bones, and Derek and her parents were asleep. Otherwise they'd help her, save her from the agony of being skinned alive. Oh God, there was no one to help—God! That was it! Something she'd read in a novel once, something she could use now.

"Don't even think of it!" the blackened mass said, delving into her thoughts. "Your God has forsaken you. He won't help."

"In the name of Jesus Christ, demon be gone!" Peggy raged, forcing the words to come out. Then she listened to the raspy laughter of the beast as it neared her face.

"I'm taking your eyes and the skin on your face first," it said. "Then I'll skin the rest of your body. It's nothing personal. I'm just in pain."

Peggy fought the aura still forming in her brain and tried to remember the phrase from the book. She was sure she had it right, but it hadn't worked, so maybe—

"Maybe nothing," the blackened beast said. "Your God has forsaken you. I told you this. He won't help."

But the beast was mistaken. Peggy wasn't a

forsaken or forgotten soul. She just had the words wrong. If she could only remember!

"It was just a book, dear, written from some writer's imagination. The chant won't work."

After hearing those words, Peggy watched in horror as the beast lifted its arms from its sides, the heavy moaning sounds it made telling her it was in pain. There was an instrument that resembled a potato peeler in one of its hands, the fingers of the beast fused and smoky. Closing her eyes against the terror she felt, she saw the white of the aura flash three times in her brain and knew a seizure was on its way. The flashing motions of the aura exploded in her brain like a bomb. Three times it had flashed. Three was the number of evil. The verse she'd spoken had to be said three times in rapid succession to nullify the powers of evil.

"In the name of Jesus Christ, demon be gone," she shouted twice more and opened her eyes. She was alone.

"What the hell's going on?" Derek said, his voice strained. Peggy shot up and saw him coming down the stairs. Rushing to her side, he wrapped her in his arms while she tearfully told of her encounter.

"Then that explains it," he said. "I tried to use the bathroom down here, but the door was jammed tight. I had to go upstairs. Those bastards jammed the door on purpose. They wanted me away from you so they could pull their nonsense, but you did good, baby, real good.''

Peggy felt the weight of his lips on hers and saw the aura dissolve in front of her. Whatever magic there was in the emotions of love, Derek was using that magic to help her control the horror in her life.

"I love you," he said. "And not just for now, for always. And I won't leave your side again until this is over. I promise."

"You may not have a choice."

Both Peggy and Derek heard the voice and turned and saw Max, his hideous form at the bottom of the stairs, his face twisted with hatred, his axe raised and ready. "If I kill you now," he hissed, "you'll spend eternity locked in an embrace in my cave, tortured beyond belief. Your promise just might come true, Derek."

Peggy trembled and drew closer to Derek, who just smiled at Max in return. "Do I have to send you away again, or will you be a good boy and go?"

"You're pushing!" Max said, his face twisted even tighter, his mouth a line of contempt. But then as quickly as Peggy could blink, Max's expression changed to one of amusement. "Maybe I won't let you stay together. Maybe I'll keep your bitch for myself. Nicole Martin was a good lay. Peggy might be even better."

Peggy dug her nails into Derek's arm. The thought of someone like Max was a nightmare.

She expected Derek to go into a rage, but he didn't. Instead, he kept calm. "I'm not falling for it," Derek said, smiling. "You want me to get mad so I'll get stupid. No way!" Moving Peggy gently aside, Derek rose and raised his arms over his head to chant. But before he could speak, the black winged beast that had tormented Peggy nights before appeared and grabbed his arms, holding them fast.

Lowering his head to Derek's shoulder, the beast revealed jagged teeth laced with yellow spittle and began to sink them into Derek's flesh. Peggy rose and struck him hard across the side of his head while her hands shook for fear she'd hit Derek instead. In shock, the beast withdrew and vanished, while Max's laughter filled the air like a blanket of torment.

"Your bitch protects you, boy," Max shouted and was gone. But not his voice. Hiding behind the guise of invisibility, Max threatened and tormented them for the better part of the night. Beasts appeared out of nowhere and threatened the lives of Charlie, Anita, and Peggy, then vanished when Derek chanted. Max was trying to wear them down, trying to exhaust Derek so he'd either give in to the demons or give up and leave.

But Derek had made a promise to help them rid their lives of Max. He also had promised to protect them until Max was gone. So Derek kept watch and kept his wits about him, always conscious of the fact that if he lost his temper and his reason, Max would be the victor. They'd have lost the battle before it began.

CHAPTER TWENTY-ONE

Peggy glanced at the full moon ringed with clouds and prayed for this to work. So many things had gone wrong it seemed their efforts were doomed before they began. Derek was upset because he hadn't fasted for seven days as per the instructions for the ceremony, but there hadn't been time. Charlie was upset because although he'd found parchment paper at Sears, it wasn't the right paper. According to the text, they should have slaughtered a lamb without blemishes and used its skin to write on.

Anita was upset because she'd gone upstairs alone to get the ouija board and Max showed up again, but Anita was crafty enough to have memorized Derek's incantations. Anita

347

kicked ass, and Max went away, only not for good.

While Peggy stood by with Anita and Charlie, Derek traced the symbol of Solomon on the ground near the swimming pool, using the wooden-handled knife. They saw him draw a six-pointed star—two triangles interlaced—and watched as he filled the outer edges of the star with Hebrew incantations.

They were in the back of the house, the only place safe from the prying eyes of neighbors because of the surrounding bushes. Peggy lit a candle and checked her watch. It was 2:53 in the morning. Derek wanted to have the ceremony in full swing by 3:00, the true hour of the prince of darkness.

"Now step over the lines," Derek told them once it was finished. "You're safer in here with me than outside."

"Yeah," Charlie said nervously, "unless one of us messes the lines and destroys the symbol. Then we're dead meat."

"Then we'll have to be careful," Anita said. "The boy is trying his best. We have to cooperate. Only there's one thing I can't understand. Max has been fairly quiet all day. Why hasn't he tried to stop us?"

"Because either he thinks we can't do the ceremony, or we'll botch it up and his friends will kill us," Derek answered. "Now, everyone stay inside the lines no matter what."

"Wait!" Peggy carefully stepped back over the line and grabbed the ouija board. "We forgot this." She was almost back inside when smoke began to rise from the board, burning her hands. She dropped it.

Anita ran to the edge of the circle and gingerly lifted the board over the line. "I'm used to handling hot stuff," she said, trying to sound nonchalant, but the crack in her voice showed how frightened she was. In fact, they were all frightened, even Derek who'd performed similar ceremonies in the past.

"Is it three yet?" he asked and began to chant when Peggy nodded. Placing three candles in a triangular pattern, Derek sprinkled salt, then incense over their flames. While he continued to do this, Peggy laid the knife and cleaver inside of the candles as Derek has instructed her to.

"Nebus, Rebellum, Mindalius. Demons from the bowels of hell, we beseech you in the name of our Lord Jesus Christ to appear. Satan, lord of fire, Lucifer, emperor of the air, Belial, beast of the earth and Leviathan, serpent of the sea—in Christ's name we ask your favors. Saraphe, Ecar, Nissam."

Peggy listened to him pray, watched him wave the branch of dogwood over the lighted candles and prayed herself that this would work. When no one appeared, Derek went to phase two of his plan—insults. According to the Key of Solomon, if cajoling didn't conjure up the demons for help, then Derek must make them mad enough to appear. Peggy shuddered.

"Lords of the elements and the black outer world of demons, cowards of all time, in the name of Christ I command you to appear. Balaam, Dagon and Mammon. In Christ's name, I order that the gates of hell be opened and you appear to accept me as your master. I command that you bestow your favors upon me!"

Peggy held onto Charlie and Anita when the ground beneath them began to rumble as if the fury of the gods of darkness had suddenly come alive. Digging her nails into Anita, she watched as one by one the demons appeared, some dressed like soldiers with jagged spears in their hands, some in the clothing of nobility of centuries past, some wearing nothing.

Yet they all had one thing in common. They were hideous and fouled the air with a stench so strong it hovered like a blanket of death. Peggy watched the beastly creatures surround Derek and wanted to die. Derek's life was in danger because of something she'd started. What a fool she was.

She listened to the creatures babbling in tongues and knew they were doing this to confuse Derek. Scanning the stinking group of bodies, she saw many two-legged creatures with taloned claws and thought of Max, who also walked on two legs. Somehow she knew that one of these creatures would have to be in charge.

"You called, human!"

Peggy followed the voice and saw two legs ending in animal hooves, a body covered with clumped fur, a face like a wolf with overly large features and a set of hairy wings. This was their leader. But was it him? Was this the king of beasts, king of the nether world of darkness? Derek said he might not come himself, that he might send an emissary.

"Your name?" Derek said, facing the beast. "I must have your name."

"I am Lycanus, Prince of werewolves and other fanged creatures. And now, what is your wish?"

This was Charlie's cue. Charlie released Anita and handed the parchment to Derek, then the quill pen, but held onto the ink bottle. Opening the cap for Derek, Charlie's hands were shaking so badly he nearly dropped it.

"Hey, guys, glad you could come. What's up, Lycanus?" Max said, his scaly, ulcer-ridden body rising from the ouija board. Seeing the hood covering his head and the axe in his hands, Charlie grew angry.

"You're the bastard who's been harassing my wife—"

"Silence!" Lycanus bellowed, opening his huge wings menacingly.

"Yes, please don't interfere and mess this up," Derek said. "This is what Max wants."

While Max stood and stared over Derek's

shoulder, Derek dipped the quill pen into the bottle of ink and wrote his demands for the demons to see. Then he handed the parchment to Lycanus, who smiled courteously, but the smile wasn't friendly.

Peggy released her grip on Anita and moved towards the candles to sprinkle more salt and incense over the flames, ignoring the growling noises that had just begun near the outer rim of the circle. It sounded like Dog, but she couldn't look, couldn't take her attention away from the task at hand.

"Dig your hole for the board," Lycanus said, his voice like thunder in the night. "We are compelled to help—"

"Hey, listen!" Max said.

"Silence!" Lycanus roared. "You know the rules. It's over, Max!" With that he held the parchment over the flaming candles and watched it burn. "As it is written, so shall it be done!" Then he turned and smiled at Max as though he'd been waiting for this for centuries, as though he wanted revenge.

Taking the hatchet by its wooden handle, Derek dug a hole and listened when Lycanus commanded Max to return to the board for burial, for all time to come.

Max's face was a mask of rage. "Where's the Black Master?" he roared. "He will not allow this!"

"The Black Master sent me," Lycanus answered, his jowls drawn back into a grin. "I won the honor this time, but only because I passed the test. Thanks, Max. You were the one who taught me trickery and deceit, and now to have won the opportunity to judge you because of what you've taught me—very ironic."

Ignoring Lycanus, Max turned towards the outer rim of the circle and mumbled some words in Latin. Peggy followed his gaze and saw that the growling noises she'd heard before had indeed come from Dog. While she watched in horror, Dog took his paw and cut a path through the symbol of Solomon, causing a break in the line, leaving the humans in danger of being destroyed.

Anita ran towards Dog as the demons of hell surrounded the rest, their talons out and ready. Peggy fought the aura forming in her brain and tried not to faint as Anita kicked Dog square in the face, sending him tumbling over sideways, his wobbly legs folding under the weight of his body.

Derek threw the wooden-handled knife over the heads of the beasts menacing him; it landed near her feet. Taking the knife in hand, Anita retraced the line and screamed when a beast dressed as a soldier grabbed her arm.

"See it, sucker!" she shouted, pointing to the line. "Now your ass is ours! And when you leave, take that fucking dog with you."

The beasts withdrew and waited while Derek

continued to dig. Once the hole was completed, Derek took the board with Max and his legion of demons inside and placed it in the hole, top side down. Derek was doing this so that, despite the crucifix, should Max ever dream of escaping, Max would go down into the bowels of hell and not up, to torment some other poor fool stupid enough to play with the ouija board.

Then Derek stopped and went into shock. "We've forgotten the most important thing—the crucifix. Oh, God! We brought everything else. How could we be so stupid."

Charlie took the branch of dogwood and used Derek's knife to cut two twigs, one long and one short. Then he sliced a piece of his shirt to join them together at the top. "No problem," he said and handed the makeshift cross to Derek. "It's not a true crucifix, but it'll have to do." Derek nodded in silent agreement.

Once the cross was placed over the ouija board, Derek used the cleaver to cover it with dirt. Then he turned to the demons he'd conjured up.

"Demons of the dark forces of the earth, in the name of our Lord Jesus Christ, we offer our gratitude for your help." Once said, the demons were gone in a burst of smoke and sulphur. It was over. Max was no more.

Peggy remembered sitting in the living room later on, drinking tea with Derek, Charlie and

Anita, all of them laughing for the first time in weeks. Max was gone, and they were free from the hauntings. It was such a wonderful feeling to know there would be no more of Max's surprises, no more fear.

"Lucky for us they took Dog," Derek said, suddenly growing serious. "Dog was outside of the circle. They weren't compelled to take him."

"So they did us a favor," Peggy said, "and threw in something extra. Maybe they're not so bad after all."

"Peggy!" Derek fumed. "Don't even think that way. They tried to kill us when Dog severed the line. Just remember how evil Max was and multiply that by one hundred. Then you'll never thank them again because that evil is them."

"Oh, hell," Charlie said, raising his cup in a toast, "this is no time to get serious. Let's drink to us and to the peaceful existence ahead."

"Before you finish," Anita said, "let me get some wine. It's not champagne but it'll do. I mean, who ever heard of a toast with tea?"

After she'd spoken, she realized what she'd said and laughed until tears streaked her face. Charlie laughed, too, as did Peggy and Derek. They were all giddy and overcome with joy because the evil in their lives was now a thing of the past, and maybe someday they'd be able to erase the horror from their memories.

Rising to get the wine, Anita fairly danced her way to the kitchen as Peggy's voice rang out behind her. "Need help, Mom?"

"No, doll, I've got everything under control," she mumbled, her words fading as she vanished out of sight. "For the first time in my life . . ."

"Derek," Charlie said, his eyes misted over, "I know this is supposed to be a happy occasion, but I'm overwhelmed. I don't know how to thank you for saving us from Max."

"No need to. It was my pleasure—"

Pleasure! The word ran through Peggy's mind as she listened to her mother screaming in the kitchen. Fighting the aura forming in front of her, Peggy tried to repair the glitch as Derek and Charlie ran to help Anita.

Anita hadn't meant to scream. In fact, when she first went into the kitchen there'd been no need.

She'd gotten the wine from the cabinet over the sink where the glasses were kept. Then she wiped the glasses and placed them on a tray next to the wine.

She then stopped to admire the scent of roses and honeysuckle being carried on the wind that made her curtains stand straight out and dance. She also stopped to marvel that her life had changed in so many ways.

And it was more than Max, more than his destruction. Anita had fallen in love with her family again. She'd regained the emotions she'd felt when Charlie placed a ring on her finger in church before God. She'd regained the emotions she felt when Peggy was first born, before she'd learned of the epilepsy.

Now her life was complete. She was happy and carefree again. She was also thankful for Derek. The boy loved Peggy so deeply.

Anita sniffed the breezes and tried to ignore the footsteps behind her. These, she knew, were all in her mind. Max was gone, and Max had been responsible for those other footsteps. But then she listened and heard deep growling noises and wondered if the beasts Derek had conjured were gone, or if one of them had lingered.

As the footsteps drew closer, she stiffened her body and slowly turned. She saw a half-rotted corpse wearing the clothing of a nobleman from ages past. He was holding a scalpel, his face twisted into what passed for a smile. Dog was at his side.

"Allow me to introduce myself, madam," he said, bowing lavishly. "I'm the Marquis de Sade, Max's replacement and avenging angel." Anita couldn't think or speak. The words were there, but they just wouldn't come out. Max was gone and his legion of demons with him. Why was this one still here? "I wasn't a part of Max, I am a separate entity. Therefore I wasn't trapped inside the board when you buried it," he said as if he'd scanned her brain and read her thoughts. "Max is gone, true, but he trained me to take his place should something happen to him."

"We got rid of him!" she spat, her anger releasing the words. "And we'll get rid of you, too!" After she'd spoken, she studied the rotting cadaver in front of her and thought how handsome Max was compared to this. Then she thought about his name—the Marquis de Sade. The word sadist came from this man; he invented torture. "We'll get rid of you, too," she repeated, but she wasn't so sure this time.

Raising her arms to shout Derek's incantation and watch him vanish, Anita realized it was useless. Her body was shackled with invisible chains; she couldn't move. Then she tried to chant but her mouth wouldn't cooperate. Somehow he'd sealed her lips, and she hadn't seen it coming.

Closing her eyes in the face of the shadow of death moving towards her, she heard this creature, the beast with the scalpel, scream for help—using her voice to do it. He was using trickery to draw the others to the kitchen. Then he'd kill them the same way he was about to kill her. She was paralyzed, struck speechless, and there was no way she could stop him.

Her life was no longer perfect. She'd lost control again.

"Help me!" he continued to scream, and Anita thought she'd go insane at the sound of her own voice coming from this beast with Peggy's dog.

"Max was too kind and arrogant. Max played

games," he said when he'd finished screaming, when the others were pounding at the door trying to get in. "Max allowed you the freedom of movement and speech. I won't make the same mistake!" Then he sliced Anita's throat with the scalpel and stood by while she gurgled and tried to swallow her own blood. But it was no use, no use at all. . . .

Peggy woke in a sweat and listened to the sound of her own moaning. Anita was at her side. "Oh God, you're alive," Peggy said holding her mother with everything in her.

With Peggy's head cradled against her neck, Anita rocked her and cooed as Peggy continued to tremble. "I heard you moaning in your sleep. These nightmares are getting out of hand," Anita said softly. "Honey, you've got to forget. Max is gone. The horror is over."

"But Mom," Peggy groaned, releasing her to make sure she was real, "this was the worst yet. You were killed by this demon—"

"Like I said, it's over. The ceremony was a success."

"But we had tea afterwards. Only you went into the kitchen for some wine and the demon killed you."

"Peggy, we had nothing, remember? We were so exhausted we went straight to bed. The dream wasn't real. Now, listen to me. Derek is down-stairs eating breakfast with your father and he's been asking for you. Why don't you get dressed?" Peggy nodded silently. "And I'll stay here until you do."

"No," Peggy insisted, feeling suddenly foolish. "I'll be okay. You go on ahead."

"You sure?"

"Yes, Mom, I'll be fine."

But she wasn't, not inside. She was still shaken from that awful dream with that awful rotted man killing Anita. As Anita closed the door behind her, Peggy rose from her bed and headed for the bathroom. She needed a shower, a long, hot, soothing one to help erase the horror.

Taking off her pajamas, she was about to step into the tub when she remembered the closet outside and the slipper chair. It was silly, but she knew she'd feel much better if the knob of the door to the closet was held fast by the chair. Besides, she'd found from past experience that her dreams had a way of coming true. If the Marquis were to come here, it would surely be through the closet.   .

She was halfway there when an awful stench struck her nostrils and made her wince. It was like having Max back again, only Max was gone. Staring at the slipper chair, she fought an aura when she saw a tattered and rotted nobleman's jacket, made of lavish, silk brocade, carelessly slung across the seat. She couldn't remember if it had been there when she went into the bathroom.

Then she found herself wondering when the Marquis would return for his jacket and when the Marquis would either haunt her dreams or kill them. He'd said he was Max's avenging angel—and her dreams *did* have a way of coming true.

AUTHOR'S NOTE: The ceremony taken from the Key of Solomon has been changed to protect those who might be tempted to use it.